THE BLACK THREE

Diane & Sophie

Great to see you!

Gene Skipworth

GENE SKIPWORTH

authorHOUSE®

AuthorHouse™
1663 Liberty Drive
Bloomington, IN 47403
www.authorhouse.com
Phone: 833-262-8899

Published by AuthorHouse 04/06/2022

ISBN: 978-1-6655-5158-8 (sc)
ISBN: 978-1-6655-5157-1 (hc)
ISBN: 978-1-6655-5156-4 (e)

Library of Congress Control Number: 2022902883

Print information available on the last page.

CONTENTS

INTRODUCTION
THE STORY WORLD

Grayville High School in Grayville, Tennessee never had a black basketball player. Now GHS has three. A new doctor moved to Grayville in August of 2020. Dr. Bokima has three sons who played basketball for Weston, Ohio High School last year and the three took Weston to the Ohio State High School basketball tournament championship. Joseph, a senior, and oldest of the three, is six feet nine inches tall and was named Most Valuable Player of the Ohio State Basketball Tournament. The other two sons are twins, Samuel and David, both juniors, are six feet six inches tall.

Dr. Hiram Bokima is from Nigeria. He was orphaned at the age of eight when his mother died of AIDS two weeks after his eighth birthday. Prior to his mother's death, just after his seventh birthday, his father also died of AIDS. He was adopted by a United Church of Christ missionary to Nigeria, Rev. Dr. William Norris and his wife, Betty. The Bokima family were members of Rev. Norris's church in the village of Opaka, Nigeria. Opaka is one of the most poverty-stricken areas of Nigeria. Rev. Norris fielded a team of agricultural experts in the area of irrigation. That was one of his first tasks as missionary, to help the indigenous develop resources for planting and growing.

Dr. Bokima, at six feet ten inches tall, played center on the Nigerian National Basketball Team during his high school years. He became very close to his adoptive parents. Rev. and Mrs. Norris contributed a great deal to the maturity and growth of Hiram. He excelled in academics and began to have a vision for himself. That vision was fulfilled as he came to America and attended Temple University where he was a pre-med major and a basketball All American his senior year.

Dr. Bokima attended John Hopkins University Medical School and did his internship at the Ohio State University Hospital in Columbus, Ohio. He left a successful practice in Weston, Ohio to move to Grayville to be near his parents who are both dealing with declining health issues due to aging. His parents retired to the Homeland Retirement Center in Pleasant Hill, just outside Grayville.

STAGE ONE

I. Grayville As a Sundown Town

When Jack Stone was a sophomore at Grayville High School in 1953, he was an usher at the Rialto Theater, the downtown theater in Grayville. His main job as an usher was to use a flashlight to help people find a seat. When blacks came to the Rialto, he led them up the narrow stairway in the back corner of the theater to the balcony. In Grayville that is where blacks had to sit when they came to see a movie, the balcony.

Grayville was one of the twenty-four "Sundown Towns" in the state of Tennessee. Sundown Towns had a sign on the outskirts of town that said, "Negros are not allowed in the city limits after sundown." Sundown Towns were also known as Sunset Towns or Gray Towns. They were all-white communities that practiced racial segregation by excluding non-whites through discrimination, local laws, intimidation, and violence. Jack Stone says he remembers seeing the Sundown sign outside town on route 70 when he was in high school.

As an usher at the Rialto, Jack didn't seat many blacks. There were very few in Grayville. The few that went to a movie went to the Saturday afternoon matinee because of the "unwritten law" that blacks were not allowed in the city limits after sundown. None of them lived in Grayville because there was another unwritten law that blacks could not live within the city limits.

A. Early History

About the year 1900 the blacks that lived in the area lived in a small settlement six miles from Grayville called Taylor Town. They had a school which was a log house that served not only as a school but also a church. There is a graveyard and there are several monuments still standing at that location. Around 1900 there were 572 blacks in Cox County, in 1910 there were just 91, and in 1920 there remained 25 blacks. In 1900 most of the blacks moved thirty miles east to Harrisburg. No one knows for sure why they moved en masse, but the suspicion is that they were forced to leave. About that time a black man was lynched at the courthouse square in Grayville. Four blacks were hung on a separate occasion near Pleasant Hill in 1920.

The few blacks who have lived in Grayville since the depression, lived outside the city limits in an area unfamiliar to most Grayville residents. It was not as far away as Taylor Town. They lived on an abandoned lot in four small run-down houses, called "coal shacks" which sat in a square lot with each house on a corner of the square. They were called "coal shacks" because once a month, summer and winter, a dump truck drove to the center of the square and dumped a load of coal in the yard for the people to use. There was not enough wood around the area to be gathered for them to burn in their stoves.

The owner of the GMC dealership in Grayville, a member of Trinity United Methodist Church, always had a dump truck drop off coal in the yard in the center of the shacks. He called it his monthly "goodwill" contribution. None of the shacks had running water. There were two outhouses located near the alley for the four shacks.

The black families that lived in those shacks didn't live there very long. Most of the time there would be one or two of the shacks empty. There would only be one or two black families at one time in Grayville following the Depression. Looking back on that time one can't imagine why any black person would want to live in Grayville. The black women that worked, usually worked as domestics. The men, if they worked, worked wherever they could find a job.

Prior to 1969, especially in the 50s, Saturday night in downtown Grayville used to be very crowded, noisy, and busy in a festive kind of way. Streets and stores were filled with people, the Rialto was full for each showing of the movie, Main Street was bumper to bumper with traffic and it was hard to find a parking place within six blocks of Main Street. Several small groups of friends, family, and acquaintances would congregate in conversation on the sidewalk on either side of Main Street.

Blacks were never seen downtown on Saturday night. In fact, there were never any blacks downtown on Main Street at any time. There was another unwritten law that blacks weren't allowed on Main Street. The lone water fountain they could use was on West Ave a block away. The outhouse they used as a public restroom was down the alley off West Ave and behind Ralph's Body Shop.

B. Wanda Phillips

The only black student during the 50s at Grayville High School was Wanda Phillips. She graduated in 1954 and never lived more than two years in Grayville. Hardly anybody knew her and if a person wanted to know her name, they would have to look through the yearbooks to find the only black girl and that would be Wanda. Very few took the time or effort to get acquainted with her. Some people feel bad that they never did. One time she came to the Rialto with her mom and dad and little sister. Jack Stone ushered them upstairs to the balcony. It didn't enter his mind to say hello to her or to ask her how she was doing. Nor did he give a second thought of how wrong it was to usher her and her family to the balcony.

When one looked back and thought about Wanda and remembered that no one ever spoke to her or ever took the time to get acquainted, they should feel very ashamed. Jack Stone expressed his shame as he thought to himself, "If I would happen to see her today, I am sure she wouldn't say a word to me and I don't blame her. I am sure she wouldn't even know me. I feel so sorry for ignoring her the way I did, the way we all did."

Jack Stone was a good Methodist boy. He went to worship and Sunday School every week, church on Sunday night, Wednesday he went to the prayer meeting, and then youth fellowship on Thursday night. Of course, the Trinity United Methodist Church was all white. Every individual that he and friends and classmates grew up with was white. They grew up culturally prejudiced and raised in a social system that fashioned a tolerance for bigotry. No wonder so many ignored Wanda when she was at GHS.

Kids growing up in Grayville during their elementary school years, learned that Grayville was a Sundown Town. Kids growing up in Grayville during their elementary school years, leaned not to associate with black people and to be afraid of them. It is called a "culturally absorbed prejudice." It is also called "a socially acquired prejudice."

The short time Wanda spent in high school must have been a terribly unhappy ordeal for her. No one befriended her or spent time with her. She was never seen at any of the football or basketball games. In fact, there was never any blacks at any of the sporting events, especially night games.

C. The 1970s

In the early 70's blacks would be seen walking along Route 70 past the Bargain Barn on their way home. Even though they were finally allowed on Main Street, there were hardly any blacks anywhere to be seen. Even though they were allowed to sit at the counter at Martin's Pharmacy, seldom did a black person get near Martin's Pharmacy. No one ever saw a black person driving a car. In most cases, they never had a car to drive.

When Jack Stone returned to Grayville for family visits or class reunions or other occasions like funerals and weddings, he seldom, if ever, saw a black person. The "Blacks Only" water fountain had been taken away. Nor did he see the outhouse behind what used to be Ralph's Body Shop.

He heard about a black woman in 1969 that sat at the counter at Martin's Pharmacy. They said that two sheriff deputies were called to tell her to leave. But she didn't. They carried her out of Martin's and took her to jail. It turned out that she was a civil rights activist from Knoxville.

Some things have changed since Jack Stone left in 1955. Blacks are able to walk on Main Street, can be seen in the city limits after sundown, and can even live in the city limits. That sounded like progress to Jack Stone.

II. University of Illinois – First Encounter with Blacks

When Jack left Grayville sixty-five years ago, he attended the University of Illinois on a football scholarship. He was, until 1968, the only recruit in the state of Tennessee to attend the University of Illinois. In 1968 a kid from Morristown received a football scholarship to Illinois because his mother happened to be an aunt of the defensive line coach at the time.

A. Three New Words

It was at the University of Illinois that his cultural bias, his prejudicial up-bringing, and the racist attitude that he absorbed in his school years, was met head-on with the concepts of respect, empathy, and compassion toward other people, especially blacks. His University of Illinois experience was a great learning experience for him.

Respect, empathy, and compassion, essentials for a solid relationship, were what he should have learned and taken in as an important part of his life. The good folk at Trinity United Methodist Church in Grayville made sure that he took in Jesus as the most important part of his life. In the first few months at Illinois, Jack began to think that Trinity UMC should have made respect, empathy, and compassion as high priorities in his life.

Respect, empathy, and compassion were concepts that were not familiar to him or a part of his vocabulary. He saw his black and white teammates show respect, empathy, and compassion to each other. He caught himself observing those relationships. They witnessed to him the great value of all three, especially when he saw black-white interaction.

Respect was never a word or concept that he was familiar with in relation to black people. He learned in third grade Sunday school at the Methodist Church we were to respect our parents. But Rochelle, who was in the Sunday school class with him, had a father who got drunk a lot and beat her. She told Mrs. Clark, the Sunday school teacher, "I don't respect my father because he beats me and my mom a lot. Am I going to hell? He should be the one who goes to hell. What can I do?" Mrs. Clark said to all of us, "We have to respect our fathers."

Empathy was a word Jack never used, and he wasn't even sure he knew what it meant. Empathy is a great word when one talks about relationships, especially when diversity is discussed. Empathy is having the capacity for sharing the feelings of another person. It has a great deal to do with understanding, being aware of, sensitive to, vicariously experiencing the feelings and thoughts of another person. Empathy would go a long way in getting rid of a lot of the prejudice toward people who are different.

Compassion was a word that most of the kids in Grayville never associated with personal relationships. Compassion was something missionaries were to preach and show to the natives of Uganda. Respect, empathy, and compassion for someone, especially a black person, was never an integrated part of Jack Stone's personality.

Jack was a halfback, and his biggest competition was from four black players. Abe Woods, Les Brothers, Harry Jackson, and the great Bobby Martin. He had never been around a black person before. In Grayville, he just saw Wanda Phillips at a distance down the hallway.

At Illinois all the stereotypes he had learned about blacks from the Cox County good o'boys got blown out of the water. He had learned back home that blacks were lazy, good dancers, too dumb to be a soldier, couldn't read or write, didn't know English, would not work, had a certain smell, and all the young black girls just wanted to have babies. The wildest stereotype he learned about black people was when he was in junior high. Billie Joe Schaeffer, the owner of Schaeffer's Shell station near the junior high school, told Jack and his friends, when they stopped in for a Nehi soda, "Nigras are all ignorant bastards. They will never count for nothin."

Abe Woods was a journalism major studying to be a TV news reporter. Les Brothers was studying aeronautical engineering. Harry Jackson was a political science major and talked about becoming a city manager. Oscar Lincoln, a black defensive lineman, was an education administration major looking to get his PhD to become a public-school administrator. Jack Stone was a physical education major.

It wasn't hard for them to figure out that Jack had no experience with black people. They had encountered people like him. They were street savvy city boys. He was from rural small-town Bible-belt Tennessee. In his first eighteen years he learned about the "colored." He knew they weren't allowed on Main Street. No one ever told him why. He knew they were not allowed to live within the city limits. No one ever told him why. He knew they had to sit in the balcony at the Rialto. No one told him why. They weren't allowed to sit at the counter at Martin's Pharmacy. No one told him why.

He thought of his job as an usher at the Rialto Theater. He wondered what would happen if he told Abe Woods or Bobby Martin they had to go up the steps to the balcony. It would never happen. They wouldn't stand for it. They would take his flashlight and threaten to ram it down his throat. He could just hear them as he flashed his light at them and tell them to follow him to the balcony. "Stone, you can take that flashlight and shove it up your ass. We are going to sit where we want to."

When he thought of all the times Wanda Phillips was ushered up those steps to the balcony, he felt ashamed and humiliated. Later on, he often said, "If only I could see her now and apologize! She too, like Les, Bobby, Harry, and Abe, had experienced enough humiliation and denial the short time she lived in Grayville." And Stone felt he had contributed to her misery.

B. Jesse Parker

The most memorable real face to face experience with a black girl, one in which Jack learned a great lesson, was from an encounter while a freshman at Illinois. It was an incident he had with Jesse Parker. Jesse was a good-looking black girl in his Spanish 101 class.

He had an injury from football practice and missed a class. A special assignment was passed out that day and he missed getting the assignment. So, he asked Jesse when he saw her in class, "I missed getting the special assignment the other day because I was laid up from an injury. If you have the assignment, could I get a copy from you?" She told him, "I have it at my sorority house. Stop by Saturday morning and I will get it for you."

Jack Stone thought this was going to be special! He was so excited. He anticipated that this was going to be a valuable experience. He was going to become acquainted with a beautiful black girl and he was going to be able to realize, for the first time, that he was becoming involved with a black person in a significant way.

He figured now he had a chance for the first time ever to have a one on one with a black girl. She seemed so nice and friendly. He imagined he would join her in the lounge of the sorority or maybe they would sit and visit in the dining room. He thought she would probably invite him to have coffee. In anticipation of that he stopped by the Spud Nut Shoppe to pick up two cinnamon rolls for them to have with the coffee.

When he got to her sorority with his two Spud Nuts, he rang the doorbell. Another black girl answered the door and asked him through the screen door, "Can I help you?" He said, "Yes, I came to see Jesse Parker." She responded, "Was she expecting you?" He answered, "Yes." She closed the door, and shortly, Jesse came and stood inside the screened door. Jack reached for the screen door handle to open it and walk in, but Jesse held it shut tight and opened it only wide enough to hand him the assignment paper. Before he could tell her he had two Spud Nuts for them to share over coffee, she completely shut the screen door tight and closed the front door without saying a word. Jack stood there on the front porch wondering what to do next. He left.

Bewildered. Confused. He asked himself, was she angry with Him? He didn't have a chance to tell her thanks. He didn't have a chance to tell her he had two Spud Nuts. What did he do wrong? He didn't say anything so it couldn't have been something he said. He headed over to Abe and Les's dorm room. He could talk to them and he is sure they would help him make sense of all this.

C. Lesson Learned

Abe and Les were in their room with Jarvis Franklin, a huge white offensive guard from Pittsburg. The guys welcomed him in, they seemed glad to see him. Especially, when he gave them the two Spud Nuts that they had to share with Jarvis. He told them everything that happened at Jesse's sorority.

Abe and Les didn't seem phased or surprised or upset or bewildered. Abe was the first to speak. He said, "Well, Jack, you expected too much. Those black girls don't take too kindly to a white cracker from Tennessee coming to the door of their sorority. Think, now. Does your fraternity welcome blacks? Does your fraternity allow blacks to become members?" He wasn't waiting for an answer, he was just making a point. "Does your fraternity invite black guys to come in to visit and have a cup of coffee? If I came to your fraternity, how welcomed would I be to come in and have coffee with you? If I came to the front door and asked to see you, do you think they would let me in to wait for you inside? If none of your brothers knew me, how would it go over if I was to walk on in?

"What did you expect at the sorority? To go in and be among all the sorority girls, have Jesse introduce you to some of them, show you around the house, sit down at the dining room table and have a cup of coffee and a Spud Nut with a beautiful black girl?"

Les chimed in with "I suppose you expected her to smile and be real friendly and welcome you in and ask you if you wanted a cup of coffee.

Hell, I am surprised she gave you the assignment sheet." Jarvis was just listening. He gave the impression he was learning something, too.

Abe started sharing again. "First of all, white guys are not welcome or invited to step foot on a black sorority's porch, let alone go inside, have coffee and a Spud Nut. You are lucky the house mother didn't come to the door and tell you to get your white ass off the porch and never come back. That girl did more than she should have done. You are lucky she even invited you to pick up the assignment paper."

Les added, "I can guarantee as a white boy you have gotten away with more than any white boy in the history of that sorority. You can bet Jesse is going to get her ass chewed out for even having you stop over there. You make sure when you see her in class that you thank her and go overboard on that. Don't dare say something stupid like, 'Jesse, I was hoping we could sit and get acquainted and have coffee. I even brought Spud Nuts.' You got more than she should have given you. So, just chalk it up as a white cracker from Tennessee got his clock cleaned by a beautiful black girl from a power-packed black sorority full of aggressive 'take no bull-shit' sorority girls." Jack had a long way to go to learn empathy.

D. Retired and Back in Grayville

After working and living in the Midwest for almost sixty-five years, Jack retired and moved back to Grayville. They say you can't go back home, and Jack found that out. One of the reasons that is true is because of the response you get from those who stayed home. He left and they thought he thought he was better than them. He left and had the opportunity to go on to bigger and better challenges and they didn't. He left and experienced change and survived it. They never tried. He witnessed what it was to grow personally and to progress and prepare for the next century. They didn't. He left to see what it is like to be a small fish in a big pond. They didn't want to. He left and he came back a different person than the Jack Stone when he left. They were afraid to.

His old high school buddies that still lived in Grayville detected that he was a different person than when he left. They saw that he was different in the first few conversations at the Grayville Coffee Shop. They didn't tell him he should never have left. They didn't tell him they were glad to see him. They didn't ask about his wife.

They tested "the waters" to see where he fit on politics, social issues and religion. In Cox County a big question to ask is, "Are you a vet?" Then if you are or are not you got a follow-up question of, "What did you and Jane Fonda do during the Viet Nam war?" A question that really draws a line in the sand is, "Do you think we ought to have a Martin Luther King Jr. Day?"

Then, there is the real defining question as to where you are with the Bible. They make a statement like, "The Bible is the breathed Word of God" and wait for your response. It is not important where you are with Jesus, just the Bible. It is not important to be logical or reasonable. Statements that make no sense are the normal. "When do you think the Rapture is going to be?" "Thank God for the book of Revelation!" "Thank God for Fox News." "Obama was the biggest lying president in history." "Are you one of those liberal assholes that kill babies?" "I have been saved, sorry about you."

Carl Hill was the senior class president and went on to start his own painting business. He also began his own church, the Church of Revelation. He asked Jack if he "knew the Lord." Jack asked him, "What do you mean, 'know' the Lord?" "Have you been saved?" replied Carl. Jack asked him, "From what?" Carl mumbled something in an agitated manner to Stan Williams sitting next to him. There were no more church or Bible related questions.

Among themselves, but so he could hear, they talked about the "damn first same sex marriage in Cox County at Downer Hills golf course. Just a bunch of perverts." He knew he should have never come back home. Things are pretty much the same as they were in the mid-50s.

A. A Pick-up Truck Mentality

There was a "pick-up truck" mentality in town that he had never grown into. He saw no need to put a Confederate Flag plate in the front license frame of his car. He saw no need to join the NRA or obscenely denounce the ACLU. He could not join in on their theology which was bent on condemning the National Council of Churches. Nor did he align himself with their placing the Second Amendment as equal to the Bible. He never shared their homophobic bent toward the LGBTQ persons.

It was very hard to get used to their nonchalant use of the N word. Jack came to know it as the most offensive and abusive expression possible when referring to a black person. Every time he heard it he thought of his black friends and colleagues back in Illinois. He just saw two of his best friends, Abe Woods and Bobby Martin, when they met last year for their sixtieth reunion of the 1959 Cotton Bowl team. To even think of the N word around them would be grossly offensive. The N word was never even thought of in his past sixty-five years. Now, in Grayville, it is as common as "Can I get you a beer?"

He started going to Glider's downtown for his coffee. Then one day he heard mentioned all the "left-wing-liberal-democrats that are ruining the country with their socialism, lies, and bull-shit." His friends around the coffee table talked about how Trump could do so much more if he didn't have to contend with radical-socialist democrats. When he had the opportunity to interject a thought on current events with some of them, he mentioned that in a democracy there was room and freedom for all kinds of political positions. They told him, "Not around here." At least he was driving a Ford.

Having grown up in the Bible-belt and having "never missed a Sunday," as they say, Jack Stone was very familiar with the theology and level of biblical knowledge of Cox County. They all knew he was a "Reverend" but he dare not say anything of his doctorate received at United Theological Seminary in Dayton, Ohio.

The last time someone brought up the subject of a doctor's degree, one of the men at breakfast told them his minister at the Grayville Four Square

Gospel Tabernacle had his doctorate. "He got it at a mail order place in Tampa for $50.00 and it took him a week to get it. Then, in a way of saying, "Can you top that, Jack?" he was asked, "Did you ever try to get a doctorate?"

Jack went ahead and told them that he too had a doctorate. "Did you get as good a deal as Ralph's minister?" "No, I got mine at United Theological Seminary in Dayton, Ohio, it took me three years, and cost $60,000 dollars." Three of the men laughed out loud and said at the same time, "Shit Jack, you should have gone to Tampa." Everybody had a good laugh.

The unwritten laws against blacks that prejudiced the young minds in the 50s do not prejudice the young minds as much today because the unwritten racist laws are seldom mentioned. There will be some people today who will reminisce and say, "That is the way it used to be" with revered nostalgia. When the more elderly folk of Cox County recount the "way things used to be" there will be a hint of pride or appreciation even though those days perpetuated segregation, prejudice, and hate.

While blacks are now allowed on Main Street, can sit at the counter at Martin's Pharmacy, can be within the city limits when the sun goes down, and can even sit on the main floor of The Rialto Theater, there are still images, words, examples of the ugly head of prejudice and hate being made evident in what people do and say.

There are those who say, "We have made a lot of progress around here. Look at all the changes that have taken place in Cox County and Grayville." Sometimes those comments serve as excuses for latent prejudice and are only lame compliments. They really mean to say, "I wish it could be like it was in the 50s."

B. The Confederate Flag

One example of the way the ugly head of prejudice and hate appear is the way the Confederate Flag is revered and made prominent by some. The day he moved back to Grayville, Jack Stone saw three pick-up trucks with two 2x4 boards anchored on the two back corners of the beds of the pickups with even bigger Confederate flags tied to each board.

The Confederate Flag is considered a treasure by many folk in Cox County as they speak of the heritage it represents, its unique history, and its grand tradition. The Confederate Flag is incredibly significant to the persons of Cox County.

For many folk in the Bible-belt, the Confederate Flag is like the Bible… it is revered, holy, and held as sacred. For many folk the Confederate Flag is held in highest esteem like the Second Amendment.

Growing up, many believed the same thing as people entered the mystical realm of romanticism and sacredness of the Confederate cause. There is the image of a young soldier in uniform going off to the unknown with a beautiful long-haired Southern belle waving a fond goodbye with tears in her eyes. Many got caught up in that image which was far from the reality of the real world at that time.

Mooresville, TN just east of Grayville, is home of the Mooresville "Rebels" with the Confederate Flag as its symbol. One year the Confederate Flag was used for the cover of the Mooresville High School yearbook. A few years ago, the student council voted to never use the Confederate Flag as the cover of the yearbook. They also voted to change the mascot name from "Rebels" to the "Eagles."

To say the Confederate Flag brings rich feelings of the sacrifice and commitment of the South's finest, it misses the mark, the truth. The truth is the Confederate Flag does represent a history, a legacy, a tradition. But that history, legacy, tradition is slavery, separation of families, oppression, injustice, hatred, pain, death, the lack of freedom, and the evil of segregation. That is why it has seen its demise from prominent places in the southeast. Its place is no longer a place of highest esteem.

C. Black Lives Matter

Donnie Joe Masters, one of the service reps at White Chevrolet, expressed his prejudice in a more subtle way by saying, "I am sick and tired of hearing about 'Black Lives Matter.'" He didn't say, "Black lives don't matter." He didn't say, "We have spent over three hundred years showing that we don't think black lives matter." He wouldn't go that far, that loud, that emphatic.

"Black Lives Matter" has been a phrase that has a lightning rod effect on people. Especially, if that person has a prejudiced bone is his body. Instead of it being a phrase that generates compassion and understanding, it has been a phrase that divides people. The problem is, the divisiveness already exists, the phrase just ignites the fire. Divisiveness runs deep within and in most cases, never comes to the surface, except when people touch the "nerve." People touch the nerve when they wave the flag of "Black Lives Matter."

When Donnie Joe said he was "sick and tired of hearing 'Black Lives Matter,'" he was shocked when Delbert Sands said, "Bull shit, black lives don't matter." Donnie Joe meant to say the same thing but it would be an indictment against him as being racist. He didn't want to be so blatant, so obvious, so he took the subtle way, the non-committal way of hiding his prejudice and hate. We have ways of hiding our true feelings about race. Some don't, like Delbert Sands.

Leroy Miller, played defensive nose tackle at GHS the same years Jack Stone played, and made the common false accusation of the "Black Lives Matter" movement by saying, "It is nothing more than a movement generated by a bunch of punks. They have no interest in racial justice. They have no interest in civil rights. All they want to do is cause riots and mayhem. All they are after is looting, destroying property, being violent, creating chaos, showing complete disregard for law and order. They all ought to be shot. Like the man said, 'Loot then shoot.'"

Shaun Black Feather, one of the few descendant families of the former Cherokee Nation who settled in Cox County, said, "An unlikely contribution of BLM has been calling attention to the American Indian. No race or ethnic group in the United States can match the horrible treatment the United States has given us. The White Supremist groups would like the black population to be dealt with like we were. Place them in far-removed-isolated areas so they will be with their own. Declare war on them. Show no respect."

Everybody likes Shaun Black Feather. Everybody is sympathetic to the American Indian. The American Indian has never tried to impose their present plight and the way they were treated through politics or bullying or social media on America. Shaun never has. But Shaun was getting fired up. He said, "We have never had a Martin Luther King Jr. Who speaks for us? Who will lead us to demonstrate to call attention to the way we were treated? Nobody."

Shaun said, at one of the earlier coffee conversations, when he stepped out of his quiet mode, "Sam mentioned the other day that some liberal democrats are pushing for reparations being made to the blacks of America. If blacks or anybody is to receive reparations, it ought to be made to the American Indian. You know the familiar cliché 'Give it back to the Indians.'"

Jack Stone thought, "Where has this guy been all this time?"

Jack overheard Thelma Lou Snider, one of the waitresses say, "I ain't gonna watch another pro basketball game because the players have "Black Lives Matter" on the back of their jerseys." Everybody laughed at her comment. Tom Wright said, "Thelma Lou, what if there was just white players?" Thelma Lou shot back, "Black Lives Matter wouldn't get off the ground."

Tom told her, and for all to hear, "There was a time, not so long ago, when the NBA was all white. What do you think about that, Thelma Lou?"

"I think that is a damn good idea."

D. National Football League

Another, not so subtle way of showing our prejudice, is when watching the NFL. The conversation got very heated on this subject. They make mention of the number of blacks on the defensive side of the ball. "My

God, all eleven players on the defensive team are black! And, they even have a black quarterback!" It was as if they were saying, "What the hell is this world coming to?" This comment was not made in a subtle or hidden fashion. It was expressed in words and manner that was pointed, loud, and daring for a counter comment. It was a blatant prejudicial comment. Nobody cared.

E. Pseudo Patriotism

Everyone at coffee this morning was in total agreement when Frank Sampson said, "I am not ever going to watch another NFL game. Those million-dollar athletes kneeling during the National Anthem, showing such disrespect to our National Anthem and Flag. It is a disgrace."

Irene Black, the pastor of the Pleasant Hill United Church of Christ, was sitting in a booth nearby and asked, "What difference does it make if they are millionaires?" She went on to say, as if daring any of the men to tell her "It is none of your business." "The only difference is that they are black. They know what it is like to face a prejudiced attitude. They know what it is like to encounter all the abuse that a black man faces in America."

There are many times we can respond with quotes from the athletes who kneel and none of them do so out of disrespect of the Flag or National Anthem. Calais Campbell, a black defensive end for the Baltimore ravens said, "People only see the action of kneeling. They don't see what is in the heart and mind. We kneel to draw attention and awareness of the injustice that black people receive. I love America. I love the American Flag. I am patriotic. I respect the National Anthem. But I want history to say I acted to bring awareness for Congress to pass the *Justice and Policeman's Act*. God gave me this platform from which to make that point." Other teammates say, "We can't continue as is, we must make changes."

No matter the quotes, no matter how many athletes say kneeling is not to oppose the Flag or National Anthem but to call attention to the injustice that exists, many fans say they still will not watch another NFL game.

The relevant questions are; Don't they want to support the voices against injustice? Don't they want to demonstrate against hate and prejudice? Don't they want to align themselves with "Black Lives Matter?" Don't they want to make a statement against police brutality and the killing of unarmed black men? Not if they have a prejudiced bone in their body.

Rev. Black, not receiving any response from anyone, pulled out a paper from her purse and said, "My seminary, in Dayton, Ohio made this statement in its last newsletter, 'The way of peace is not dispassionate or passive in the face of injustice or deeply held beliefs. The way of peace calls us beyond ourselves, it disturbs deep-seated prejudice or destructive habits and invites us to active discernment.' She put the paper back in her purse and said, "In summary, what the article says is 'Think.'"

Since Rev. Black was speaking so openly and freely, with no hostile rebuttals, the lady sitting with Rev. Black chimed in on the topic. "It is clear why they say they don't want to watch NFL or NBA games anymore. It has to do with 'pseudo-patriotism.' It is like all the politicians wearing that famous and popular flag lapel pin. It makes them look patriotic. Not watching the NFL games because they are reacting to the players kneeling during the playing of the National Anthem? That is a big crock! It all depends on who is playing quarterback that day. And it depends on which two teams are playing." With that comment both ladies got up from their booth and walked out in such a way that one would think they just delivered a lecture.

IV. The New Challenge

Grayville is facing a new challenge. It is not only new but, considering local history, may be an insurmountable challenge. The historic lineage of Grayville and Cox County and their treatment of blacks, the periodic embracement of and attachment to the KKK, being a former Sundown Town, and the place of respect in which Cox County holds the Confederate flag has been confronted and challenged with a critical racial reality. To those factors, we add two more that make an impact; one is blacks never had a presence in athletics at Grayville High School but now they do; the second is it has always been a rarity that blacks lived in the city limits of Grayville but now they do. Grayville High School and Grayville are going to experience a new and unique challenge.

A. Dr. Bokima

Dr. Hiram Bokima and his wife Deloris have three boys. The oldest is Joseph who is a senior at Grayville High School. Samuel, and his twin brother David are juniors at GHS.

Dr. Bokima had developed a solid, reputable, and enduring patient base in Weston, Ohio. His reputation as an unselfish and compassionate community leader was unwavering. He was the team doctor for the Weston High School athletic teams and volunteered as a "doctor-in-house" at the homeless shelter in Columbus two days each month.

The Bokima family attended the Calvary United Methodist Church in Weston, one of the few African American UMC churches in the greater Columbus area. It was at Calvary Church that Dr. Bokima became known for his civil rights work on behalf of the black community of Franklyn County. He and Rev. Clarence Jordan became known as leaders in making sure the black voice was being heard, that the black needs were being met fairly, and that instances of racial intolerance and injustice were being addressed.

Doris Bokima spent most of her time raising the three boys while Hiram was in medical school and as he began his practice in Weston. Doris studied architecture at Temple and worked part-time for the architecture firm in Columbus of Wright and Barber. At six feet two inches, Mrs. Bokima played center for the Temple University women's basketball team.

In Grayville, Mrs. Bokima, who appeared in many musical dramas at Temple, is also a seasoned actor and volunteer in the musical productions at the Community Playhouse. She is a valued volunteer at the Playhouse because of her experience at Temple and her ability to mentor and assist in the training of some of the young talent from Grayville. She especially is credited for the progress and talent of her son David, one of the six foot six twins who is a regular cast member in the musical productions at the Playhouse. David dances, plays three musical instruments, acts, and sings.

B. David and Lisa

It was through the activities of the Playhouse that David became involved in a relationship with Lisa Bennett. Lisa and David have much in common. Both were juniors at GHS, Lisa is the captain of the GHS cheerleaders for the basketball team, she has danced and sang in productions at Community Playhouse. She also plays three instruments, and like David, her parents were former college basketball players.

Lisa and David began to develop a relationship into something more than just friends. He is black and Lisa being white was not an issue with either set of parents. Lisa's fellow cheerleaders also do not make an issue of it. Some students did make an issue of the relationship Lisa had with David.

A Christian youth group in the school, *Warriors for Jesus* took upon themselves to initiate the shunning and targeting of David and Lisa. The *Warriors for Jesus* would place notes in places where David and Lisa would find them. Notes that said, "God's wrath awaits you as you denigrate his word and son, Jesus Christ." One note was placed in an envelope and taped to the door of David's locker. It said, "Unequal's yoked together are an abomination unto the Lord. His fire of hell will consume your soul for eternity. Be saved by the blood of Jesus Christ that you might yet live in His Glory."

Warriors for Jesus gave themselves the responsibility to uphold the Christian virtues for the school. Couples yoked together as a mixed couple were not one of the virtues they fought to uphold. Another virtue they were adamant about was to get rid of women ministers. One of the United Methodist Churches in Cox County had a woman minister. Rev. Louder had a daughter who was a junior at Grayville High School. *Warriors for Jesus* made her life miserable by the constant harassment of following her in the hallway and telling her that her mother was going to go to hell for disobeying the Word of God. They would tell her, "You have got to tell your mother to repent and believe in the breathed Word of God. Otherwise, both of you will experience the fires and pain of hell."

As the GHS basketball team's success became more and more established, and as the unique racial makeup that defined the team was becoming noted throughout the country, David and Lisa's relationship became a factor of interest. Three black players dominating the high school basketball landscape in a historically all white high school basketball program, was an interesting story in itself. And to have one of its star players involved with the white head cheerleader made an interesting story much more intriguing.

That factor raised an interesting question, "Who will the other two black players date?" The school's holiday dance is coming soon. The Valentine's Day dance will be coming soon. What about the prom? How will the dating be structured then? Will David and Lisa blaze the trail by opening the door to future possibilities? Will they lessen the stigma of a "mixed couple?"

Lisa and David, their parents, and most of the school do not make an issue of it. They have been careful not to draw attention to themselves. They do nothing to create conversation or scuttlebutt. They keep their public appearances to a minimum.

In the Bible-belt, a mixed couple not only was defined by the black and white difference, but if one in the couple is Roman Catholic and one is Protestant, it was a mixed couple. In the Bible-belt if one is a church goer and the other a non-church goer, they are a mixed couple. That just could not take place. Rev. Jack Stone was asked to officiate at a wedding at one of the local churches because the pastor would not officiate because the groom was not "saved" or at least not a member of his church.

Lisa's parents were educated, had lived in more progressive communities, had relationships that were open to new experiences, and are not confined or afraid of a new social challenge. Their relationship to David was an extension of a solid and meaningful relationship with David's parents, Hiram and Deloris.

C. Opponents Reaction to the Black Three

For the 2020-2021 basketball season at GHS, the Bokima boys are in the starting five of the GHS basketball team. In the first four games of the season, GHS is 4 – 0 in the 3 A Dist 7 class. They average 76 points per game and have allowed the opponents an average of 39 points per game. Joseph Bokima, the six-nine center, is ranked second in the state of Tennessee in scoring with an average of 35 points per game. Joseph's main contribution to the team is the number of blocked shots per game with an average of 13.

The Grayville basketball team has attracted the attention of most sports media outlets throughout the southeastern United States. The popularity of the team has not only been their undefeated record and the margin of winning, but also the unique fact that of the five starters, three are brothers. For many folks, especially around Cox County, the interest and attention to the GHS basketball team, which never had any blacks play basketball in all its history, is centered on the three blacks in the starting lineup. It is also interesting to note that last year, the three Bokima boys led their High School team to the state championship in Ohio.

The three Bokima brothers are excellent basketball players and that is what really draws the attention of so many folks in central Tennessee. But their race also draws attention from the fans. When teams in this part of the state play each other, there never has been any racial issues or problems because no teams had a black player. But when the first four teams played Grayville to start the season, there were instances of cautionary remarks and questions from different community sources.

The police chief of Duncan called the police chief of Grayville to ask if there had been any racial strife since GHS has three blacks starting for their basketball team. He told the Duncan chief there were no problems. He asked, "Why are you asking?" The Duncan chief said he had several phone calls asking if he was going to allow those niggers from Grayville to enter the city limits. He told the Grayville chief that he would make special precautions to try to avert any trouble when GHS came to Duncan for the game. GHS won the game 78 to 33. There was no trouble.

The pastor of Ambrose Independent Bible Fellowship in Ambrose, TN called Coach Montgomery to tell him that several of his church members suggested he not bring the black three to Ambrose for their scheduled game. Coach Montgomery told the minister, "Rev., on road trips we like to leave early from school to have dinner together before the game. Sometimes we have had churches host a dinner for us. It provides us with a real good chance to get acquainted and have fellowship. Would your church ladies like to host the team from Grayville?"

The coach said the minister told him, "I tried to warn you." The minister hung up on him. GHS beat Ambrose 79 to 39 before a packed and standing room only Ambrose crowd. There were no problems.

Two schools that were scheduled long before the 2021 season, cancelled their games with GHS. Both schools cited problems with the lighting and ventilation of their gyms. One of the scheduled games was at GHS.

The third game was against a long-time rival, Morrisville. The only reaction to that scheduled game came from three fathers of three players from Morrisville. The three fathers told the Morrisville coach to tell the GHS coach not to bring the three black players or cancel the game all together. If not, they would not allow their sons to dress for the game. The Morrisville coach told the fathers that if they did not allow their boys to dress for the game with GHS, they would no longer be on the team. The three boys dressed and played and there were no problems while GHS was in Morrisville. GHS won the game 81 to 40.

The fourth game was a game that Coach Montgomery rescheduled of one of the two cancelled games. He scheduled St. Teresa, a Catholic high school in Knoxville. St. Teresa is coached by Tom Dempsey, a friend of Coach Montgomery and former college basketball rival of Dr. Bokima. He is a black coach who played basketball at West Virginia and played against Dr. Bokima when he played at Temple. When coach told Dr. Bokima of the scheduled game and who the coach was, Dr. Bokima said he wouldn't miss this game for anything.

The trip to St. Teresa was one of the longest road trips that GHS had ever made. But, due to the circumstances and the relationship of Dempsey, Montgomery, and Dr. Bokima, the trip was a joint venture of having a good time, renewing valued relationships, and facing a tough opponent. The game was made a big issue by several newspapers and Knoxville TV stations. St. Teresa's gym was packed. Of the four games played so far, this was the toughest. GHS won by the score of 66 to 46.

GHS was scheduled to play Bakersfield as one of the early games of the season. Bakersfield is located near the training facility of the only identifiable extremist militant group in the southeast US that claims ties to Neo-Nazism. When the leadership of the group heard about the makeup of the GHS team, they sent a warning to the principal of Bakersfield High School. The warning stated, "If the black three of Grayville High School came to play the scheduled game, there would be protests and demonstrations that may get out of hand and be harmful to some persons."

That was the essence of the first warning two weeks before the scheduled game. The second warning sent to the principal was also sent to the basketball coach of Bakersfield. The second warning said, "If the scheduled game with Grayville High School is not canceled in two days, one of your starting five will have an injury."

To add a sense of credibility to the warnings, several members of the Neo-Nazi group called WMP (White Mega Power), patrolled the main street of Bakersfield dressed in military garb and armed with large automatic rifles. It was if they were saying, "There will be no threat of blacks interrupting our traditional pattern of living and display of sports as we have known it to be all these years."

The principal of Bakersfield High School called the principal of GHS, Mr. Thomas Gammon, to convey to him the threats made by the WMP and the resultant board of education decision to cancel the GHS game. He told Mr. Gammons that the White Mega Power group has so far refrained from any demonstration that could bring harm or physical damage to Bakersfield persons or property. He further added that "At this time the WMP has not been a problem to our community, and until we can determine legal action to limit their presence, we will have to cancel the Grayville basketball game to avoid any challenge or risk to the safety of our players and yours and individuals in our community."

It was difficult for Mr. Gammon to discuss politics and political policy on the phone but he did tell the principal of Bakersfield, "In a democracy we shouldn't have to have our freedoms usurped by any group or individual. I am sorry you have made this decision. Once the WMP knows you have let them dictate what will go on at the high school, what will be their next demand? I hope you haven't given them a green light to exercise more control. Good luck."

At the fifth game, against Shelby, TV, radio, and several sporting news agencies from all over the country were evident in the parking lot with TV and radio apparatus and vans. Representatives from several different news services came from distant markets to see the GHS basketball team. The gymnasium at the Grayville High School was filling up fast. The black three play for a school which never had a black basketball player in the history of the school. Now the black three have taken over as the spectacle of high school basketball in the country, not just TN.

A. Gary Patterson

Even though the different schools had problems with the black players from Grayville High School, there were students in GHS who could not pass up the opportunity to blurt out currish and disdainful words of hate and contempt at one of the four black students who often got harassed as he walked the hallways of GHS. He is a sophomore and has lived in Grayville since 2018 when he and his mom moved from Iowa.

Gary Patterson's mom is white and is from a Quaker family with roots in academia circles in Pennsylvania. Her father was a former colleague of Dr. Elton Trueblood the great contemporary Quaker theologian and writer. Her father was on the staff and taught theology at Earlham College in Richmond, Indiana with Dr. Trueblood. Gary's mother's parents are retired and live in Fairfield Glade.

Mrs. Patterson taught nursing at William Penn University in Oskaloosa, Iowa, a Quaker university and one of the most respected smaller universities in the United States. Gary's father was black and died of leukemia when Gary was in the seventh grade.

Gary, his mother, and grandparents attend the Quaker Meeting in Pleasant Hill held at the library in Fisher House. Gary's mother is the director of nursing at the Grayville Medical Center. They moved to Tennessee to be with her aging parents as her mother is in the early stages of Alzheimer's.

Gary is a friend of Lisa Bennett and David Bokima because he too, like Lesa and David is a talented vocal and instrumental musician and thespian who spends a lot of time at the Community Playhouse. He has acted alongside Lisa and David on many productions at the Community Playhouse. He plans to attend Earlham College in Richmond, Indiana and study musical drama.

Gary is a good friend also of David's brother Samuel through a very unusual circumstance. Gary is 5 feet 7 inches tall and weighs 130lbs. He is a light complexion black kid with sharp features and wears his hair in a unique pony-tail-bob. He has been bullied, intimidated, harassed, and physically abused by some of the insecure "jocks" in the school because they have labeled Gary as gay. His quietness and non-aggressive demeanor along with his drama and musical talent have given some of the homophobic macho athletes a license to harass and verbally abuse him. But with the new principal at GHS, Gary has found an ally in the emphasis against bullying.

Wednesday before the Friday night Shelby game, Gary had the occasion to make the acquaintance of Samuel Bokima. During school that Wednesday, just after lunch, Gary picked up some books from his locker. He shut the door to his locker and as he was about to lock it, two boys, both much bigger than him, shoved him hard against his locker, grabbed his hair and slammed his face against the locker and started calling him names. They called him "Gary the fairy" and "faggot." To make the most derisive epitaph, they got close and yelled into his ear, "you no good f----N---r." Then they proceeded to knock the books from his arms and punched him in the stomach, hit him in the face repeatedly with their fists, and before he fell to the floor, one of them smashed his face against the locker again causing a great deal of blood to come from his nose. When he fell to the floor, he seemed to be unconscious and one of them kicked him in the side. Several students witnessed the abuse, but no one tried to stop it.

Then along came Samuel Bokima, one of the three new big black male students in school. Samuel is not only six feet six inches tall; he also has a mature physique for a junior in high school. Samuel yelled at the several students standing around, "What is wrong with you people? You are going to just stand there and let these two jerks beat on this little guy?" With that Samuel grabbed one of the thugs and threw him across the hallway where he crashed into the lockers on the other side. As he did so, some of the students who were watching got knocked down when the guy got thrown against the lockers.

Both of the attackers are juniors. One was Charles Jackson, the starting center on the football team. The other bully, who was thrown against the lockers, is Tony Pirello. Tony is captain of the wrestling team and qualified for the state wrestling tournament last year as a sophomore in the 180-pound class.

After he aggressively smashed the one bully against the lockers, Samuel took the other bully and rammed his head against Gary's locker, took his arm and twisted it behind his back, and slammed him against the locker. He told him, "Tell this kid you are sorry." At that time, a teacher came out of his classroom just a few feet away and gave a frantic yell, "What is going on?" Samuel rammed the bully he was holding into the lockers again and then yanked his head to face the teacher and told him, "Tell the teacher what you were doing to this little kid."

Instead of him telling the teacher, Gary spoke up with a bloody split lip, bruised eye, and blood running out of his nose and getting all over his "Go Eagles" T-shirt. "These two guys jumped me and started hitting me. But this guy, (pointing to Samuel) stepped in. He saved me from getting beat up real bad."

The teacher said, "It looks like you still got beat up really bad." The teacher said to a student standing nearby, "Go to my room and get in my middle desk drawer and get the towel that is there. This young man needs the towel to control the bleeding." Then he tells Gary, "After we stop the bleeding you go down to the nurse's office. And would you go with him?" as he nodded to Samuel. I will make sure you get written excuses for the classes you will miss. I will have to drag these two to the principal's office because I don't believe they can walk."

That was the start of a solid and meaningful relationship between Gary and Samuel. As they were walking down the hall to the nurse's office, Gary said, through the towel he was holding against his face, "My name is Gary Patterson. Who are you?"

"My name is Samuel Bokima. My brothers and I are new here in Grayville."

"I am really glad that you are so big. You took care of those bullies. How tall are you?"

"6'6" but my older brother is 6'9" and my twin brother is also 6'6.""

"My God, you ought to be basketball players!"

"We are."

When they arrived at the nurse's office, Mrs. Hurt took one look at Gary and said, "What happened to you?"

Samuel said, "Two bullies, much bigger than him, beat him up. It happened just down the hallway."

Gary said, "And Sam here broke it up or I would have really been broken up."

Mrs. Hurt said, "Well, Gary, I am afraid you did get broken up. I have seen many broken noses in my life, and you have a good one." As she attempted to stop the bleeding, she confirmed that it was indeed a broken nose.

"We are going to have to get your nose taken care of and that busted lip will have to have some stitches. I will call your parents and they can take you to the emergency room."

Gary told her that he doesn't have a dad and his mom works at the hospital and it would be almost impossible to get her to come to the school to pick him up. Gary said, "I will just get a cab to take me to the hospital."

Samuel asked the nurse, "Why can't I just take him to Dr. Bokima's office? He could get in right away and have it taken care of."

"I'm afraid going to a doctor's office would be too long a wait. Gary has to get stiches in his lip soon. He is bleeding too much for a long wait. And he has a cut below his left ear lobe, and it is bleeding too."

Samuel said, "Dr. Bokima is my dad and I am sure he will see Gary right away. If he doesn't, his assistant will."

"Your dad is Dr. Bokima? I know him well. He has been very helpful to the school and the students we have sent him. He is very accommodating. Yes, you take Gary to your dad's office."

"Will I need you to write an excuse for the classes I am missing this afternoon?

"I will be glad to give you and Gary excuses. I will also stop in the principal's office and report to him what has taken place and where you are taking Gary. I want him to know what those two bullies did to Gary. He is going to have to do something about it. I will see to that."

"Gary was beaten up right outside a classroom. The teacher came out in the hallway after I stopped them from beating Gary. He said he would take the two guys to the office. So, they may still be down there when you get there. I will take Gary to my car and we will leave right away."

She reached into a small freezer, "Before you leave, take this ice pack. Gary, make sure you keep it on the left side of your face. Your eye is starting to swell shut and that ear needs attention too."

It didn't take long to get to Dr. Bokima's office. As they went in, there were patients waiting in the waiting room. They all saw the swollen eye, the ice pack, bloody face, cut lip, bloody ear and a white towel covering a large portion of his face turned red with blood. As the boys walked in, the nursed entered the waiting room to call a patient. She saw Samuel and did a double take on Gary, "Oh my, Mrs. Lewis, you are next, but do you mind if I take this young man in right now?" Mrs. Lewis, seated near the receptionist window, with a look of shock, said, "By all means, this young man looks like he needs help right away." "Samuel, bring your friend in. I will get your dad."

Samuel and Gary both told Mrs. Lewis, "Thanks."

As the nurse pointed them to an examination room, Samuel heard the nurse tell his dad, "Doctor, your son Samuel is here in room three. He needs to see you." Then the nurse joined them and began to tend to Gary's wounds. She began to treat the cut lip and checked his eye which had swollen almost shut.

Soon, Dr. Bokima entered the room and began to put the picture together of what had happened. Samuel explained everything while Dr. Bokima began to care for Gary's broken nose. After about thirty minutes, the nose was set, the lip was stitched, the ear was stitched, a patch was placed over the eye to keep it from being further irritated, and an ice pack was held by Gary to the side of his face and swollen eye.

The nurse came back into the room and Dr. Bokima told her, "Tell Ruth (the secretary/receptionist) to call the school and talk to the principal. Tell her to identify herself and the extent of Gary Patterson's injuries and the reason for the injuries. Tell the principal that I will see to it that he receives a full medical report. Tell him that as a parent of three African American boys I am very concerned about the safety and security in his school for the black students."

Then, Dr. Bokima said, "Samuel, thanks for coming to Gary's rescue. Gary, I am sure you could have handled the situations just fine, but it was nice to have Samuel show up anyhow. Now you go home, lay down, and get some rest. Put an ice pack on that lip and eye." "In fact," he said with a grin, "put ice on your whole face!"

Gary said, "I can't do that just now. I have a rehearsal at the Playhouse at seven and I have to be there. I have a lead part in the next production. So, I was going to hang around school until time to go to the playhouse. My mom is working until midnight."

Dr. Bokima asked Gary, "What is the production you are rehearsing for? Tonight my son is also rehearsing for an upcoming production."

"'*The Winds of March*' is the name of the production. Who is your son?"

Samuel interrupted and said, "Remember that I told you about my twin brother who is also 6'6"? Well, he is also active at the Playhouse. His name is David."

"I know David!"

Dr. Bokima told Samuel, "Samuel, I am putting you in charge of Gary. Maybe he can hang out at practice and then take him home with you. You can all get a bite to eat before everyone has to go to rehearsal. Also, try to get some ice on Gary's face."

Dr. Bokima asked him where his mother works. "She is the director of nursing at the hospital."

"Norma Patterson?" "Yes."

"I know Mrs. Patterson. She has helped with a few of my patients."

Right after practice, all the boys, including Gary, went to the Bokima home to get a quick bite to eat. Then David and Gary went to rehearsal. Gary's participation in the rehearsal would not be a smooth or enjoyable experience. He could only see out of one eye; his lip was numb and swollen, and the pain in his nose was beginning to become constant and throbbing. But, as David encouraged him, "The show must go on!"

B. The Six White Players

Before the start of the fifth game with Shelby, the six white players who were the nucleus of the team last year, were in the locker room changing into their uniforms. One of the players was Chad Morgan, a senior. Last year Chad, who is six feet tall, was the starting guard and was the leading scorer. He is the son of the most well-known minister in town, Rev. Dr. Talbert Morgan.

Rev. Morgan has been the pastor of Faith Baptist Church, the largest church in the area, for twelve years.

Chad does not fit the typical "preacher's kid" stereotype in that he does not have the reputation in school as a problem or troublemaker. He is an excellent student ranking third in a class of two hundred eighty. Upon graduation he is expected to earn an academic scholarship to Belmont University, in Nashville. He has also been invited to be a walk-on with the Belmont University basketball team.

Chad is an Eagle Scout and has been a volunteer at the Hope for Life Homeless Shelter. At the homeless shelter he helps twice a week with the evening meals after the basketball season. Members of his father's church and the faculty and staff at Grayville High School consider Chad a model student. Chad and his father were among the first persons from Grayville to welcome Dr. Bokima and his family when they first moved to town..

A few Sundays ago, as Chad was walking down the hallway at church, two junior high boys passed him and called him "pressy pants." At first, that upset Chad. Then he began to think about the image he has been projecting.

Chad told his girlfriend, "I really don't like the image that I have as a senior in high school. The image that was placed on me was OK when I was in junior high, but I am too uncomfortable with it now. I come off a being a 'sissy,' or 'goody two-shoes.' It seems I have two lives. One is within the church and the other when I am outside the church. I have to find out which is me."

Another white player is Tom Bledsoe, also a senior. Tom is an average student and an average basketball player. What Tom lacks in basketball skills he makes up with his strong leadership and motivational skills. Last year he was a valuable team player because he seemed to make the team perform at its best. At six feet two inches tall, he was a steady rebounder and contributed to scoring constantly when the team needed a boost. He regularly active in the youth fellowship of the Trinity United Methodist Church in Grayville. It is in the youth program of the church where he also exhibits his leadership skills.

Tom is a handsome kid and is popular with students from all backgrounds, regardless of economic status or social standing. He is a very compassionate young man, and that characteristic is evident in his spending time as a volunteer at the Cox County Animal Shelter.

Although he is an average student, he is one of the more responsible seniors and is well respected by the teachers and his fellow classmates. The family could be a centerfold for the "perfect family" because his mother and father symbolize the model for the middle-class family. They are good protestant church goers, moderate in their political interests, and don't tend toward straying from "the box."

Tom is a good friend of Chad's and they have shared their mutual frustration of being placed with a certain image. Tom has talked about the "box" in which he and his family have been placed. "Sometimes I just want to say, 'screw the church.' It seems I spend more time there than at home. And that just makes my image more make-believe. Sometimes I don't know who the hell I am."

Mack Diles is another senior and was instrumental in the team's success of last season. Mack played football his first three years at GHS but made the decision to concentrate on basketball his last year of high school. His size of five feet ten inches and a solid two hundred pounds made him ideal for the good high school football player he was. But, in the last three games last season, he played in spite of a knee injury. After several off-season visits and therapy sessions with a sports medicine specialist, he was told physical contact to the knee will create permanent damage. So, the decision to concentrate on basketball.

His speed and quickness are very evident on the basketball court as he is outstanding defensively. His hustle and drive are very contagious to the rest of his teammates. He is probably the best all-around athlete on the team.

Mack would often be seen with his dad who is on disability after having a serious back injury while working at the Crab Orchard Stone Quarry. His dad is a graduate of Grayville High School. The Diles are members of the Church of God in Crab Orchard. His mother is a department manager at Cox County Community Co Op.

Mack is the only white basketball player who drives a pickup truck. He is built like his dad, muscular, and has a flat-top haircut like his dad. Although his dad is on disability, they spend a lot of time hunting as both own several shotguns and hunting gear. Mack will often be seen wearing fatigues and boots at school as if he was anticipating his dad saying, "Let's go out and see if we can get some pheasants."

Ronnie Miller is a junior and one of the smaller players on the team. He is a bit shorter than Mack Diles at five feet nine inches. But Ronnie Miller is another all-around athlete on the team. He, like Mack, is a two-sport athlete at GHS. His other sport is baseball, and his position is pitcher. He had a 9 – 4 record as a sophomore but toward the end of the season he developed a curve ball which helped him win the last four games he pitched. The tennis coach and the golf coach have both tried to get him to participate in their sports.

Ronnie's dad left his mom when Ronnie was one year old. He has never seen his father and never heard from him. His mother, Linda Miller, is a nurse's aide at the Remington Senior Facility. She is from Nashville and lived in government housing with her mother and Ronnie in a mostly black complex. Ronnie is one of the few students at Grayville High School that has any exposure or experience with blacks.

Ronnie's world revolves around his mom. He has few friends outside his involvement in sports. His closest friend is Tony Pirello, the captain of the wrestling team. Ronnie is not involved in a church, he has no girlfriend, has no car, and seldom is seen apart from his mom. He has not talked much about his plans or vision for his future. He seems to be very tied to his mom. He seldom has talked about plans after high school.

Wes Carter is a senior and was the center on last year's team. He stands six three and in most of the games last year was the tallest player on the floor. Wes is not a good student. He is not dumb, as he says, "I just don't have time for studies." He says the only book he has ever read was the *Gene Autrey Story* when he was in the sixth grade.

Wes spends a lot of his time bringing up trivial issues and making them sound like major topics of discussion of importance. He adds to this put-on humor by acting like he is a learned person on those topics. He might ask the question, "How do they shell the Brazilian nuts to make them come out in such good pieces?" Then he proceeds to explain in detail how it is done when he has no idea. His creative thinking is always interesting as he draws people into his phantasy world. He is always thinking what to do to play a prank on someone. His friends often say that "Wes doesn't have a serious bone in his body."

Wes is very popular with his classmates. His greatest joy is making people laugh. Last year he was "The Man" on the basketball team. It was during games that he would really "shine." He was the focus of activity on the court but the black three took over that role. And Wes misses being the focus of activity.

The final white player is Mark Evans. Last year Mark was one of the top three-point shooters in Tennessee high school basketball. Mark is the least one on the team that fits the image of an athlete. It is not his size that does not fit the image. Mark stands at six feet. He has an excellent build for a junior in high school.

The way he stands out from the athletic image has to do with his interests. On the team bus after an away game, while it is dark, Mark will often be using a flashlight to read a book. If he is not reading a book, he has his headphones on to listen to classical music.

Having a black family move into Grayville was an event that really perked his interest. Coming from a very culturally and racially diverse school in Cincinnati, he was used to and familiar with racial diversity. His interest in the Bokima family moving to Grayville was hopeful and a "wait and see" moment.

Mark is labeled as a scholar and gentleman. In addition to being an athlete he also has the talent and interest in music, dancing, singing, and acting. He has been an active participant at the Community Playhouse since the Evans family moved here from Cincinnati, Ohio in 2016. He plays the trumpet and drums, as well as sing, dance, and act.

With the coming of the Bokima family, Mark has become best of friends with David, one of the twins, who also is an active participant at the Community Playhouse. They both have been featured actors and musicians in several music productions.

C. The Racist Comments

As the six white players were getting dressed for the game, they were having casual conversation among themselves. The Bokima brothers entered the locker room and overheard their white teammates talking. The casual conversation they heard took on a more serious tone. The black three realized the subject of their conversation was them. They stopped while behind a row of lockers and listened. The comments were denigrating and belittling. The black three were shocked and surprised as the comments became more degrading and caustic. They couldn't make out who said it, but someone said, in response to another comment, "That's just like a bunch of niggers."

They made out the voice of the Baptist preacher's kid, Chad when he said, "This town and school was a lot better off before those black assholes came to town." Most everything that was being said came out clear except when their voices trailed off to a mumble. The Bokima boys began to listen carefully to the comments being made. They heard Chad continue. "They have taken over basketball and now they think they are going to take over the whole damn town." They could hear Chad mumble something under his breath, "Just like a ...." But they couldn't hear what he said, but they imagined.

The white players continued their diatribe. Samuel recognized Tom Bledsoe's voice, "We need to have things like they used to be. This is all bullshit. I don't know how, but somehow, they need to know they are not welcome here. We never invited them here."

Samuel was taking it all in and looked up at his brothers and mouthed quietly, "This is sick."

The black three continued to be still and did not move. They listened to more. They couldn't believe what was being said about them....by their own teammates! They were surprised and shocked! They never realized the white players had any such feelings about them.

Mack Diles said, "They don't belong here. Why in the hell did they move here, anyway? My daddy said 'niggers don't belong here.' When they moved in, my daddy said nothing but bad stuff will happen. They got coach sucked into this whole thing. I hate to say it, but he has become a nigger lover."

Ronnie Miller said, "This kind of talk makes me feel uncomfortable. I don't think we should be talking like this. They are our teammates. What if someone hears us?"

"To hell with it, it is a free country." None of the Bokima boys could make out who said that.

As the Bokima boys listened, they got more discouraged. They felt less like playing basketball even with a gym full of fans. What thoughts do all these comments create in the minds of black teenagers hearing such horrible non-thinking-lightening-rod rhetoric about them?

They made out Wes's voice. He said, "I told you that when they moved in, nobody knows what to expect. This is the first time I ever heard of black people living in Grayville. I wish we could just play basketball. We sure as hell don't want the coach to hear us talk like this."

The sixth white player, Mark, never said a word during all the exchange the other white players made. He seemed to be listening at a distance. Was he the only mature one? Was he the only one with a moral bone in his body?

Mark was already dressed in his uniform. He looked like he was anxious to play basketball. He walked to the middle of the other players and said, "You know that David and I are good friends. I am really sorry to hear you talk about him and his brothers like you have. Is it because they are black? David is not a nigger. His brothers are not either. In fact, I have never heard that word used in my whole life, until tonight, just now." With that Mark walked over to the water cooler and just stood there. Everyone was quiet. Where were the black three?

Joseph had heard enough. He gestured for his brothers to back up and silently leave the locker room. Trying to be nonchalant and not raise suspicions from fans entering the gym and walking through the parking lot, they made it to their mom's SUV and drove away. On their way home, Joseph called his dad. Their dad and mom were just then getting into the car in the garage to come to the game. Joseph told his dad and mom not to come to the game because they were coming home. "Dad, we need to talk."

D. At the Bokima Home

On the way home, the three brothers did not say a word. Disappointment and anger took the place of any conversation. Joseph, driving his mom's

Honda CRV, spoke for all of them as he whispered to himself over and over, "I can't believe this shit."

Their mom and dad heard them pull into the driveway. Dr. Bokima said to his wife, "The most talked about players in the country left a packed gym full of excited fans with news reporters rushing around for news bits." To no one in particular he raised the question, "What the hell happened tonight?"

After they parked the car, they entered the house. No one said anything. The parents just stood there looking at them for any sign that would help them make sense of the quandary. Mrs. Bokima broke through the discomfort as the boys made their way into the house by asking if everyone wanted to sit in the living room or gather in the kitchen. Samuel led the way to the kitchen and the rest followed still not saying a word. Samuel opened the refrigerator door, took out a Dr. Pepper and said, "You won't believe what happened tonight."

Dr. Bokima asked, "OK, who is going to fill us in on what has happened? Why are you here and not at the gym?" David made a suggestion, "Since Joseph is the oldest, he should start the discussion. We will chime in when we need to add something."

Joseph spoke up and began at the beginning about them walking into the locker room and being confronted with all the shocking words and name calling about them. He said, "They even used the nigger word to describe us." David spoke up next and was quick to add, "They didn't know we were in the locker room. They didn't know we overheard every word. But we didn't say or do anything. When we heard enough of that crap, we left very quietly. We walked past the crowd as they were coming into the gym. They didn't suspect anything, they just said stuff like, 'Good luck tonight guys. We are looking forward to seeing the game. We know you will do good.' Then we got in the car and came home. We're sure that some of the fans who saw us drive off are wondering what's going on."

David continued, but he was trying to use the right words to describe the language the players used. "After hearing all the terrible things they said about us, none of us felt like playing basketball. Not with them. Not tonight. Not ever! As far as I am concerned, the basketball season is over for me."

Samuel added, "If I ever play basketball at Grayville High School again, there will have to be some really big changes and not only in who the players are. I am not talking just about those guys in the locker room. I am talking about all the others in this town that agree with them, and I am sure there are some. But, considering all the rotten things said about us tonight, it is going to take a long time and a lot of changes to make things right."

Joseph was quick to add, "Three guys did most of the talking. Ronnie said he felt uncomfortable with this kind of talk. Wes didn't say anything really bad. Mark told them he was surprised they talked about us like they did. He told them, "David is not a N . None of his brothers are. He said, 'In fact, I never heard the Nword until just now.' I know he felt very uncomfortable hearing all the stuff that was said."

V. The Issue

Back in the locker room at the gym the players who had made the racist comments about the black three had no idea they had been overheard by the Bokima boys. As they finished putting on their uniforms they began to settle down. In walked the basketball coach, Mike Montgomery.

A. Where Are the Black Three?

He said, "Someone just told me that they saw Joseph and his brothers walking through the parking lot. They said they got in a car and left. Do you know why?"

The white players looked at each other. Their eyes gave a look of shock and surprise. They were stunned by what the coach said. They knew exactly why the black three left. Mack quietly said, "Oh shit."

Tom said, "Oh shit is right. The whole damn town is going to find out."

They hoped the shocked look would be interpreted as being shocked that the black three left like they did. Tom feigned confusion, "Why would they leave? This is one of the biggest games and certainly by far the biggest crowd this town has ever seen."

Chad chimed in, "It doesn't make sense. Maybe they forgot something. Or maybe one of them got sick and they had to take him home." He tried to convey complete surprise and confusion on the question of where the guys went. Mark, Ronnie, and Wes who did not say anything about the black players, did not offer any word as to the whereabouts of the three players. They just feigned being confused and perplexed by the turn of events.

Coach Montgomery said, "Well, we have a game to play and we have a big crowd that came to see us play. We will go ahead and warm-up and see what happens. Hopefully, the boys will show up." With that, the six players lined up and jogged out onto the floor. The crowd erupted in applause and cheers. The crowd expected to see the black three lead them out onto the floor and when they didn't the applause and cheering tailed off. One could see people in the crowd looking at each other with a big question mark on their faces. "Where are the black three?"

Each of the guys warming up were trying their best to look like they were really into the warm-ups. But each one knew what had happened to the black three and why. They went through the warm-ups with no expressions on their faces, hoping to hide the guilt they felt and fear of what people will say after they find out why the black three left.

They knew they were in deep trouble and there was no way to deny what happened or make excuses. Even as they were active physically during the warm-ups, they experienced a great deal of anxiety wondering what reaction the coach would have once he found out why the Bokima brothers left. They wanted the warm-ups to end and get out from under the scrutiny they felt from the fans even though the fans knew nothing of the truth.

They wanted to get out of the gym! They didn't want to be around the coach, especially when he finds out why the Bokima brothers left.

While the six white players were going through the drills of warming up, Lisa was leading the crowd in cheering the team as the team came onto the floor. But, like everyone else, she didn't see David and his two brothers. She became very upset. She tried to lead the cheerleaders in choreographing the crowd, but she kept looking over her shoulder to see if David was going to appear. She looked up in the stands to where her parents were seated to see if they could give any sign of knowledge of what was going on. No one knew anything. There was no one for her to grab and ask, "OK, what is going on?"

After the short time when the teams took the floor for the warm-ups, Coach Montgomery who had been standing near the sideline, had the players return to the locker room. All the time he stood on the sideline watching his team, people kept eyeing him for some hint as to why something was amiss. He tried to show a demeanor of being stoic and in charge when he felt things were crumbling under his feet. He waited a while before he went to the locker room hoping that he would see the three boys return to the gym.

After time spend in the warm-ups, there was still no idea of where the black three were. There was a heavy mood of confusion and a long litany of unsettled questions. That confusion among the crowd grew even more as Shelby continued their warm-ups.

As they settled in the locker room, there was a general mood of guilt that seemed to hang over the players for being responsible for creating a very disappointing experience for a lot of people. They realized the Bokima brothers must feel disappointment, disillusioned with their teammates, and even abused. Chad quietly spoke for everyone as they took a seat on the benches, "This is a perfect case of the horrible pain of prejudice. At least I am beginning to feel the pain."

They could not escape the reality of the stands being filled with the biggest crowd ever at Grayville while under a thick cloud of intensity around the question of "Where are the black three?" The question would not go away, the predicament they were in would not go away. They wished they could make a quick exit from the locker room without being detected by anybody.

Before the coach came back to the locker room, Chad gathered everybody around him. He spoke in a quiet voice with a heavy statement to the players. "What we have said and done here is going to make the news, big time! We have attracted a lot of attention and publicity because of our winning record. But now, we are going to get a different kind of publicity. We are going to be made out as irresponsible red-neck racists. Grayville is going to be made out as the new "Clinton, TN" and "Selma," and "Little Rock," and "Birmingham." The country will identify us as the new faces of hate, prejudice and bigotry. Six white basketball players at Grayville, TN high school clearly defined the lines of hate and evil. We really screwed up." Mark was quick to respond with a correction to Chad's comment when he said, "Three white basketball players."

B. Coach Calls Dr. Bokima

When the coach entered the locker room there was no conversation among the players. Everyone kept to themselves. They looked down at the floor. They breathed quietly. A cough was stifled. No one reached for the water bottles. No one moved. No one raised his head or looked toward the coach. No one wanted to make eye contact with him. The only movement was Coach Montgomery as he walked into the locker room. He had his phone out. He said, "I am going to call Dr. Bokima to see what happened to the boys."

Lisa could not stand the anxiety, the uncertainty. She thought to herself, this is not like David. He is the most responsible boy I have ever met. Something terrible has happened for this to be going on. Is it him who is sick or in trouble? After each cheer she looked up to her parents for some sign of an answer. She saw nothing but confused looks on their faces. Amidst the cheering she could detect the crowd in great dismay as if to ask, "Why weren't the black three in pre-game warm-ups?"

Lisa couldn't stand the anxiety any longer. She left the other cheerleaders, ran out of the gym and went to her locker down the hallway and got her phone. She called David. He had his phone in his hand expecting Lisa to call him and he expected her to be upset because it was about game time, and they weren't there.

"David, are you OK? Where are you? What has happened?" David told her, "Just relax. We are all OK. Here is what happened." Then he told Lisa everything that was said and who said it. While David was on the phone to Lisa, Dr. Bokima's phone rang. When his phone rang, everyone stopped talking and what they were doing and became quiet. Everyone expected a phone call to one of them from someone at the gym. They all expected it to be the coach. It was Coach Montgomery. David put Lisa on speaker. They both were going to listen to what Dr. Bokima was going to say to the coach.

When the coach walked to the other side of the locker room to call Dr. Bokima, the players became quiet and dead serious. They were tuned in to what reaction the coach was going to have. They anticipated the worse.

As he stood in the kitchen with the phone in his hand, Dr. Bokima began explaining to the coach what had happened and why the boys left the gym. He told the coach which player said what. Although the turn of events was very unsettling, he did not express any anger. He chose his words well so as not to convey or sound like he was going to insist the coach take some drastic action. He wanted to stay away from any words or tone that pointed to a harsh judgment of the players, the school, the coach, or community. Dr. Bokima did not want the coach to think he was out to seek revenge.

He told the coach how surprised he and his wife were of the offensive language used by the boys. He said, "My wife and I have been realistic about the possibilities that we would be the target of hateful words and expressions of prejudice moving into this area. After the boys told us what they had experienced tonight and the words they heard about them, we are surprised that it occurred in this situation with their teammates.

Coach, we are not angry nor are we going to make a big deal of this to the media or insist that the school board take some punitive action. We are just hurt and disappointed, especially for the our sons. We also realize how serious this incident is for you, the school, and community. You can trust us that we will do all we can to keep a lid on what has happened. Right now, we are all experiencing dismay. All we want at this moment is to have some family time to talk it over, especially what this all means to us about living in Grayville. We need to ask the question, what now? What can be done and by whom to correct a wrong that affects us in a very personal way. And we need to pray."

The coach asked if they would mind if he stopped over in a little while. Dr. Bokima said he would be welcomed to come over, that they would all appreciate it. Before Coach Montgomery hung up the phone, he said he had to go back in the gym and announce that the game had been cancelled. "Then, the players are waiting here in the locker room. I told them I want to talk to them which I will do before I come over. I have no idea what might result from that conversation. I have no idea what to expect. After that, I have to talk to some of the parents and fans and some of the television reporters who are waiting outside the locker room wanting to know what has happened." After Dr. Bokima hung up the phone, the room became quiet.

David broke the silence. He seemed to be dwelling more over the past proceedings than the others. He told everyone, "I am really concerned, worried, and uncertain about what is going to be the attitude toward us now. How will this affect our presence in school? When we walked away from the game did that jeopardize our relationship to the students, fans, and school administrators? Will the people understand? Will they show empathy? Will they turn against us? Will we be labeled as troublemakers?"

C. Reactions of the Black Three

Joseph said, without waiting for his dad to speak about the phone call from the coach, "I have made up my mind. I am going to find out about the possibility of transferring to Caseyville because I want to get out of this cess-pool. I want to play basketball."

His brother Samuel said, "I am staying. Nobody is going to use name calling to intimidate me. I am going to play basketball here whether they like it or not. I am going to show these people I am the best basketball player they ever saw in Grayville. I am going to show everybody who has a prejudiced bone, that I am somebody, I am not going away because I have every right to be here. I am going to show them all that I am not just a basketball player, but a special somebody."

Samuel's twin brother, David, spoke again, "I am staying too. I am going to show everybody what kind of person I am. I am a good basketball player, but they are going to see that I can do lots of other things too. They may try but they will never get rid of me. No ignorant prejudiced person is going to use their hate to drive me out of town. Any ignorant prejudiced person better not try to drive me out of school. Nobody should ever try to keep me from doing what I want to do. I am staying and people are going to have to accept that."

VI. The Coach Forfeits the Game

After talking on the phone to Dr. Bokima, the coach came back to where the players were seated and told them he was going back in the gym to announce the game has been called off. He said to them, "You stay here. I will be back. We need to talk."

The coach took the mike from the announcer and made this announcement, "Due to circumstances beyond our control, Grayville High School will have to forfeit tonight's game to Shelby. Thank you for coming." With that he left to return to the locker room and the players.

No one suspected that the game would be called off. Everybody suspected the cancellation had to do with the absence of the black three. People still were wondering what happened to them. Whatever it was, why would it cause the cancellation of the game? The fans and players from Shelby, the basketball officials, the principal, and the school board members in attendance couldn't imagine why the game was called off. Something serious must have happened to the black three to have the game called off.

Coach Montgomery had never faced such a perplexing situation. Never had he experienced everything around him to get so unraveled. Never had he experienced something he was responsible for to become so ruined.

A. The Coach

Mike Montgomery graduated from Grayville High School in 1995. Mike was one of the few talented basketball players to come out of GHS. He received a few basketball scholarship offers from smaller colleges in Tennessee. Carson-Newman, Tennessee Tech, Middle Tennessee State, Belmont, University of Tennessee in Chattanooga were some of the more solid offers.

Jack Stone knew Mike and his family very well and he knew of his excellent career as a high scoring guard for Grayville. Stone was going to see if he could pull any strings with his contacts in the Midwest for any additional offers of a college basketball scholarship. The first person he called was a fraternity brother, and good friend, Steve Thompson, who lived in Bloomington, Illinois and was a fireman for the Normal Fire Department. Steve was probably the number one athletic supporter for Illinois State University. He was a good friend of the ISU basketball coach. He attended every home basketball game and some away games, traveling with the team.

The two of them got together in Bloomington and tried to weave a plan to invite Mike Montgomery to consider coming to Illinois State.

Steve approached the head coach at ISU on Mike's behalf. ISU showed some interest and asked for some tapes of Mike playing in a few games. They agreed to invite Mike for a visit. Mike came for a visit and the rest is history.

Mike was physical education major and through Stone's contacts arranged for him to do his student teaching at Champaign Central High School. At Champaign Central his supervisor would be Stan Cabelli the head basketball coach at Central. For over thirty years, Stan Cabelli was one of the winningest high school basketball coaches in the state of Illinois. Studying and learning under Coach Cabelli would be great on Mike's resume.

After a successful experience of student teaching which also included serving as an assistant coach with Cabelli, Mike was invited to join the staff full time at Champaign Central. Following graduation from ISU in 1999 Mike spent three years at Champaign Central teaching physical education and serving as an assistant basketball coach.

With the recommendation from Coach Cabilli, Mike was hired as head basketball coach at Park Manual High School where he coached from 2002 to 2008. As a result of a successful coaching experience at Champaign Central and at Park Manual, Mike became sensitive to and knowledgeable of the black athlete's participation in sports. He became aware of this own social and cultural perspective toward minorities. Like Jack Stone, college exposed Mike to their need to examine their attitudes toward black persons and all minority groups.

After his successful experience at Park Manuel, he was offered the head basketball coaching position at Chicago's St. Joseph High School, one of the most noted and accomplished basketball programs in the state of Illinois. He was at St. Joseph's from 2008 to 2012.

Mike's journey to Illinois and his experience there really prepared him for this new challenging experience in Grayville. He had his attitude toward blacks exposed with all the prejudices that came with it. He learned about diversity. He took on the characteristics of being tolerant and compassionate. He became acquainted with the importance of empathy.

He got rid of a lot of baggage that would keep him from being open and accepting and understanding. With his knowledge of the racial history of Cox County, the present uncertainty of having three black basketball players playing for a school which never had a black basketball player, and his experience as a high school basketball coach with racially mixed teams, he was the right man for the job.

B. The Coach Expresses His Feelings

After he announced the cancellation of the game, the coach returned to where the six players were still waiting in the locker room. For what seemed a long time to the players, he just stood there in front of them, leaning his back against the lockers. He was trying to find the right words to say. Finally, looking in the direction of a couple of the boys, he said, "Can one of you tell me, why?" Then, he shifted his focus on the floor in front of him.

"Can any one of you tell me why such hateful and vitriol talk came from you about your three teammates?" He paused for a moment. "When did you begin to have these feelings? Where have these feelings been hidden? You sure kept them from me. What button was pushed that caused them to come out like they did? Mean spirited. Hateful. Insensitive." After each word, there was a long pause.

He raised the questions rhetorically, looking at no one in particular, not expecting an answer. After each question he would pause for a while to let them fully absorb it. "Do you know what vitriol means? It means making cruel statements toward someone. Cruel! It means harsh insulting language about someone."

There was another long period of silence. He just looked at the floor, not expecting any responses or conversation. "I will tell you how I feel. I feel broken. I am forty-three years old. This evening I feel more disappointed than I have ever felt in my life. Shocked! Sad. Surprised." After each word, there was a pause as he looked at them one at a time. "Never in my life have I experienced anything as terrible and hurtful as this."

"What is bad is that what took place here tonight will have repercussions and fallout all over the country. Not just Grayville! Then a long pause. Not just Cox County! You indicted me. You indicted yourselves. You indicted the school. You indicted Grayville. It makes me raise the question to myself, 'Will I still have the desire to coach after this whole experience has run its course?'

I actually thought you liked each other. Talk about naïve. You had me fooled. I thought we were getting along fine as a team, getting along as individuals. Man was I wrong.

I am sure, that Joseph, Samuel, and David are speechless, dumbfounded. I know they never realized you had these feelings. I never realized you had these feelings. It is very unsettling to me to discover this side of you. I had no idea it existed. You did a job on me!"

With that, he turned and started for the door to talk to some of the parents and many others who were waiting outside the locker room for some word. School administrators and several of the fans also lingered around in the gym and hallway waiting for some word from someone for an explanation. He had to provide some comment to the press and television reporters. He didn't know what to say.

C. Player Confessions

As he started for the door, he turned and said, "There are several people waiting outside the locker room. I have to go and tell them something. I have never experienced anything like this, so I am not sure what to do or say." When he turned away from them and headed toward the door Chad Morgan got up from the bench and with hesitation in his voice, spoke up to get the coach's attention, "Coach, wait, I need to tell you something." Chad looked into the eyes of Coach Montgomery for a moment, not saying a word. It was as if he was struggling to think of what he should say. Finally, Chad was able to say in a halting nervous way, 'I am the one who caused the problem. I am the one who made the derogatory and insulting comments." Chad could hardly be heard. It seemed difficult for each sword to come out. It was as if he was facing the three brothers and trying to explain to them why he used the words he did.

"These other guys are innocent." He nodded his head toward them and then he looked at the coach. "I am the guilty one and whatever the discipline you and the school think I should get, that's the way it should be. I am sure that what was said here will get to my dad. I have created a big problem for him. I have become a big embarrassment to my church. I turned my three teammates against me, guys I really cared about. I failed you." At this point Chad is standing in front of everyone and begins to cry unashamedly. "The greatest hurt to me is that I have been unfaithful to my Lord and Savior Jesus Christ."

As Chad sat down, Wes, probably the one player considered the leader of the six white players, stood up and walked toward coach Montgomery. "Coach, Chad is lying. He is not the only one who caused the problem. I was in on it too. I don't know why. Those three guys are great guys." After a pause he said again, "I could have told everybody to knock off the racist talk, but I didn't. I don't know why. Whatever the consequences are for what I said or didn't say, I deserve." Then, he sat down.

Mack stayed seated and started talking right away in a quiet voice. "That makes three of us. I said some bad things too. They always treated us OK."

At that point Ronnie and Tom go up at the same time and Ronnie spoke first. "I don't know about Tom or anybody else, what was said, was all uncalled for. There was no reason for it. It was very immature and irresponsible." They both stood there facing the coach, not defiantly, but as if they were willing to take a verbal thrashing.

Tom spoke next and said, "It was all stupid talk. It was hateful talk." Then he got very quiet, "There is no place for that kind of talk. Especially, on a basketball team. Especially, this team. Especially from me."

Tom said very slowly, trying to make an emphatic point, "Coach, it is very important that you know that Mark never said a word." Tom walked over to where Mark was sitting, stood behind him, laid both hands on Mark's shoulders and said, "He is the only mature one of us. He is the most responsible one. He never went to the gutter like we did." Here is where Tom spoke with clarity and punctuation. "Please take our word, Mark is innocent. We know that Mark is a good friend of David's and he wouldn't say anything against his friend.

Three of us did the talking and deserve whatever you think we ought to get. Please don't mention Mark's name when you talk about us creating this problem." With that, Tom took his hands off Mark's shoulders and walked toward the coach, "I speak for all three of us, Chad, Tom, and me, we are sorry and we're ashamed. I have no idea where such shit came from. Maybe deep within. Maybe stuff we grew up with. Whatever, it was wrong, and we all confess to it. We will do whatever you say to make things right."

Then he paused and did not say anything. He just stood there as if he was putting something together in his mind. Then he spoke slowly as he said, "I ask Jesus to forgive us. We ask you to forgive us. But we really hope our teammates forgive us."

Tom had a hard time holding back the tears as he sat back down. Mark leaned over and he put his hand on Tom's shoulder and didn't' say anything. Then Mark and everyone else was facing the coach. They had a look of relief on their faces. The worst was over. Admitting to the truth was exceedingly difficult to do. Admitting to the truth meant that now they would face the reactions and judgements of people from all over, not just the local voices.

Those who were guilty had just experienced what most people never have to encounter. They had bared their souls. They had to confess that they had committed a terrible wrong. No one told how wrong it was at the time. They had confessed to participating in one of the most damaging ways of denigrating an individual. No one tried to stop it. They confessed to putting in place one of the most sordid injustices which will designate Grayville as a place on the map of intolerance and prejudice.

As they sat on the benches, Coach Montgomery told them how he appreciated their honesty and their feelings of regret about the way they talked about their black teammates. He also told them, "I have not experienced anything like this. I am not sure of my responsibility in all this. I don't know what the consequences will be. I don't know if the school administration or the school board will take action. If it gets out, it is going to make the news all over. I don't know what the Bokima family will do or say. They have been severely disappointed and hurt."

"Just get dressed and go on home. I will be getting back to you after we have some time to think about all this. I would imagine in the next few days I will be meeting with the school administration. We will wait and see what is decided."

VII. The Coach Speaks to Those Waiting Outside the Locker Room

Coach Montgomery still had to step outside the locker room to talk to those who were waiting. He hesitated as long as he could. What would he tell them? "We have a black/white issue here. We have five boys who made some very racist comments about their black teammates?" or would he repeat what he said when he told the people in the gym that the game had been called off? "Due to circumstances…"

Four parents of the players, the Bledsoe's, Evan's, Carter's, and Mrs. Miller were waiting outside the locker room door to hear what the coach might say. The Diles were not there. Rev. and Mrs. Morgan had briefly spoken to the coach just before the team and coach met in the locker room. The principal and superintendent were also there, as well as four television crews and several newspaper reporters. Some curious fans were also waiting to hear what had happened.

Lisa and her parents were standing around in the hallway off the gym not far from the locker room, with several others from the crowd. Everyone was looking for the answer to the question, "what happened to the black three?"

Earlier, he had told the assistant coach and the manager to go on home. They had come to the locker room soon after the black players left. They were glad to make the exit.

Coach Montgomery stepped out of the locker room into the hallway and met all those who were waiting. He took a deep breath and said to them, "I have never experienced anything like I have experienced tonight. I was not prepared for such a turn of events. I don't know the correct way, the appropriate way, the fair way to handle it. I don't know what or how to explain it to you. You will find out as time goes on. I should probably say that a terrible injustice has taken place. Thoughtless words of disrespect and hate have been made toward our three black players. Those who are guilty showed a complete lack of empathy, compassion, and respect.

"Because this has taken place, Grayville is going to suffer." He repeated it again, "Grayville is going to suffer. We all are going to suffer. Then we have to ask, 'What can we do? What can we do to make things right? What can be done to make changes for the better?'" The coach then became silent. No one made a response. It was as if they understood completely the dilemma the coach was going through. Then he continued, "I don't know what else to say."

Mr. Bledsoe was one of the parents who immediately asked a question of the coach. He asked if his boy Tom was one of the boys that made the derogatory comments about the black three. Coach Montgomery responded to Mr. Bledsoe, "Tom did say some hateful things. As I implied, there were others. But yes, Tom did make some inappropriate hurtful comments. But they all confessed and were very sorry. When they made their comments about Joseph, Samuel, and David they didn't know that the three boys were just arriving and were behind a row of lockers and heard everything. When I confronted them, they were sorry for such behavior. I was impressed by their genuine and sincere honesty and confession. They admitted freely and were ashamed of the things they said. They have a wholehearted desire to reconcile with the black players. So, to each of you parents, don't be too harsh with them."

"They realize there will be repercussion from all this, not only here in Grayville, but all over the country. They realize they really blew it."

"Mr. and Mrs. Evans, I wanted to tell you both, that the players made it a point to tell me that Mark did not say a word. The one exception to all this was Mark, who didn't say anything. They were very emphatic about that. They made sure I knew that Mark Evans was innocent. It was just three of them that said the things that the black players overheard as they came in the locker room. They emphasized the relationship Mark has with David and he would say nothing bad about David or David's brothers."

"Any more questions? If so, don't hesitate to call me. Right now, I am going over to the Bokima home where they are all gathered. I am not sure what they will say or what they think, but I know they are terribly hurt and disappointed."

As he looked at the other parents, he noticed the Carter's standing off to the side. He went over to them and quietly told them, "Wes didn't say any inappropriate comments. He was very responsible."

As he was about to leave, Mrs. Miller said to him, with tears in her eyes, "Please tell Dr. and Mrs. Bokima and the boys, we are terribly sorry. And, that we will do anything we can to make up for this evening's bad experience for them. We feel so badly."

"I will be sure to tell them, and they will be glad to know that." Then the coach came closer to Mrs. Miller and told her, "Ronnie was one of the three who didn't make any derogatory remarks about the Bokima brothers. I want you to know that."

"Thank you for telling me. I am so relieved."

VIII. Gathering at the Bokima Home

After speaking to those who had waited outside the locker room, Coach Montgomery went to his car and headed for the Bokima home. He was going to talk to the Bokimas and their boys.

Lisa called David and told him that she and her parents wanted to come to his house to be there for support and encouragement. She told him, "My dad said that what has happened is going to impact the community in a big way and create news about Grayville to be looked at by the whole country. He said we should be there for you and your family. They need to know that they have our support. Mom and Dad have become friends to your parents, and they feel they should be with them at this time."

David said they would all be welcomed to come over and spend this time with them. He told Lisa, "It is close to being like a funeral here. Everybody feels a big loss. I feel like I stepped in a big dark hole. I will be glad to see you."

A. Mark and David

David called Mark. Mark was leaving the gym to get into his car to go home. David was curious how Mark maneuvered through all the terrible comments made about him and his brothers. He was also curious about the response from the coach. "Where are you right now?" Mark said he was in the car ready to go home.

Mark and David are both juniors. It is Mark's second year on the varsity. He was doing a good job as a sub for David. David was deadly from three-point range. That was also the strong point of Mark's game, the three-point shot. When David was taken out of the game because Grayville was so far ahead in scoring, Mark took his place. However, Mark would fire and continue to build the score from three-point range.

In spite of the color difference, David and Mark found a kind of chemistry that drew them together. They had similar tastes in so many unique ways and enjoyed many of the same things. Both liked to read. Both liked classical music. As far as church figured in the picture, they both liked traditional church music; the organ, choir, traditional hymns, and instruments such as the oboe and flute. Those unique interests are the makings of a special friendship, especially in teenage boys.

Mark had a hard time when his family moved to Grayville four years ago. His dad was transferred by his employer, the Keebler Company, which is a subsidiary of Debbie Bakery. His dad is an engineer and does systems analysis for quality control in production and product development for Debbie Bakery.

They moved from the Sinclair School System in Mercer, Ohio. Sinclair is a large suburban school system just northeast of Cincinnati in the suburb of Mercer. Sinclair is one of the most reputable high schools in the metropolitan area of Cincinnati. It ranks as one of the most productive and accomplished high schools in southwest Ohio. Its main strength is academics. As far as athletics go, it is known for its "mind-sports." Such as soccer, golf, water polo, swimming, volleyball, fencing, and lacrosse.

The student population at Sinclair is very diverse. The student body is not only made up of a significant number of African Americans, but also students of Indian (India), Iranian, Japanese, Korean, and Mexican descent. Mark thrived on this diversity. He developed relationships which enabled him to learn to tolerate, assimilate, respect, and develop the gift of acceptance.

At Sinclair he never encountered the debilitating effect of racism because the many foreign students defused that potential problem. He seldom witnessed the hurtful results of prejudice. He never knew of anyone being left out or neglected. The pockets, clicks, camps, or bands were made up of students of different colors and languages.

When he got to Grayville High School, he saw a different make-up of the clicks, bands, and groups of students. There were no foreign students to band together with white students and no African American students to share time and conversation in a pocket of friends which would include whites.

While at Sinclair, Mark learned the characteristics of the students' attitude toward minority groups. He learned that there were some who had little empathy or ready acceptance of anyone of color. He became familiar with the languages used by some of the foreign students, their behavior, and their values. He believed that is what enabled him to develop tolerance and acceptance of people different than him.

When the Bokima family moved to Grayville, Mark became very skeptical of this new dynamic where three black students who had experienced inclusion and acceptance in their old school would now experience less assimilation and diversity in their new environment. After just the first day of basketball practice, it was obvious to everyone that the black three were tremendous players. They were very skilled in every aspect of the game, and one could see they were well coached. As basketball players, they were dominant because of their experience as state basketball tournament players.

Mark told his mom, "having a black family may be too much for Grayville to handle. Having three black students coming into Grayville High School may be too much for the school to handle. Since the three are very good at basketball, I am not sure if that will be of help to them or just make the situation worse."

David told him to stop over at the house before he went home.

B. Mark and Post-Forfeit

When Mark arrived at the Bokima home, David met him at the door with a smile on his face. "Guess what," he said to Mark, "everyone who went to the game is here," he joked as he gave him a shoulder/chest-bump-hug. He also wanted Mark not to feel uncomfortable since he was privy to all that had happened and all that was said.

When Mark entered the house, Samuel and Joseph came to greet him. They each gave him a bump-hug and asked, "Ok, what did you bring to eat? We are starving here."

As they were walking toward the kitchen, David asked Mark if they could go to the living room and talk. The two of them headed for the living room where they would have a chance to have conversation in a quieter setting. Mark sat on the couch and David pulled up a chair and asked Mark, "What did you think when Chad began to talk about us?"

"First of all, I was really surprised. Here is the son of a Baptist minister talking like he did. I was surprised at the language he used but I was more surprised that he would even speak of you and your brothers with such prejudicial and bigoted language. I was thinking, 'This is a Christian attitude? Don't they teach that this kind of racial talk is not Christ-like?'

But after he finished, I thought 'Surely the better side of Chad will take over and he will come to his senses.' Well, it happened. As coach was about to go to the people waiting outside the locker room, Chad's true colors began to shine. He called to the coach to stop, he wanted to speak to him. He profusely apologized to the coach; he broke down and cried. He felt so ashamed. He told the coach, he was especially sorry for how he let down his Lord and Savior Jesus Christ."

David told him, "I heard you never said a word during the time the other guys talked about us. What was going through your head?"

"One thing kept going through my mind as I heard those guys say all those terrible things. That was, 'This can't be the last word from these guys. Surely, they will come to their senses and realize how stupid they sound. This can't be the last word they utter. There has to be some kind of revelation that they have gone too far.' I just kept that in my mind. What was going on and being said was not like anything I have ever heard from any of them. So, I just put it all on hold and decided to wait it out."

And it happened. When Chad made his confession to the coach, and as he started to cry, everyone else seemed to come to their senses. Practically everyone was in tears. Genuinely sorry and ashamed of themselves. The revelation I was hoping for, was realized. They all went home with their tails up their asses because they were going to get run through the ringers by their parents, basketball fans, students, and friends of you guys. They also knew they were going to be judged by people in other corners of the country. Right now, they are getting the first bit of pain as the ringer starts in on them by their parents. Everybody who gets word of what they said are going to put them through the ringer.

Mrs. Bokima peeked in and said, "We have refreshments in the kitchen. Help yourselves." Mark and David got up and went to join everyone in the kitchen.

While the Bennett and the Bokima families dealt with the cancelled game and the reason why, the boys who made comments about the black three, will have to answer to their parents. For some that will be a problem because some of the parents do not have a tolerance for prejudice or divisive and inflammatory talk. For others, that will not be a significant problem because some of them grew up and absorbed the cultural prejudice of this part of Tennessee.

The coach had arrived before Mark. As Mark entered the kitchen, coach seemed surprised to see him. He set down his cup of coffee and embraced Mark. Nothing was said as they held the embrace and patted each other on the back. One could detect that their emotional response to each other was from the ordeal of the last two hours. The coach said to Mark, and for everyone to hear, "This has been one hell of an evening. And you never made one three-point shot." With that comment everyone laughed; they all needed a good laugh.

Lisa, her parents, Dr. and Mrs. Bokima all came over to Mark and hugged him and said they were glad to see him. Mrs. Bokima went over to the stove and said the pizzas were about to be ready to come out of the oven. Dr. Bokima said, "Whoever doesn't have a drink, check out the refrigerator in the garage and pick one out. If we don't have what you want, tough it out."

STAGE TWO

IX. The White Five at Home After Post-Forfeit

A. Bledsoe at Home After Post-Forfeit

When the Bledsoe's got home after talking to Coach Montgomery, Tom was already there. He was sitting at the kitchen table eating a bowl of tapioca. Mr. Bledsoe came into the kitchen and stood next to the table where Tom was sitting and said, "After the coach and you boys had your talk, he came outside the locker room and talked to us. What the hell was all that bad mouth you guys gave the Bokima boys?" Then he sat down, and Mrs. Bledsoe joined them at the table.

Before Tom could respond to his dad, Mr. Bledsoe continued. "The coach told us what you said and that the Bokima boys overheard you. That is why they left." His became louder and angrier in his tone. "You should have figured that out!" No telling what that family and those three boys think of you and your teammates, and us, as your parents! You boys have really put Grayville on the map! Everyone is going to think we are a bunch of racist red-necks!"

With that, Mr. Bledsoe got up and walked over to the refrigerator. He opened the door and pulled out a can of Coors. Tom, without thinking, in purely an instinctively forgetful moment, asked his dad, "Could I have a drink?" His dad yelled, "No! You've got a lot more explaining to do!"

"I want to know why?" Mr. Bledsoe got louder. "Why the hell all that racist bull-shit?" Mrs. Bledsoe told her husband, "James, take it easy. You don't need to yell. You don't need to cuss. We have a serious issue here, let's try to work it out."

Tom had stopped eating his tapioca when his dad started talking. Now he was just sitting there not saying a word. He began to hold back the tears, put his elbows on the table and his head in his hands. After a while, he said, amidst the sobs, "I said some terrible things. I have lost everything tonight."

His mother said, "What do you mean, you lost everything tonight?"

His dad sat back down at the table.

Tom straightened up. Put his hands in his lap. He tried to look into his mom's eyes but had to wipe back the tears. "Sherri will never speak to me again." Sherri has been his girlfriend for the past year. They both are active in the Trinity United Methodist Church Youth Fellowship. This past summer they went on a church youth mission trip together to the Kentucky mission, Red Bird, a United Methodist mission in Eastern Kentucky. Since they both are seniors, they are recognized as the leaders of the youth group. "It will get out and everyone will know exactly what I said, and she will be done with me as well as everyone in the youth group. The whole church will be done with me."

His dad raised the question again, only this time quieter and in more control. "Why, Tom? Where did all those words come from?"

"I don't know. Others made all kinds of comments. I never heard them talk like that. They never heard me talk like that. For a couple of days, we heard different guys talk that way at school. Seemed like every place we went, people were talking about the three black players. We just got kind of tired of it."

His dad responded, "That's no excuse. In fact, that is a bunch of bull. No matter how much you heard it, it is wrong. What did the coach say he was going to do to all of you?"

"Nothing, yet. Joe, Samuel, and David will have nothing to do with me and I don't blame them. (He mentioned their names slowly and paused between each one as if he were picturing them in his mind as if he was talking to them.) Their parents are really going to be ticked off. Everybody is going to be ticked off." He paused for a time and said, "And, you're ticked off." With that he began to cry openly and took out his handkerchief to wipe the tears and blow his nose.

His mom and dad let him cry and no one spoke a word. His mom reached over and put her hand on his arm and said, "Tom, we are disappointed, and it is something we will have to work through. But it is going to be okay. I think you boys learned a big lesson tonight."

"I know. I know I really screwed up. A lot of damage. Did a lot of damage." He spoke through deep sobs. After a few moments he composed himself and said, as if he was delivering a lecture to the youth group, "I need to talk to Joe, Sam and David. I've got to do that. No use for me to pray about it. My prayer wouldn't get off the ground." Then he began to cry again. He got up from the table and said he was going to his room.

Mrs. Bledsoe whispered to her husband, "Let's just leave him along. Maybe we can talk some more in the morning."

B. Diles at Home After Post-Forfeit

Mack Diles drove his pickup home after he left the locker room. Mack didn't know if his parents were at the game or not. Seldom do they go to the games. Since the black three were starters, his dad didn't see much reason to go to the games even though Mack was a senior.

Mack learned from his dad how much he and many of his friends appreciated the way things were in decades past in Cox County in reference to blacks. Mack had a sticker on the bumper of his pickup that aligns him more with the locker room talk. The bumper sticker says, *It will be a cold day in hell when you take my gun from me!* He had a couple of second amendment stickers on his pickup, as well.

Of the boys who felt remorse and shame for what was said in the locker room, Mack's confession was less heartfelt and seemed less sincere than the others. One could say he hid his being sorry very well. Mack would feel no loss if the black three left and never came back.

His sister, who was two years younger than Mack, always said that their dad had a great deal to do with Mack's attitude toward blacks, guns, Mexicans, homosexuals, and women truck drivers.

Mack gave the impression he was rock-solid and unwavering in his stance against black people. He never offered a word of sympathy when he heard of a black being discriminated against. He stayed clear of any of the blacks he encountered. He kept clear so he would not have to engage in conversation with them. That included the black three.

He and his dad were very close, and they spent a lot of time together . His dad was prejudiced so he was too. His dad seemed to be obsessed with "the way things were." His dad would talk down any suggestion that required or would bring about change. His dad's brother was a Viet Nam vet and Mack's dad had the same mindset and "hawkish" attitude about the military. When Mack learned about George Wallace in civics class, he told some in his class, "My dad is just like George Wallace."

One day after school, an older white gentleman picked up David Bokima and drove off. Mack asked Ronnie Miller who the white guy was. Ronnie told him, "That's his grandpa. He lives in Pleasant Hill."

"That white guy is his grandpa? You got to be kidding!"

"That's true."

All of a sudden, Mack was speechless. It was as if a switch was flipped in his head. He mumbled to Ronnie, not caring if he heard, "This world is getting more confusing all the time."

C. Miller at Home After Post-Forfeit

Ronnie's dad left his mom when Ronnie was just one year old. He has never seen his dad and has never heard from him. Maybe that is why he seems like he is always mad or in a bad mood. His world revolves around his mom, his few friends, and sports. He is very close to his mom and is not embarrassed to be with her like some of his friends are with their mom and dad.

Ronnie is a better baseball player than a basketball player. Ronnie Miller is small for a basketball player. At least he is not the smallest player on the basketball team. For a baseball pitcher he was average size at 5'10" and 170 lbs. But Ronnie is very well built and strong for a boy his size. His best friend is captain of the wrestling team and the wrestling coach has tried to talk Ronnie into coming out for wrestling.

Ronnie was never a good student. He has never been involved in school extracurricular activities. Linda Miller works days and could work overtime some evenings and weekends. With just the two of them they do okay as far as finances. At least Ronnie has never had to say he couldn't go or do anything most of his friends did because of money.

Ronnie's biggest flaw is his rather naïve attitude toward blacks. He always was a quiet kid and sometimes came off as a loner. His only outlet or involvement socially has been his involvement with sports. His attitude toward blacks usually expressed in rhetoric that shows little understanding or knowledge. It all comes from observance and rare moments like the conversation the players had in the locker room. It is unique that such a quiet person expressed himself as he did in the locker room by telling them how uncomfortable he felt from their comments. "What if someone hears us?"

D. Carter at Home After Post-Forfeit

Wes Carter seemed to be one who had the least amount of derogatory verbiage toward the black players. He mentioned how things could go wrong when a black family moved in. What he said was expressed in the most thoughtless, simplistic, and meaningless words. He mentioned that Grayville now has its first black family. What did he imply with that? Such a statement raises a lot of questions. If one were to ask him to define all that he said, it would be interesting to hear how he would answer it. "First black family?" The response would be an interesting answer for a student to a test from a sociology teacher.

Wes is a very popular kid with his classmates. He comes off as being a white Will Smith since he looks like a white Will Smith. He is tall like Will Smith, always trying to get a laugh like Will Smith, and has a girlfriend who is pretty like Will Smith's wife. He is always trying to make people laugh as he likes the limelight. Teachers have a hard time disciplining him because he makes them become part of the pranks he pulls. In basketball this year he is not the "man" he was last year. Last year he was usually the tallest player on the court. Not this year. This year in school he shines more in the classroom as the class clown than he does on the basketball court.

E. Chad at Home Post-Forfeit

Chad was already home when his dad and mom arrived. The first thing Chad said to his folks, when they walked in the door was, "Did you talk to the coach?" "Yes, after we talked to him, he said he was going to the Bokima home. I don't envy him at all. Going to talk to the Bokima family will be a real challenge. I can't imagine how the boys feel. I am sure Dr. Bokima and Mrs. Bokima are very disappointed, angry, and they must be trying to figure out what to do next. I should call Dr. Bokima to find out if I could go over there and talk to them. I don't look forward to that at all."

Chad was sitting in the chair with his head down. He was silently sobbing. He told his parents, "I have no excuses. Everything you heard is true. One of the things I should do, is talk to Joe, Sam, and David. That is one thing I need to do. And then I have to tell the church that I am sorry. But the most important thing is for me to tell you is I am sorry. I am sorry for this evening. I am sorry I embarrassed you. I am sorry I failed you. I didn't mean to hurt you. Dad, if you go to see Dr. Bokima, please tell them all how sorry I am. And, if Joe, or Sam, or David will talk to me, I want to talk to them." With that, Chad left and went to his room.

B. Dr. Bokima Receives Call from Rev. Morgan Post-Forfeit

When everyone gathered at the Bokima home after the game was cancelled, the mood and conversation was subdued, quiet, anger and disillusionment lingered in the air. As time went on the conversation became less intense, more lighthearted, nondescript, and not as discouraging as when people first arrived.

Interrupting the conversations was a phone call. Everyone became quiet. Everyone was curious because one would expect the phone to really ring off the hook at the home of the black three. Was it a phone call from a disgruntled fan to voice their contempt that the game did not go off as planned? What it be a phone call from a fan who was concerned about the black three?

Dr. Bokima answered the call and after listening for a minute, he turned to his wife. "It is Rev. Morgan, Chad's father. He wants to know if he could stop over in the morning. Yes, that would be fine. We will be glad to see you. Thank you for calling." When he hung up the phone, the whole room became very quiet as they looked at Dr. Bokima for some indication of a response.

Mark was the first to speak, "I better get home. I called my parents earlier to explain as much as I could. I have to let them in on all that has happened. Thank you all very much. David, maybe we can get together tomorrow. I will call you in the morning. See you all later."

Coach followed Mark to the door and said, "I will have to be leaving also. I left my phone in the car because I didn't want to be on the phone while I was here with you all. No telling who has been calling."

After a few goodbyes, Lisa and her parents began to make their way toward the door. "Mrs. Bokima, thank you for the pizza and your hospitality. It was good to be with you all tonight. Hope this weekend is good to everybody. Good night." Lisa gave David a short wave and a longer look to let him know how sorry she was and how much she cared.

After everyone had left, Mrs. Bokima asked Hiram, "What do you think Reverend Morgan wants to see you about?" Hiram replied, "He may come in loaded down with guilt. He may be very sorry that his son started this whole fiasco. Or, he may say that his boy said our boys lied, that his boy and the others never said anything like what was reported they said. That would be a tough thing for us to swallow. I have met Reverend Morgan and he doesn't seem like that kind of fellow. We will see."

The next morning, the doorbell rang. It was Reverend Morgan. Greetings were made and words of welcome exchanged. Dr. Bokima directed the Reverend Morgan to the living room. Reverend Morgan sat on the end of the couch and Hiram pulled a chair up close for conversation.

Reverend Morgan began immediately, by saying, "Please call me Talbert, especially now, because I don't feel very reverent." Dr. Bokima said that would be fine and he added, "Please call me Hiram."

Talbert brought up the subject right away. "Last night, I heard directly from Coach Montgomery that my son Chad was the one who initiated the unfortunate discourse in the locker room." At that time Mrs. Bokima entered the room, apologized for interrupting, and said, "Rev. Morgan, good morning. Could I get some coffee or a pastry for you gentlemen?" They both replied, "No thank you." She left without saying a word.

Rev. Morgan continued, "I want you to know that my wife and I are humiliated, embarrassed, and shamed by our son's comments about your sons. His words were deplorable, degrading, and hurtful. We can't express the words to tell you how sorry we are."

Dr. Bokima responded, "We understand. We would feel the same way if the roles were reversed." With a smile he went on, "Our sons have put us in some very unusual and uncomfortable situations. I can imagine it was extremely uncomfortable for you to come over here this morning. I am so glad you did. Please convey to your wife that we harbor no ill will, no hard feelings, no anger, or animosity. Honestly, we were surprised, because we thought the boys got along fine with each other and that they made a good team."

Dr. Bokima continued, "When we found out that Chad made some of the comments, I immediately thought of the consequences with the congregation at Faith Church if they found out. And, I thought of you, and how this might impact you and your ministry. But the more I thought about it, the more I saw the possibility that some good can come out of all this. To tap my meager attempt at theology I could see where this could be a great exercise of confession and redemption. An example of brokenness and healing. A place and time when the Good Shepherd initiates change from divisiveness to harmony. In this day and age of racial unrest, it could be the catalyst to show the power of love over hate. And being a black man who has experienced racial prejudice and hate, it could be a great time to see and feel the power of respect, empathy, and compassion."

Rev. Morgan became more relaxed and animated in what he said, "Dr. Bokima, would you come and preach for me next Sunday and give the fantastic sermon you just gave? What you said was no meager attempt at theology, it was the "Message," with a capital M. It would be wonderful if we could take this experience and make it a blessing and witness to the community. I will do all I can to bring about this redemption and healing and harmony you so eloquently defined. I know others that will make that their calling. What an effect that would have on the community!"

Dr. Bokima asked, "What have you heard from individuals in your congregation since last night? Have you heard of any fall out or criticism, or voices of concern?"

"I have heard from three persons. Each one did not know or even suspect that Chad had a role in the comments made about your boys. I left it at that. They will hear just like everyone else as time goes on. At that time, I will deal with it.

"But I feel I need to tell you a little about me and the church." He started his response very deliberately, slowly as if to make sure he was understood. "My parents were missionaries to the Philippines. They went there in 1961. I was born in Manila in 1966. I have an older brother and sister. When I was five years old, my parents adopted a boy whose mother was a member of my dad's congregation. She died of polio when Julius was two. So, my parents adopted Julius. Julius is black. We never met his father. From the beginning, Julius has always been one of the Morgan children.

"Julius, officially, is my stepbrother. We are very close. I have known him mostly as my best friend and more so, as my brother. He currently is a member of the faculty of Iowa State University in Ames, Iowa. He is a professor of mathematics.

" Chad knows how close I am to Julius. Chad and his uncle Julius are close. That is why this has been so difficult for us. It just seems so impossible and so unlikely that Chad would use any racist language given the makeup of our family.

"I feel the need to tell you about Faith Baptist Church. Unlike some Baptist Churches, we seek to be a church that is open and affirming. We are a church that is tolerant and accepting of all persons.

"We make the statement expressed by the more progressive United Church of Christ, 'No matter where you are on life's journey, you are welcome here.' We have a sign in front of the church that says, 'Everyone Welcome' and then we define everyone; 'Everyone of any race, color, creed, sexual orientation, economic status, age, or disability.' Our mission statement says, *We believe everyone is of sacred worth and created in God's image. We are inclusive of every race, ethnicity, age, sexual orientation, gender identity, marital status, physical or mental ability, economic status or political position.'"*

"So, as a church, we are really taken a back with what has taken place. Chad has put us in a quandary. What took place last night reflects a great deal on us as a church and that is so unfortunate considering all we do to try to break down walls of prejudice and hate."

Dr. Bokima replied, "I can see how what happened last night would weigh heavily on the church. We will not say or do anything to add to the weight you feel." He added more words of assurance, "What we will do and say is that Faith Church, because of its commitment to diversity, makes us feel the spirit of your unconditional love."

Rev Morgan, with his head down and speaking in a voice of resignation, said, "But, the fact remains, my son is guilty of using language so contrary to what we, as a family, as a church, could ever imagine. My wife and I are having a hard time deciding on how best to handle this." He then looked in the face of Dr. Bokima, as if looking for advice, "We just don't know how to handle this."

"What did Chad say last night when he got home?" asked Dr. Bokima.

"He asked me if I had talked to the coach. I told him 'yes.' I told him that the coach told me all that was said and who said it. The coach told me he was going to the Bokima house to talk with the family. That is when my wife and I sank to the deepest depth of despair and disappointment. I can't begin to tell you how terrified we felt. We felt terribly ashamed."

Rev. Morgan continued, "After our son told us what happened, he became very emotional. He gave no excuses. He did not try to lie to get out of it. He said the most important thing he wanted to do was talk to your boys. But he didn't think your boys would want to talk to him. He was still shedding tears when he went to his room. That is when I called you.

He seemed very remorseful. As I said, my wife and I are not sure how to handle this. We want to do what is right – to him and to you, to everyone. We don't know what to do."

Rev. Morgan stood and as he was about to walk to the door, he asked if he might offer a prayer. "By all means, please do," Dr. Bokima answered as he reached for the hand of Rev Morgan. Rev. Morgan paused for a moment and began to pray slowly expressing each word in such a meaningful way that the prayer was one of thoughtfulness and not one just thrown together. "Our Father, we ask for your wisdom during this difficult time. May your love guide us to use the right words as we seek to share that love. As parents, be the Good Shepherd to guide us that we make the right decisions for we want to do the right thing. We ask all of this that you might be glorified. Amen."

Rev. Morgan added, "I am curious about the other four boys and their parents. I am curious how they have been dealing with this. I don't know what to do so I am a not a good person to offer advice." Then with a smile on his face, he said, "I also don't know the general mood or response of my congregation. I'm sure I will be hearing from them soon. You might say a prayer for me in that regard!"

C. Joseph and Chad

That morning Joseph, Samuel, and David went to talk to their dad. They asked what Rev. Morgan said about Chad. Instead of answering, it was as if Dr. Bokima was not paying any attention. Like he had been concentrating on another question. He asked the boys, "Which of you was closest to Chad?" Joseph said he was, that they were both seniors and seemed to have more in common than Samuel and David.

Dr. Bokima asked, "What else besides being seniors do you have in common?" Joseph thought for a moment and said, "It is not so much what we have in common, he just asks me questions about stuff. Chad has asked me questions about Pleasant Hill Community Church. He knows we go there. He said he saw members of the church, older people who were dressed like they just came from church, smiling and waving, and carrying signs about immigration, how God blesses all people, not just the USA, and Black Lives Matter. All this on the courthouse lawn. He was just curious and asked about it.

He saw my tee shirt about the state basketball tournament, and he asked about that a few times. We talk a lot about basketball. He thought he might get a basketball scholarship to that Baptist College in Nashville, Belmont. Stuff like that."

Dr. Bokima spoke to all three boys. "Joseph, I wonder if maybe you ought to stop over and see Chad. It might be too intimidating to have all three of you stop over. But maybe you. Would you be up to it?"

"I guess so. What would I say to him? Do you think he will want to see me?"

"His dad said he wants to see you. He may feel very uncomfortable at first, but when he knows you just stopped over to see how he is doing and that we aren't angry with him, maybe he will open up and have something to say."

Dr. Bokima went on to say, "It is important that you know that what came out of Chad's mouth is not his true feelings. I have no idea why he said the things he did and his father and mother are equally perplexed by it all. He is seventeen years old and no one knows what to predict from you seventeen-year-olds. From what Rev Morgan said, Chad is very sorry, remorseful, and downright ashamed of himself. So, I think he is going to be willing to see you and talk to you."

"When should I go over to his house?"

"Anytime. You might do it pretty soon just to keep him and his folks from fretting too much."

Joseph left to go over to the Morgan house to see Chad. He rang the doorbell and after a short wait, Chad came to the door. When he saw it was Joseph, he hesitated before he even said hello. Then he said, "Would you like to come in?"

Joseph stepped into the house and asked, "How you doin'?" And, with a smile and the impulsive not-sure-what-to-say comment, said, "Last night was some crazy night, wasn't it?" Chad gave a timid smile back and with a trembling voice said, "Yea, crazy alright. Stupid is a better word. I created the problem, Joe. I'm really sorry."

Joseph said, "Forget it. That's what my brothers would say. Things are okay." With that, he stuck out his hand to Chad. As they shook hands a sense of relief took over both.

Chad directed Joseph to the living room here they sat down and could take the time to more seriously discuss the "verbal stream of abuse" more seriously (as Rev. Morgan called it) that Chad and the others directed toward the black three last evening. Dr. Bokima told Joseph that hopefully there would be the opportunity to sit down with Chad and really try to come to some understanding for the reasons for such hurtful statements.

They began a conversation, but it did not deal with the "verbal stream of abuse." Chad began to ask questions that really were directed to engage Joseph. He really wanted to get acquainted with Joseph. He was interested in Joseph. Seldom do teenagers take an interest in someone other than themselves.

Some of the questions Chad asked Joseph were "Who have you gotten acquainted with at school that you would say is your friend? What is it like to have twin brothers? What is it like to be six feet nine inches tall? When did you stop growing? Or have you? Do you have a special bed? When is your birthday? Do you like to read? What do you like to read? Are you going to play basketball in college? Where do you want to go to college? What do you want to study in college?"

Chad was truly interested. They exchanged verbal bios and the conversation took on a healthy and meaningful direction. Relationships are very important these days of divisiveness and mistrust between people. It was very refreshing to see two people take on the task of getting absorbed in each other, especially teenagers.

Earlier, the advice that Dr. Bokima gave Joseph was to just sit and listen and let Chad do the talking. "Don't volunteer any comments, just let Chad do the talking. Chad has more than just his own personal need to confess and admit his guilt. He has his mother and father and their image in the community which Chad has tarnished and must, somehow, recover. Chad has the added burden of renewing trust and respect to himself from the congregation."

"Last night I don't know why I said what I did. My uncle is black and he and I are very close. I've been on mission trips to Haiti with my dad. I have never used the 'N' word in my life. I find it reprehensible. I don't know what is wrong with me."

Joseph gave a big laugh and said, "Your uncle is black! My grandpa is white! Now figure that!

"There is nothing wrong with you." Joseph was going to say more but he remembered what his dad said, "Don't talk too much, let Chad talk. Don't enable him by speaking for him. Let him get all his feelings out." Joseph only added, "We all screw up. Just chalk it up as you just blew it." Joseph thought he had said enough but he couldn't pass up the chance for a little put-on-humor, "I don't see anything wrong with you, except you're a Baptist." Joseph laughed out loud. Chad took it as intended and gave a smile and chuckle.

"Your Grandpa is white? I don't understand."

"When my dad's mom and dad died of AIDS he was only about nine years old. My grandpa was a missionary to Nigeria and parents belonged to his church. After his parents died, my grandparents adopted Dad. He was able to get Dad a basketball scholarship to Temple University in Philadelphia. And you know the rest of the story.

"Joe, you're right, I really blew it. I blew it big time. Joe, I am really sorry. I know you're never supposed to say 'never' but it will never happen again. The fact is, this is going to be more than a huge bad memory. It is a scar I have to carry with me all my life."

"We won't carry it with us, and we don't expect you to."

Chad asked Joseph, "Would you mind if we go talk to my Dad and Mom? They don't know you're here. Dad is in his study and Mom is in the back room. I want them to know we talked."

"Sure."

Joseph followed Chad to the back of the house. They came to his mom and when she saw Joseph she gave him an enthusiastic greeting and hug. She said, "Joseph, this is a pleasant surprise. We are so glad to see you." Chad asked her if she would join them in his dad's study.

As they entered the study, and Chad's dad saw Joseph, there was a look of surprise on his face. He got up from his desk and greeted Joseph with a handshake and a smile. Rev. Morgan put everyone in a comfortable mood with his words of welcome to Joseph. Chad began the conversation by telling his mom and dad that he and Joseph had talked, and Joseph assured him that things were okay between him and his brothers.

Chad asked Joseph if he had anything to add. Again, Joseph remembered his dad's advice, "Don't say too much." Joseph simply said, "We just want to get back to basketball."

X. Signing Individual Pledges – A Team Commitment

Rev. and Mrs. Morgan gave a hearty "Thank goodness!" after they heard from Chad and Joseph that things were okay in their relationship. Mrs. Morgan said to Joseph, "We are so glad to have you in our home. We have been so worried, so ashamed. Talbert said your father was so gracious and kind this morning when he went to see him. You and your family would have every right to be upset with us. You have every right to wish to never see us. This had been an exceedingly difficult time for all of us. And we want to do everything we can to right this wrong. We love your family very much." With that she gave Joseph a hug.

Rev. Morgan said, "Joe, you have been very gracious coming here to see Chad. You have been very gracious in telling him you just want to get back to basketball. That is a beautiful message. It is a powerful example of forgiveness. It is a great message of reconciliation, and it will go a long way in getting people to examine their own prejudice. We thank you very much."

Chad and Joseph's conversation was good because it put things right and with no hard feelings between them. When Chad asked Joseph what he would suggest they do next, Joseph said, "We need to get all the guys together, just us nine, and try to see if we can work through all that was said and get back to being a team. A lot depends on what happens at the meeting tomorrow with Coach Montgomery. Some things should be discussed. Like where does the name calling come from? Are we really hated? Why did it happen? How does everybody feel about it? I know how you feel, but how do they feel?"

"Joe, trust me. All of us have done an about-face on what we said last night. I know that the guys are sick, truly sick for what they said. Even Mack, who I know is the most red neck on the team, is sorry and wants very much to have a good relationship with you and your brothers. I think your idea of a meeting of just us nine, is a great idea."

"Joe, if you could have been in the dressing room last night before everyone went home, you would have seen each guy drowned in tears. Tears of shame. Tears of sorrow. Tears of confession. Tears that come from having failed. I really want you to believe me when I tell you we really regret, we are truly sorry for what we said."

"I believe you. I appreciate what you have told me. I don't want any bad feelings between us and there are none. I know that my brothers feel the same way. Here is my thought about a meeting of just us nine players. I suggest we put together an oath or pledge that we sign as a commitment or promise to each other. If everybody signed the pledge, we would really be ready to play basketball. If each of us signed a pledge or oath, and made it known to the public, I think it would be a great message to convey to the people.

The pledge we would sign and the message we would make to everyone is that with us there is no room for prejudice, hate, or discrimination. By signing our pledge there is no room for prejudicial thoughts or any racially denigrating comments. Signing the pledge is about building relationships. Signing the pledge is affirming no racial issues. Signing the pledge is about putting away the past and starting anew."

Rev. and Mrs. Morgan were still in the study as the conversation between Chad and Joseph continued. Mrs. Morgan asked if she could say something even though she said it was none of her business. She went on to say that she thought getting just the team together was an excellent idea and the oath or pledge was an even better idea.

She went on to justify her comments. "What took place last night is going to be the subject of discussion in most every town and school all over the country. It won't take long for it to be spread all over. It presents a difficult challenge to make this terrible wrong come out right. But, if you two can get everyone to really talk about it, be honest with their feelings, and want to do what is right, a wonderful message will come from it all."

Joseph said, "Consider it done. Chad and I will make that our job. When we get everybody together, Chad can preach to them." With that Mrs. Morgan laughed out loud. Rev. Morgan said, "That is a sermon I want to hear!"

Chad asked, "Do you have a model or sample of the oath or pledge?"

Joseph said, "I have been caring around a copy of something that deals with diversity. I got it from a book written by Rev. Jack Stone. He is from here in Grayville, played football for the University of Illinois, and was a United Methodist Minister in Ohio for forty-one years.

His book had to do with making choices. I took the liberty to add some of my own choices to it. Choices which would fit us. From them I wrote out a pledge for us to consider. It is something we should discuss at the very beginning of our meeting when we get together. Let me read some of the points I used for the oath.

"The points are: *'Are we willing to accept each other or reject? Are we willing to forgive or hold grudges? Are we willing to give unselfishly, or are we out to get? Are we willing to play basketball, or stay a prejudiced person? Are we willing to love and not hate? Are we willing to be about reconciliation or have hard feelings? Are we willing to forget Friday Night's forfeit? Or stay angry? Are we willing to give affirmation to each other or criticize? Are we willing to show empathy or be selfish? Are we willing to show compassion or not care? Are we willing to care or be insensitive? Are we willing to show maturity or be irresponsible? Are we willing to be a thinking person or have no interest?'"*

After Rev Morgan listened to Joseph read the points to be made, he said, "Joseph, I really like the way you are suggesting using these points. They represent a very solid foundation for a pledge or oath. Having the individual team members sign that pledge will make a wonderful statement for all to see. The several points are a statement in themselves and is an incredibly significant statement. I am sure that it represents the message Coach Montgomery wants the team to share with the community."

"Thanks. Here is a sample of the pledge that the players would sign." Joseph hands the pledge to Rev. Morgan.

*As a member of the 2020 Grayville High School basketball team, I make this pledge as my commitment to give not only to my teammates but to all persons, regardless of race, ethnicity, age, sexual orientation, physical or mental ability, or economic status, **respect, compassion, empathy and love.***

...I accept each person as sacred worth, created in God's image.
...I seek to forgive, and not hold a grudge.
...I seek to give unselfishly, and not take.
...I seek to play basketball and not let prejudice stand in the way
...I seek to love and not hate
...I seek to forget Friday's forfeit, and not be angry
...I seek to affirm each other, not criticize.
...I seek to show empathy, and not be selfish.
...I seek to show compassion, and not indifference.
...I seek to care, not be insensitive.
...I seek to show maturity and not be irresponsible.
...I seek to think, and not appear uninterested.

_____*Signature*_____*date*

After he read it, he kept looking at the paper, then he lifted his head and said, "Joseph, this is very good. It says everything you would want said. If the public knew this was the pledge made by each member of the team, it would go a long way in people forgetting what took place last night. I hope you boys make good use of this. It is a job well done, Joseph.

Joseph had a look of embarrassment from the compliment of Rev. Morgan. He simply said "Thank you."

Mrs. Morgan said, "Thanks for these words Joseph, I believe you boys are on the right track." Chad told his parents that he and Joseph were going to discuss the plans for the meeting with the team.

"First let's call the guys and make sure they can all make it tomorrow. Probably about 5:30? I will call my brothers. And I will help you call the others. Then if everyone can make it, we can call our moms and ask them to fix us a light dinner."

After a few phone calls were made the plans were all in place for what could be the most important meeting since Friday's forfeit.

A. The Shelby Forfeit Hits the Streets

The Grayville Dispatch and the Cookeville Tribune were not the only newspapers that picked up on the forfeit. The forfeit made news all over where the "watch" was going on. The "watch" was the community and thousands of people all over who were monitoring, observing, surveilling, keeping a close eye on the Grayville basketball team. People were "watching" to see how the black three would fare in a high school that never had a single black basketball player. The "watch" was to see how long it would take before the race issue would raise its ugly head. After several weeks of "watching" and anticipating a reaction, it finally happened.

Once the forfeit was announced, investigative reporters began to ask a lot of questions. The common denominator of the questions was, "What finally took place that the perfect basketball season of 4 and 0 came to an end?" Sports writers, fans of all positions on race relations, the people of Grayville, the students of GHS, basketball fans throughout the southeast all anticipated an "incident" which would reveal the true colors.

People were surprised that the white teammates of the black three caused the racial lid to blow. Most believed it would come from a demonstration of some "white power" outside the school in the form of a parade in downtown Grayville with pickup trucks and their confederate flags. The Tennessee hate groups, the two white power militant groups, and assorted individuals who like to parade with flags and banners which defined "our linage and historical pattern toward black people" had expressed a desire to hit the streets of Grayville.

Many believed, and hoped, that some extremist white militant hate group would blow the lid off. After all, Tennessee had several hate groups and ever since the Bokima's arrived in Grayville, Grayville High School had every indication of becoming a potential target. There were some from some churches that saw three blacks on a basketball team fly in the face of God's Word. Considering the racial history of Cox County, it was not hard to imagine some expression of "enough is enough" to confront the black three.

No matter the cause for the split to have occurred, it was completely unexpected to have that expression be from the white teammates. With a record of 4 and 0 there was no hint of a problem. When the fans watched the team play, they saw finely tuned teamwork. Nothing was ever seen of behavior that looked like it came from prejudice, hatred, or animosity.

B. Coach Meets With the Players

Coach Montgomery called a meeting of the nine players to take place on Sunday afternoon at 3:00 at a familiar site. The place determined by Coach was the locker room.

The meeting was to begin at 3:00 P.M. on Sunday following the Friday cancelled game. The coach had one of the custodians join him early in the afternoon to set the benches up in a particular order to provide comfort, the chance for eye contact, and proximity to each other to enhance conversation. The players would take a place on the benches which were placed in a horseshoe shape.

The coach was the first to arrive. Soon, the nine players began to arrive. It was the first time they had seen each other since classes ended

Friday afternoon. For each boy there was a great deal of uncertainty about the meeting. They had a lot of questions. What does the coach want of me? Where am I supposed to sit? Do I sit with the good guys? Am I supposed to talk? What am I supposed to say? Who goes first? What does he mean, "honest sharing?" How will I know when to talk? What if nobody talks? What if I don't want to talk?

As the boys came into the locker room, they saw the benches in a horseshoe shape and began to consider where to sit. When Chad saw Joseph, they moved toward each other, gave a silent bump hug and sat down next to each other, not saying a word but with slightly nervous smiles on their faces. They both realized they had a big jump on the rest of the players because they had the good fortune of their previous conversation to mend the brokenness.

As if on que, Samuel and Tom gave a nod to each other and sat near Chad and Joseph. Some of the others stood looking around, not sure where to go or where to sit or sit with whom. Wes went over and sat down next to Joseph since Chad was on the other side. When Mack came in he looked around at the others, not sure if he was supposed to sit in a certain place. Sam looked at him, caught his eye and pointed to the place next to him. Ronnie came right behind Mack and followed him in and sat next to him.

Mark saw David and the two nodded at each other and sat down next to each other. They gave a knuckle greeting to each other. Eventually, everyone found a seat. No one smiled or made recognition of the others. No one said anything. The coach was seated off to the side on a stool. He never said a word, just watched a bunch of nervous teenage boys.

When everyone was seated and seemed to be settled down, Coach stayed seated on his stool and spoke to them. He mentioned to them the purpose of the meeting was very simple; "We are going to try to salvage the season through honest sharing and try to come to a resolution, an agreement of respect, empathy, compassion for each other. If we can't do it, it doesn't mean we didn't try."

Coach said he had a vision for the meeting with the boys. "My vision comes from the conversation we had just after I cancelled the game with Shelby. I am taking seriously your confessions. I am taking seriously that you regret your hateful words, I am taking your word that you were sincere. And, because I trust you, we have a real positive future as a team. As I said, I am taking you seriously. Therefore, my vision for us is to become a witness to our community and country, that having created a wrong, we will correct that wrong because of our love for each other.

"Now, I realize I am dealing with sixteen, seventeen, and eighteen-year-old boys. People will think I am being very naïve. You may think I am being very naïve. Regardless of what you think about my vision, if we don't' do our best to make it a reality, we are in deep trouble. We have a lot of people watching to see if we can make a terrible wrong, right. We have a lot of people praying and hoping we succeed. We also, and I repeat, we also have a lot of other people hoping we fail.

"I have four expectations for our being together. First, I hope that each of you (he paused at this point to see if he had their attention), each of you who made the inappropriate and hateful comments would explain, as best you can, why?" He waited for a while to let the first point be thought through. Then he repeated, "As best as you can, explain why."

Then he went on. "Secondly, I hope that Joseph, Samuel, and David will feel comfortable in telling us how they feel. It is very important that we understand how they feel." Again, he waited for that second point to sink in.

"Thirdly, I hope, I really hope that we can think (here he paused again) of what we can say or do to show respect and compassion to each other. We have to use some creative thinking, show some empathy of what ways we can show appreciation to each other."

"Finally, can we, each of us, be agents of change? Can we, as individuals, make it happen? Can all of us together, make it happen? Can we move from a position of prejudice and hate to a position of empathy and love?"

"The most important points are the last two. How can we show respect and compassion for each other? And can we be agents of change going from expressions of prejudice to expressions of love? Now, those are my expectations. If they are not your expectations, you are free to leave at this time and the basketball season will be over for you. I won't waste anymore of your time."

Then coach became silent. Those were the only instructions given.

No one got up to leave.

After a long silence, and enough time for anyone to get up and leave if that was their choice, the coach said, "Okay, you have a general idea of what we need to discuss. The ball is in your court."

Tom reacted immediately but stood up slowly. "I've been agonizing over this from the very first. Agonizing over facing my teammates. I want to get it over with." Pausing after each name, tears welling up in his eyes, "Joseph. Sam. David." He looked at them directly. "I honestly don't remember what I said last Friday night. People may have told you what I said. I don't remember. I know it wasn't good. It was bad, I am sure. It was certainly uncalled for. I can't tell you how sorry I am for what I said."

He began to sob. "I am asking you to forgive me. That is more important to me than ever playing basketball again." He kept standing as if he was going to say more. Immediately, Joseph, Samuel and David got up and lined up in front of Tom and each one gave him a big hug and smile. After each one had hugged Tom, they each said something in his ear. Then he sat down. Joseph, before he sat down, said, "Hey man, we are going to play basketball!"

No one said anything. Chad was next to stand. "Yesterday, Joseph came to my house." There was a long pause. "Can you believe that? I should have gone to his house. But he came to mine." Chad starts to cry and had a hard time going on with his comments. "Here he is standing in our doorway, all six feet nine inches. I thought he came to punch my face in. (Long pause with some muted chuckles) He came to see how I was doing." At this Chad starts to cry openly. Joseph stands next to him and gives him a big hug. Then they both sit down.

Coach Montgomery had tears welling up in his eyes.

Mack was next to speak. He stood up and said, "I know exactly what I said Friday night. I said, 'Niggers don't belong here.' Can you think of anything more stupid than that?" After a long pause Mack went on. "I have heard people say that kind of shit most of my life. I have heard my dad say it, I don't know how many times. That is where I got it. Not only is it a stupid thing to say but it was even more stupid for me to say it. Guys, I'm really sorry."

David got up and walked over to Mack before he could sit down. He drew him in for a bump-hug as they shook hands. David said, "As Joe said, 'It is time to play some basketball.' You are a good man, Mack. And you are not stupid." Then he sat down.

Ronnie was next to speak. He rose slowly from the bench as if he didn't really want to say anything. He paused and did not want to make eye contact with anyone. He said, "Let me tell you about stupid. Stupid is when you should speak up when bad stuff is going on. I am just as guilty as anybody. I am surprised I got invited to this meeting. Can a person forgive stupid? I told my mom how stupid I felt because I didn't say anything to stop the bad comments. When I told her about this meeting, she said 'Will they let stupid people attend the meeting?'" At this point everyone laughed. "Here I am," he shrugged. Before he sat down, he said, "Joseph, Samuel, David, I am sorry I didn't have the balls to stand up for you to say the right thing." Then Ronnie sat down.

Wes was next to talk. "I should have kept my mouth shut the other night. I didn't say anything that made sense. I am sure my words were offensive and derogatory. They were words that were just kind of thrown out there to make noise. I am sure they sounded hateful, but I do not hate anyone. I am a senior for Christ's sake! I am eighteen years old! I sounded like a junior high jerk. Ronnie, you talked about being stupid. You don't come close to my stupid stuff."

Wes continued as he looked each Bokima brother in their eyes, really trying to get their attention. "I tell you what, Joe, Sam, and David. I want to be your teammate." His voice became quieter and he enunciated each word very carefully, "I want to be a GOOD teammate. I want to play with you guys. I hope y'all will give me a second chance."

After he sat down, Joseph, Samuel, and David went over to him, Wes stood up to greet them and they did a three-man group hug. At six feet three inches, Wes was the shortest. They said nothing and then just sat down.

Everything got quiet. No one moved. It seemed like minutes went by. Coach Montgomery just sat on his stool. Samuel got up and stood at the opening of the horseshoe. He looked bigger than six feet six inches. He looked even broader. It seems like every time something intelligent must be said, Samuel says it. For instance, every time someone makes some all-inclusive, all-encompassing generalization remark like, "Everybody does it." Samuel steps in and says, "Everybody? You sure about that?" or when someone says something that seems like an exaggeration, he will ask, "Where did you get that information?" or he will say, "Can you document that?"

Samuel looked at everyone with a smile on his face and said, "Does it feel like we are in church?" By this time, everyone who had tears in his eyes, welcomed the change of pace that the comment gave. At Samuel's remark, they all laughed. They were glad, in what was a tense situation, to have a chance to laugh.

In the mood that made everyone feel relaxed, Samuel continued to speak. "I had no idea what we were going to do here or say or what would be the general conversation. I will tell you; I really appreciate all that has been said. My brothers and I feel like a big weight is off our shoulders. And we are really looking forward to the game with Clifton. We will be putting a good team on the floor. Coach, you are not only a super good coach, but you are a smart man. You ought to be a psychiatrist. But wait 'til after we all graduate." With that closing remark, everyone gave Coach a standing applause, with hugs and smiles all around.

Coach Montgomery smiled, nodded his head in thanks, and returned to his seat.

Ronnie, who had spoken earlier, got up and went to the open end of the horseshoe. "I don't know if you know it or not, but last week Samuel came to the rescue of the only other black kid in the school beside the Bokima boys."

"This kid, Gary Patterson, was getting beaten up by two of our star athletes. Two of our big athletes beat up one small black kid. One of the athletes is Charles Jackson, the center on the football team. He is six two and two twenty-five. The other, and a good friend of mine, well, he is no longer a good friend, Tony Perillo, the captain of the wrestling team. Six feet tall and one eighty. Charlie and Tony, both good sized athletes, were BOTH beating on Gary Patterson, all 130 pounds of him."

"Then Samuel shows up. All six feet six inches! In just seconds, Samuel not only stopped Gary from getting beaten up, but he also took out the two bullies. I mean he really took them out! He roughed them up and they were scared to death. They had to think, 'where did this big black dude come from?' I just wanted you to know that I am going to choose my friends better. I want to count all of you as my best friends."

Silence seemed to be the next order of business. No one wanted to break it. Finally, the coach rose up from his stool and said, "I don't know where it came from, but I saw and heard a lot of maturity and thoughtfulness and caring here this afternoon. What you have done is put together a powerful message for a lot of people. The message that is centered on caring, compassion, empathy, reconciliation, and love. People all over the country will have heard of the forfeit to Shelby last Friday night. Now, we have a new message for them. Now, we have a very powerful message for them. Thank you."

Before the coach dismissed everyone, he said, "Before we leave, would anyone like to offer a prayer?" Chad stepped forward and said, "I will." Everyone got silent. After a long pause, Chad said, "I can't, Coach." Tears were streaming down his face. Coach picks it up, "My prayer is a thanks to all of you. Thanks for allowing me to see this side of you that is your best self. Thanks for the chance to be your coach. My prayer is that God's blessings go with each of us the rest of the day to give us peace and joy. Amen."

"Practice regular time tomorrow. Don't be late. Thursday night is Clifton. Joe, Sam, and David don't know about Clifton. For your information, we haven't done well against Clifton in ten years."

C. The Player's Meeting and Pledge

The players arrived at the Morgan house on time, 5:30 P.M. Of course, telling them there would be food was a big incentive. Mrs. Morgan and Mrs. Bokima really set out a spread on the dining room table. The boys were going to meet in the living room, and they had free reign for a buffet set up on the dining room table. Chad and Joseph were well prepared hosts.

Before they ate from the "buffet," Chad made sure everyone was comfortable in their places and ready to listen. He began.

"Joe and I had a big agenda set up for this evening. We were going to cover what it means to really be honest with each other. Really express our feelings. Don't hold back. Say what is on your mind. Truth is very important. But after our meeting with Coach two hours ago, we don't need to be told to be honest and express our feelings. We know how to do that. No basketball team in the country is as good at it as we are!

Another thing that Joe and I wanted to emphasize was how we need to start our season all over. Start from the very beginning. We wanted to emphasize that our 4 and 0 record is a thing of the past. We want to commit to a new beginning. Make it a fresh start. And to borrow one of my dad's theological terms, 'renewed.' Be renewed.

We hit the bottom Friday night. No, let me rephrase that, I hit the bottom. I understand that Sam had the right words to describe our stupidity, to describe our words from hell. After the Bokima boys left the gym Friday night and went home, I heard that Sam said, 'I can't believe this shit!'" Everyone had a big laugh at that statement. "But after our meeting two hours ago, we don't need to worry about starting over again. We already are."

The last thing on the agenda for this evening was we wanted to deal with the purpose of our meeting today. Something terrible happened at the Shelby game. A terrible wrong must be made right. That was to be our purpose tonight. To right a wrong. As Coach Montgomery said, 'We have a message to give.' A lot of people are watching. That is why we need to get together as a team. To send a positive and hopeful message. A terrible wrong must be made right. We are on our way with that one too.

The only things left to discuss, or at least deal with, is something Joes prepared. Joe."

Joseph said, "I read something that Rev. Jack Stone wrote about diversity. It had to do with choices. I took the liberty to add some of my own choices to it, choices that would fit us. I want to read some of the points that Rev. Stone used in his article and some that I added for the pledge or oath that I want to introduce.

The points are: *Are we willing to accept each other or reject? Are we willing to forgive or hold grudges? Are we willing to give unselfishly, or are we out to get? Are we willing to play basketball, or stay a prejudiced person? Are we willing to love and not hate? Are we willing to be about reconciliation or have hard feelings? Are we willing to forget Dark Friday Night? Or stay angry? Are we willing to give affirmation to each other or criticize? Are we willing to show empathy or be selfish? Are we willing to show compassion or not care? Are we willing to care or be insensitive? Are we willing to show maturity or be irresponsible? Are we willing to be a thinking person or have no interest?*

They represent a very solid foundation to fashion a commitment, to make a pledge, an oath. Having each of us sign that pledge will make a wonderful statement for everyone to see. The several points are a statement in themselves and it is a very significant statement. I am sure that it represents the message Coach wants us to make.

Here is a sample of the pledge that each of us would sign." At this point Joe passes out a copy of the pledge to each player and a pen.

> *As a member of the 2020 Grayville High School basketball team, I make this pledge as my commitment to give not only to my teammates but to all persons, regardless of race, ethnicity, age, sexual orientation, physical or mental ability, or economic status, respect, compassion, empathy and love.*
>
> *…I accept each person as sacred worth, created in God's image.*
> *…I seek to forgive, and not hold a grudge.*
> *…I seek to give unselfishly, and not take.*
> *…I seek to play basketball and not let prejudice stand in the way*
> *…I seek to love and not hate*
> *…I seek to forget Dark Friday Night, and not be angry*
> *…I seek to affirm each other, not criticize.*
> *…I seek to show empathy, and not be selfish.*
> *…I seek to show compassion, and not indifferent.*
> *…I seek to care, not be insensitive.*
> *…I seek to show maturity and not be irresponsible.*
> *…I seek to think, and not appear uninterested.*
> _____*Signature*_____*date*

"Look at the list of choices and if you have a question, let's discuss it. I hope you find they provide a sense of direction because we want our intentions to be very clear.

"If we discuss these choices and if we sign the pledge, we would be able to really send, what coach called, a significant and meaningful message to a lot of people. A message of reconciliation, grace, forgiveness, and love. We will be like missionaries!"

Without hesitation, each player signed the pledge sheet and passed them back to Joseph. Wes said for everyone to hear, "I'm glad I don't play for Clifton. They are going to wish they never came to our gym. This whole week is going to be a fun week. And the Clifton game is going to be a fun game. Talk about a new beginning!"

"So, what's left? To eat! How about we think on these things over something to eat."

XI. Fragile Peace in "Post-Shelby" Grayville

So, the hallways at GHS are not completely safe for a frail black student. The hallways of GHS and streets of Grayville could be very intimidating for some people who don't belong to the all-white-evangelical-protestant-conservative-second amendment-pro-gun-pro-life-anti-immigrant-pro-conservative-Republican crowd and does not have a pickup truck flying the Confederate flag and a banner that says, "Black lives suck."

A. Expression of Hate

Those kind of folk in Cox County give high-fives to show agreement and approval every time someone repeats one of the white players comments about their black teammates. Several "good o'boys" were glad to see the black three leave the gym, hoping they would never come back. Many said, in regard to David and Lisa, "Now that the black boys quit basketball, maybe that white girl's parents will talk some sense into her to dump that black kid."

Comments reigned down about putting the blacks in their place. People wanted to know, "Why on earth would a black family move to Grayville?" One reason might be that a new, competent, and dedicated doctor has come to share his skill and commitment to healing.

The hard-core racial slurs that divide and hurt became more vocal, loud, more intense, and more often after the canceled Shelby game. Some folk saw the Shelby game as a starting point for a new found opportunity to discriminate and harass. A certain element of the community made excuses for the boys' racial attitudes by implying the black players deserved it.

Some people were very indifferent and thought nothing of the grossly irresponsible verbiage directed at the three black boys. Dangerous camps began to be fashioned around prejudice and hate which established a polarization and segregation of people into sides that alienate, create divisiveness, and build walls of animosity and mistrust.

Many made the excuse of such unthinking denigrating rhetoric by saying, "boys will be boys." A culturally induced prejudicial mindset had become the only expression for some to articulate. One begins to think that to make a change of hearts and minds seems to be nearly impossible. To disrupt their comfort and ease of holding a prejudicial attitude would create a great deal of discomfort. To perpetuate the Cox County legacy that blacks don't belong, excuses one from thinking or having to deal with one's own prejudice and hate. As Lyle Schaller, noted church consultant said in his book, 44 Steps Up Off the Plateau, *"The comfortable plateau has a broader appeal than change."*

The depth and seriousness of the hate and prejudice that many held was expressed in accusations that the black three lied when they said derogatory and prejudicial words were spoken about them. Despite the confessions of the five white players that they did indeed say such hateful words, many did not and would not accept that as true. This became a conspiracy among those people which was their argument to make accusations against the three black players.

With such a distortion of the truth and with unhinged persons acting out with undisciplined behavior, the Bokima family began to be concerned about their own wellbeing. The incidents of verbal and mental abuse of their boys at school increased. Anonymous and threatening phone calls placed the family in constant fear and anxiety. The Bokimas had a cross burned in their yard. The N word was written on the walls in the restrooms and hallways at school and as graffiti in different places in the community, including the water tower! Hate mail was a constant reminder that they were not welcome.

Dr. Bokima received hate mail at his office. A poster was put on his door to his office that said, "Black lives don't matter." He hired a plain clothes police officer to patrol in front of his office.

Cars drove by the Bokima home in the wee hours of the morning, honking, squealing tires, causing damage by driving into their yard and throwing trash in their yard. At the park near their home, an effigy of a black man was hung from a tree. A neighbor saw the spectacle and attempted to cut it down. As he was standing on his ladder to cut the hanging rope, three young men came and knocked the ladder out from under him. As he fell to the ground, they kicked him in the face and told him if he interfered again, they would knock out all the windows of his house.

"White power," "KKK," and "APB" were spray painted on the Bokima's driveway, on the side of the house, and on the sidewalk on Main Street in front of Glider's.

B. The Upside

The upside within these troublesome expressions of hate, was a land-swell of people's responses that came pouring in from the community, from all over the state and beyond, with the intent of giving support and a shepherding hand to the Bokima and Patterson families. Letters, cards, emails, text messages, and phone calls were great sources of encouragement. A total of sixteen churches and one hundred forty-one volunteers over a period of two months made their way to Grayville, TN to lend a hand. They took up sections of the motels in the area, camped out on the lawns, parked their fifth wheelers and RVs at local trailer parks and camped out at the Cox County State Park.

For eight weeks, beginning as early as Saturday evening after the Shelby game was called off, volunteers throughout TN and the Midwest, were scheduled for two weeks each to cover eight weeks of shepherding care twenty-four hours a day, seven days a week. Some of the volunteers extended their stay for than two weeks.

Eight men from the United Methodist Men's Breakfast group from Hope UMC in Nashville, called themselves the "Guardian Angels," were included in that list of sixteen churches. And those men were some of those volunteers that stayed "at their posts" to provide surveillance and a watchful eye more than the expected two weeks.

Julie Dempsey, a professor at Chandler School of Theology and her husband from Atlanta, GA assumed the responsibility of developing and coordinating a schedule of the sixteen churches and one hundred forty-one volunteers. She spent her two-week vacation in a fifth wheeler parked at one of the local campgrounds near Grayville which also served as the "office" or as one person called it, "the base of operations." She developed a daily/weekly schedule which included each of the sixteen churches of their "responsibilities," locations, route when it called for transportation, time required, and how many volunteers were needed. When she had to return to her teaching, her husband stayed until the eight weeks were completed.

The schedule of the churches that were a part of the surveillance that was put in place included the First Avenue Church of Christ from Evansville, Indiana. They didn't make a phone call to inquire "What can we do to help?" They just came as a caravan of five cars to Grayville, TN. They came to serve as escorts, security aids, monitors, surveillance eyes, watchmen, buffers, and "gofers" to the Bokima boys and their parents, and Gary and his mother, in any way they could be of use. They came because they were needed. For two weeks the five Indiana license plates were spotted all around town.

Mrs. Bokima, David, Lisa, and Gary spent a good deal of time going to rehearsals and staff meetings at the Cox County Playhouse. In those many forty-mile round trips, they became acquainted with four couples who were scheduled specifically to take turns accompanying them as their "security." The four couples were from the Third Ave. Nazarene Church in Collinsville, Illinois and Bethel Christian Church in Alton Illinois.

Two volunteer couples from Broad Street United Methodist Church in Memphis were scheduled to be "on-watch" at the park for a week in case there would be another move to intimidate with another effigy hanging. Three other volunteer couples from Memphis "set up camp" in the Bokima's yard to serve notice to anyone who wanted to cause trouble that they were present. For two weeks, 24/7 volunteers from the Cookeville Church of Christ accompanied members of the Bokima Family as they went from their home to office, to the grocery store, school, work and a host of other errands and side trips.

The First Baptist Church of Clarksville, TN provided volunteers for the same kind of surveillance. For two weeks, starting since Saturday noon, after the cancelled game on Friday, they have kept "watch" twenty-four hours a day, seven days a week. When asked about the duration of this task, they said, "We are committed to the long haul." As one volunteer from First Baptist said, "We are here until we see and experience light bulbs going off in the heads of those who are not thinking right now."

The Rev. Dr. William Norris, the missionary to Nigeria, and who is the father of Dr. Bokima, gathered several members of the Pleasant Hill Community Church to serve as "monitors" to the Bokima family. Rev. Norris was assigned the responsibility to keep close surveillance on the schedule of Dr. and Mrs. Bokima.

The day of a doctor's appointment in Cookeville, Mrs. Bokima was followed, in a very menacing way, by a pickup truck. In the pickup were three young men who were intent on harassing and intimidation. The back of the pickup displayed a large Confederate flag. On this occasion a couple from Pleasant Hill drove their car between Mrs. Bokima and the pickup truck with the intent to become a nuisance to the three young men. The men wouldn't back off, so the Sheriff was called, and the young men were arrested for intimidation and harassing.

When the agitators realized that there were people committed to providing support and company to the family for the long term, and as some of the agitators were encountered by the police, the incidents of harassment became fewer and less intent.

It seems that the efforts of so many who came so far to provide security and care became the unspoken message the two black families needed. The bottom line of those several weeks of demonstrations of support and encouragement, motivated from the desire for reconciliation and the protection of civil rights, introduced the notion that the prospects for positive change was possible.

As the community witnessed the outpouring of love and support from so many from around the country, there came a movement of many persons in Grayville to augment the spirit of advocacy. Many clergy of the county provided mobilization to convene a common effort to combat evil, hate, and harassment that certain elements of the county expressed. The president of the Grayville Clergy Association said, "We are not going to allow that element to step one foot in the door. We are not going to allow those bullies room to breathe."

Not only did the clergy join in the voice of reconciliation and advocacy, but the Chamber of Commerce spoke of the need for Grayville and Cox County to take a new direction, fashion a new initiative to counter the legacy and tradition of racism characterized by Cox County of years past.

C. The Bullies

When the players had the specially called meeting with Coach Montgomery, he stopped Samuel and asked him about the latest news about Gary and the two boys who were suspended that beat him up. Samuel said he had not heard anything after they were suspended indefinitely. "I know my dad is very concerned that a small frail black kid got beaten up in the hallway at school by two big white boys. He sent a medical report to the principal. There is going to be a hearing at the principal's office tomorrow morning, with those two, their parents, me, dad, Mr. Gammon, Mr. Foster, Gary, and his mother.

Monday morning, Dr. Bokima and Samuel arrived at the principal's office five minutes early for the meeting in the conference room just off Mr. Gammon's office. Mr. Foster was already there and shortly after, Charles and Tony arrived. Only Tony Pirello's mother came. Charles's parents never showed up. When everyone was being seated, Gary and his mother were escorted in by Mr. Gammon's secretary.

Everyone was seated around a large rectangular conference table. Mr. Gammon had name cards on the table in front of the chair designating where each person was to be seated. Charles and Tony were seated next to each other at the end of the table. Tony's mother was seated near the corner next to Tony.

Mr. Gammon was seated at the other end of the table opposite Charles and Tony. Gary and his mother to Mr. Gammon's right on the same side of the table as Mrs. Pirello. Dr. Bokima and Samuel were seated on the left facing the Patterson's and Mrs. Pirello. Mr. Foster sat off to the side near the corner of the room.

Mr. Gammon began by stating the purpose of the meeting. "It has been seven days since Mr. Patterson was brutally attacked by Charles Jackson and Tony Pirello. In accordance with the policy of conduct on school property, Charles and Tony were suspended that day. School policy dealing with violent behavior on school property and especially, while school is in session, is very clear. Such behavior has a zero tolerance. Such a violation of this school policy is an automatic suspension. We are here today to make certain that is understood. That being the case, we are going to do our best to take appropriate action to see that such criminal behavior (a pause is taken here as Mr. Gammon looks directly at the boys at the other end of the table) will never take place in the school again."

At this point, Mr. Gammon opened the letter from Dr. Bokima and read only parts of it. The letter spoke of the extent of the injuries to

Gary Patterson and statement of personal concern for the welfare of black students attending Cox County High School. It was a personal expression of recognition for security for the black students. "I wanted to share a portion of this letter from Dr. Bokima to emphasize the need for sensitivity to the issue of violence and abuse toward black students in the school. This letter has two intentions – to note specifically, the seriousness of the morally bankrupt behavior of Charles Jackson and Tony Pirello which cost Gary Patterson a significant amount of pain, time, humiliation, inconvenience, and money; and to help determine the discipline to realistically fit the irresponsible behavior of Charles Jackson and Tony Pirello."

Then Mr. Gammon asks the two boys at the end of the table, "First of all, Mr. Jackson, do you know the extent of Mr. Patterson's injuries? Do you have an idea of the medical cost of Mr. Patterson's injuries?"

After a long pause, Mr. Gammon addresses him again, "Mr. Jackson?"

It appears that Mr. Jackson is not listening. He asks, "What is the first thing you asked?"

The extent of Mr. Patterson's injuries. Do you know what they were?"

"No."

"Do you care?"

"No."

"Mr. Pirello, do you know the extent of Mr. Patterson's injuries?"

"I heard he had a broken nose."

"Did you do that? Do you remember hitting him in the face hard enough to cause an injury like a broken nose?"

"No, I didn't hit him hard enough to break anything."

"Mr. Jackson, I suppose you never hit Gary hard enough to break anything."

"That's right!"

"In the letter from Dr. Bokima, he describes the injuries to Gary Patterson. He states, 'Mr. Patterson has a broken nose, lacerated lip requiring six stitches, cut ear requiring three stitches, two chipped teeth, bruised left cheek bone, injured retina in the right eye, bruised phalanx bone over the right eye. And two skin lacerations of the left side of his face including a tear near the left ear lobe.' We know how Mr. Patterson received these injuries. You are both responsible. What I personally find hard to understand is why it took two of you to attack Mr. Patterson. You are both leading athletes at GHS, involved in contact sports. You are used to being physical in your respective sports. You each outweigh Mr. Patterson by thirty-five to almost a hundred pounds. You stand taller than him by eight inches. Could you answer my question, why? Mr. Pirello?"

"I don't know."

"Mr. Jackson?"

"I don't know."

"Samuel Bokima, did you see these boys hitting Gary Patterson?"

"Yes."

"If you hadn't intervened, would they have done more damage to Gary Patterson?"

"Very much so."

"Did you get the impression that the two were enjoying beating Gary Patterson?"

"Yes."

D. The Sentence

"Mrs. Pirello, would you like to make any comment?" She shook her head 'no.'

"Mrs. Patterson, do you have anything to ask or would you like to make any comment?" She also shook her head 'no.'

"Gentlemen, any comment?" At this point, Mr. Gammon gave time for each boy to respond if they wanted. "If not, I am ready to read the sentence, the penalties, for your assault on Mr. Gary Patterson. The President of the Cox County School Board, Mr. Josh Stackhouse, the Superintendent of Schools, Mrs. Joy Chambers, the Principal of GHS, and I have made the following determination for disciplinary action to be taken, with the concurring opinion of Dr. Bokima and Mrs. Norma Patterson.

1. You both are responsible for the payment of the medical bill of $1500.00 to Dr. Bokima.

2. **Due November 23** – Each of you will write an essay of 50-words on the value of DIVERSITY IN A COMMUNITY. The essay will be presented to Dr. Timothy Blackmon, professor of sociology at Rhone State. He will judge the essay as either PASS or FAIL. If FAIL, you have one week to rewrite.

3. **Due November 30** – Each of you will write a 100-word review of the Frederick Douglass Essay of 1852, *"What, to the Slave, is the Fourth of July?"* The review will be presented to Rev. Dr. Jack Stone for editing. If he finds your review lacking, you will have one week for rewrite.

4. **Due December 14** – Each of you will write a 500-word essay on: The thoughts the American Indian had when they heard the Pilgrims say, when they landed on Plymouth Rock, "Thank you God, for this land that you have given us." The essays will be presented to Rev. Dr. Talbert Morgan for review. If they do not meet the standards of justice and moral sensitivity, they will be returned for rewrite within one week.

5. Each of you will be required to spend four hours each week, for three months, at the school bus barn cleaning out buses. Scheduling work hours will be through the bus barn director, Tom Harris. He will also evaluate your efforts.

6. You are both required to report to me, Thomas Gammon, each Friday after school for a progress report on the effectiveness of carrying out the requirements of the eight disciplines.

7. Your future participation in your sport will be dependent on when and if the suspension is lifted and how well the requirements have been met. The final decision when the suspension is lifted will be in the hands of the superintendent of schools, the athletic director,

and the coach of your respective sport. A great deal depends on your achievement on the above seven disciplines as to whether you will be participating in the sport.

8. On December 15, meet with me, Samuel Bokima, and Gary Patterson in my office for a review of the above seven disciplines the reinstatement of you being students at Grayville High School is dependent on the review results of the December 15 meeting.

"Mr. Jackson, Mr. Pirello, Mrs. Pirello, do you have any questions or comments?" Mrs. Pirello shook her head 'no.' The two boys did not make any gesture or show any sign of physical anxiety or anger. Their faces reflected no emotion. They did not make any comment.

"It is important that both of you are aware of the most important requirement in addition to the eight requirements, and that is; There will be the imposition of a Restraining Order on both Charles Jackson and Tony Pirello. Under no circumstances are you to have any kind of communication, or physical presence near Mr. Patterson for the remainder of this school year. If you are in violation of this restraining order of a physical presence to Mr. Patterson, or if you make any gesture of intimidation or threat to Mr. Patterson, you will not only be expelled from school, but you will also face a conviction which would lead to imprisonment. Hate crimes are not taken lightly in this state in this time."

Mr. Gammon made a final statement. "Mr. Jackson and Mr. Pirello, we expect these disciplinary actions to be carried out starting at the conclusion of this meeting. Does anyone wish to make any comment?" After a pause, Mr. Gammon said, "Very well, this meeting is adjourned."

E. Post Sentence Happenings

Jon Meacham, biographer, historian, and professor at Vanderbilt University, writes in his book *The Soul of America,* a 1903 Quotes from W.E.B. DuBois, scholar, historian, and activist,

"The problem of the Twentieth Century is the problem of the color-line" Meacham goes on to say, "and, while DuBois was surely right, it is correct, too, to say that color in some ways remains the problem of American history as a whole. Such talk is uncomfortable in the twenty-first century. After King, after Rosa Parks, after John Lewis, after the watershed legislative work of Lyndon B. Johnson in passing the civil rights bills of he mid-1960s, many Americans are less than eager to acknowledge that our national greatness was built on explicit and implicit apartheid. Yet for all the United States has accomplished, and we have been a country that people take pains to come to, not to leave, we remain an imperfect union."

Charles Jackson and Tony Pirello would certainly agree "That color in some ways remains a problem of American history," For them, and others like them beating up a smaller boy of color is their way of handling the problem. The persons attending the meeting at the principal's office saw the reaction, or lack of reaction, of Charles and Tony. They expressed no emotion, gave no visible response to the eight disciplines laid out by Mr. Gammon. Their facial expressions were stoic, with no hint of remorse or anger, just a glazed look of unconcern.

As they were leaving, Mrs. Pirello said little to her son, just a wave goodbye. Tony got in Charles' car and they drove off. Tony was the first to respond to the action taken at the meeting, "I have never heard such bullshit in my life. 500-word essay! My ass! What the fuckin' Indians said when the Pilgrims stuck a pole in the ground? Gimme a break!"

They both had a big laugh at that comment.

Charles expressed similar thoughts as he referred to the 100-word essay, "Who the fuck is this Douglas guy? And, if we don't get it right, we write it over again? Fat chance. It is like they are giving assignments to a girl scout troop. That was a wasted hour. Gammon said the eight things we have to do are all required. What the hell is he talking about?"

F. Jake

Charles said, "Jake wanted us to come over to the Broken Drum to see him and tell him what went on at the meeting. We can tell him that a goddamn farce took place." The Broken Drum is a small, dark, and dingy sports bar on the edge of town where Charles and Tony spend a lot of time and where they will likely spend most of the time while on suspension.

Tony asked "What are we going to do about all those things we are supposed to do? They are required! And, what about this bullshit that we may not get to play our sport next year? What the hell is he talking about? Listen to this," (Tony reads from the sheet that defined the penalties.) 'Your future participation in your sport will depend on your achievement on the above disciplines.' I am not going to wrestle next year? I should dominate my weight class next year. And, Charlie, you have the chance to go to Middle Tennessee State on a football scholarship. What is he trying to do to us? I would like to hear what Jake says about all this."

They arrived at the Broken Drum and immediately went to see Jake. The first thing Jake asked them was, "Tell me about this student you beat up. That is what I am interested in. Why did it take both of you to beat him up? Who was he?

"He is one of the four blacks at school."

Jake asked again, "Why did it take both of you to do it? He must be a monster!

Tony said, "We want to tell you about the requirements Gammon gave us to do to get off suspension. You won't believe this shit."

Jake pushed hard this time. "I asked you about this kid you beat up. Tell me about this kid. Tell me the truth."

Charles spoke up, "He was a black dude. He had it coming to him."

"Alright, tell me why. And tell me about him?" Charles and Tony looked at each other and resigned themselves that they had to tell Jake all about Gary Patterson.

Charles started by making the excuse why two-star Grayville athletes beat up a small frail weak young black student. "We don't need no n------s living in Grayville. So, what the hell happens? We got two goddamn black ass families in Grayville. For the past two or three months I have been hearing from the people who know that we have to do something about it. They can't just come in here and take over."

Jake interrupts Charles. "Are you talking about that bunch of Nazi's? Those thugs filled with hate and violence that you have been hanging out with? Those are your 'people who know?' Charles, if I had a horse whip, I would use it on you. That is the dumbest thing you have ever said. I can't tell you how sorry I am to hear you lost your mind like that."

"I have learned a lot from them. Do you know that in a few years the whole white race will be the minority? What are you going to do then? They are going to take over."

Jake jumped in on that by asking, "So, the solution is to beat up a helpless little black kid. That will stop the white race from being taken over? Charles, you are making dumber statements as we go along. You have got to get your sorry-head out of your ass."

Jake turns his attention to Tony who has been sitting off to the side with a wide-eyed-look on his face. As if he too can't believe what he hears from Charles. "Tony, what do you have to say for yourself, one of Grayville high school's best wrestlers in its history of wrestling. You certainly showed that black kid how good an athlete you are."

"I don't know him. I just saw him for the second time when we met in Gammon's office. I saw his mom that day also. I don't know him." Tony, who can be heard most of the time he talks, could hardly be heard. It was as if he was trying to distance himself from Charles. He never looked at Charles and he never looked at Jake. One would get the idea that his mother was sitting next to him.

Jake exploded. "What the hell were you two thinking? You should have had the book thrown at you. Beating up on a small frail kid! As far as I'm concerned, you can leave and never come back until you grow up. I don't believe you two."

Jake is twenty-two years old. He played football at GHS and got acquainted with Charles when Charles was in junior high football through the Football Boosters Club. But Jake dropped out of school when he was nineteen years old when he got Marilyn Jones pregnant. He had just started his senior year. Marilyn was a sophomore and her dad sent her off to Holy Cross Academy in Indiana to have the baby and finish her sophomore year.

Jake had everything going against him so he just up and quit school. He wasn't good at football or school. He had no family to encourage him or support him. He wasn't even any good for Marilyn Jones. After he dropped out of high school, he worked around Grayville at different places and with different jobs. When he wasn't working at one of the odd jobs he managed to find, he was hanging out at the Broken Drum. Finally, the owner just asked Jake if he would like to work for him at the Broken Drum. "You are here all the time, you know where everything is, you can run the bar and cash register, and you can take care of things while I have to be away for a while. What do you say?" So, Jake became a full-time employee of the Broken Drum.

After a while, Jake cooled off, but was still upset with Charles and Tony. "Whatever you have to do to get off suspension, it isn't enough. You should have been expelled."

After they told Jake what the requirements were, and that they had to do essays and report them to different people "to see how we are doing," Jake asked them, "What choice do you have but to do what they told you to do?"

Charles said, "What choice do we have? You kid'n me! Hell, we don't need to do any of that shit!"

Jake said, "It sounds like you do, and it sounds like you better. If I were you, I would start right away by going to see this kid you beat up and his parents. He is going to determine a lot about how you come out of this. Tony, if you want to wrestle next year, this kid may be your only hope."

Tony said, "We are ordered to stay away from the kid. Gammon said we will be expelled if we go near him. So, that is out. Now, you're saying we should do all those things we were told we have to do?"

"If you don't, what is going to happen to you? What is going to happen if you don't pay the doctor's bill? What are you going to do about that? How are you going to pay it off? What did they say it was?"

"$1500.00"

"Jesus, you better go talk to the doctor, too. Hell, no telling how many people you have to talk to."

"You mentioned a big black kid at the meeting? Why was he there?"

Tony answered him, "He is the doctor's son. He stopped us when we were beating on Gary."

"He is another person you ought to see and talk to. I don't believe it, you guys have a lot of people you have to make contact to! If I were you, I would go see him right away. I would see him before you do anything. And, if you get the chance, talk to him about you going with him to see this kid you beat up. Is he one of the black three basketball players? If he is, he is the one you need to see. You better get on his good side.

You two have some changes to make and I sure hope you can. Man, you have a lot of people to see! Even if you talk to all those people, there are so many more that you have offended. If you don't do some fence-mending, and it has to be serious fence-mending, you may not even graduate. Being an athlete at GHS may be a thing of the past for both of you." Jake didn't sound like a twenty-two-year-old high school dropout. He sounded more like a parent. In fact, he is one! His word to Charles and Tony may be very prophetic, "You two have some changes to make. Big time changes."

"Here is my assessment. I really don't give a damn if you like it or not. But, if no one has told you, I will. Listen to this; 'Two big star athletes beat up a small frail black student in the school hallway.' Do you see that headline in the newspaper? Do you know what people will think? People who are mature, thinking, responsible, intelligent, and decent people? Law abiding citizens.? Here is what they will say, 'What kind of red-neck, bigoted, hate filled, no good ignorant punk would do such a thing?' Then you two appear. You two have some changes to make."

G. Tony Meets Gary

When Tony got home it was still early evening. His mom was sitting at the kitchen table having a cup of coffee. He sat down and talked to her. He asked her what she thought about the meeting earlier in the day. She told him he ought to start the next day doing the things they said he should do. She told him he should do it on his own and forget about Charles and what he does or doesn't do.

She told him she was ashamed of him and sorry for the boy he beat up. She said, "How could you do such a thing? It embarrassed me to sit there today in front of his mother and listen to what you did to that poor boy. After the meeting I wanted to talk to her but I was too ashamed. I am very sorry that there is a restraining order that you have to stay away from the Patterson boy. You really need to talk to him. But he probably would not talk to you. I am sure he is afraid of you."

Tony promised his mom that tomorrow, first thing in the morning, he would send a note of apology to the boy he beat up at school. He figured a note of apology would not violate the "no communication" statement in the restraining order.

"Tony, I have a better idea. I want us to go over to their house and talk to them. Tonight. I need to talk to her. Would you please do that for me? I am willing to take the chance that our going to the Patterson's with an apology will not violate the intent of that restraining order. I am sure that with both mothers present that would not violate the restraining order. In fact, I will take full responsibility for the risk since it is my idea, not yours."

Then Tony remembered what Jake told him just an hour ago, "If I were you, I would start right away by going to see this kid you beat up. He is going to determine a great deal how you come out of this. Tony, if you want to wrestle next year, this kid may be your only hope." Tony thought that if his mother was with him, and Gary's mother was present when he and Gary met, the physical presence order should be excused.

Tony and his mom walked up to the door of Gary Patterson's house. It was a small house not far from the high school. Mrs. Pirello knocked on the door. Mrs. Patterson opened the door. She seemed surprised but in a pleasant way. She smiled at Tony and his mom. Mrs. Pirello spoke first, "Tony and I talked this evening and I told him how ashamed I was over what has happened. I was so ashamed I couldn't even talk to you this morning after the meeting. I told Tony that we just had to come over tonight and tell you how sorry we are."

At this time, Gary came to the door and stood behind his mom. He stopped all of a sudden as he approached the open door and saw Tony. Gary heard his mom invite them in. When Tony and his mom walked in the house, Gary backed up not sure of what to expect from this surprise entrance. Suddenly, Tony felt the fear in Gary and the shock Gary must have felt. Immediately, Tony held out his hand to shake Gary's. Gary looked down at Tony's hand and then automatically stuck out his hand and they shook hands. Nothing was said as they shook hands. Mrs. Patterson invited them all to the living room. Gary, all five feet seven inches, followed the six-foot Tony into the living room.

Mrs. Pirello spoke first as they all sat down. "Gary, I am truly sorry for what has happened. I am ashamed and embarrassed. Mrs. Patterson..."

"My first name is Darla." She interrupted with a smile.

"Darla, I wanted to speak to you this morning after the meeting, but I was too embarrassed. I don't know what I can do to make things better. I know what Tony has to do, but I want to know what I can do."

Darla replied, "You and your son coming here tonight is something I would have never expected. We are very surprised, but I am so glad you did. I have no idea how this is going to work out but now I think things will work out fine. Gary and I haven't even talked about it much. We haven't been able to make much sense out of it all. We didn't realize there was such racial animosity in the school. We certainly didn't think we would ever have the chance to talk to you or Tony or Charles."

Mrs. Pirello said, "We don't know about Charles. I told Tony he is responsible for doing what Mr. Gammon told him to do. I told him to forget about Charles. Charles is the reason he got in trouble in the first place."

Tony finally spoke up. "Gary, I'm sorry for what happened. Mom blames Charles for getting me in trouble doing what I did. But I am not going to blame Charlie for what I did. I should have known better. I am really sorry."

"I am glad you came over tonight. I was really afraid of what might happen when we saw each other again, even with the physical presence restraining order."

"You don't need to be afraid of me. I am really sorry for what I did. I made a big mistake listening to Charles. Talk about being afraid. I was afraid of him. I should have never followed along after him. I am really sorry, Gary.

As mom said, I am going to do what I am supposed to do to get back in school. I want to do all I can to make it up to you. I don't care if Charles follows through or not. I am going to. I deserved to get suspended. I am going to do all the things I am supposed to do. I want to get back in school."

Gary asked Tony, "What if the two of us went to see Mr. Gammon? We could tell him that you and your mom came to our house to visit. We could tell him that we want the restraining order lifted. I will ask him if I can help you with all the requirements. We will tell him that our goal is to get you back in school and back to wrestling."

Tony was taken a back. "Really? You would tell Gammon that you want to help me? Why? Why would you help me after what I did to you?"

"It's the right thing to do. And I know that Samuel would want to help, too."

"You kidding? Are you sure? Samuel would help me? What the hell do you mean, 'the right thing to do'?" Tony shakes his head back and forth, then kind of hangs his head, looking down and softly says to himself, "The right thing to do."

"There is enough strife and chaos in this world. There is too much hate and animosity. It is time people do the right thing of helping and comforting people. At least that is what my mom and I believe."

"Samuel would want to help me, too? I can't imagine you guys wanting to help me. I can't imagine anybody wanting to help me."

There was a long pause. No one said anything. It was as if everybody knew Tony wasn't through talking. He was looking straight into the eyes of Gary. "Especially you two guys."

Tony continued speaking as if trying to make sense of what Gary said, "I know one thing for sure, I need help. But you two guys? My mom has told me over and over, I just don't make the right decisions. She says I make stupid choices. Everything I do, I prove her right.

Gary, if you and Samuel will help me, whatever you want me to do, I will do. You know more about what is right than I do. It sounds like you know this Samuel pretty well. I would like to meet him. I need to apologize to him."

Gary told Tony that he hasn't known Sam very long. "I just met him when you and Charles jumped me. He broke up the fight. That is when I met him."

"I also need to talk to the doctor. Did someone say he is Samuel's dad? If so, I have to talk to him too. In fact, Oh God." Tony seeming overwhelmed, let out a big sigh. "I have a lot of people to talk to if I want to get back in school. I may have gotten myself too deep in trouble to get out. I sure let my mom down."

H. Tony Meets Samuel

Gary Called Samuel and arranged a meeting with the three of them. The three of them would meet after basketball practice Tuesday at Glider's. Gary and Tony picked a table in an area where there was some privacy and quiet enough to talk. Gary and Tony were the first to arrive and as soon as Samuel came in, they waved him over where they were seated.

Tony was anxious and somewhat intimidated as Samuel approached them. He had no idea what he would get from Samuel. He had no idea Sam was as big as he is. Would Samuel say something like, "So, you are a big bad wrestler who picks on people who don't come close to your size." Or, "Gary, why in the world would you want to hang out with someone like this?"

What Tony got from Samuel as he greeted them at the table, was a big smile and warm greeting. "Hi Tony, it is nice to meet you like this and not in the hallway with all kinds of stuff going on. It is good to meet you. As Samuel placed his backpack on the table, he continued, "I didn't have a chance to meet you or talk to you at our meeting with Mr. Gammon the other day. Gary, how are you guys doing?"

Tony immediately offered an apology to Samuel for the trouble he caused. He said, "I am the one you threw across the hallway and slammed against the lockers."

Samuel said, "And here we are having coffee. Things sure do change, don't they? I appreciate the chance to meet you like this with Gary. Who would have ever thought?"

Tony was speechless. Gary stepped in and said, "In answer to your question, we are doing fine. Tony and I have been going over some strategy in preparation to seeing Mr. Gammon. We need your help. The main thing is to convince Gammon to drop the restraining order he imposed on Tony. We don't need the restraining order. Especially if I am going to help Tony."

Samuel said, "Should we all three go see Gammon since I am going to be helping with the eight requirements? I think it would be a good idea if I go along. Gary, you and I have a lot at stake in all this. We want to be successful in getting Tony back on the wrestling team."

Tony had not said a word as Gary and Samuel talked back and forth in making plans and forming strategy. Now, he saw the need to speak but had a hard time. "Guys, I really appreciate what you all are saying. I know my mom, especially appreciates all you are doing. She is so encouraged and enthused about Gary making this gesture of helping me out. And Samuel, she speaks of you like you are the next favorite student in the whole high school. But I don't know what to think. I don't understand all that is happening. I don't understand why you are doing all this. It is as if there was some catch to it all."

Samuel said, "The only catch is that we are going to help you get off suspension, back in school, and back on the wrestling team. That is the catch. Truth is very important here. And the truth is Gary and I want to help you meet the eight requirements. It is an absolutely sure thing if Gammon will OK us helping you. But even if Gammon says no way, the truth is we still are going to help you. There is no catch to it. We are doing it because we care. That is the truth."

Samuel continued on, "Gary may not be very big but he has a big heart. And he has lots of guts. The day you guys beat him up he had an important rehearsal at the Playhouse that evening. He went and did his part and really made a big impression on everyone by his display of guts. It was a display of what is called 'working through the pain.' The guy had dried blood all over his face and clothes. His face was swollen like a ripe cantaloupe from all the bruises and stitches. His eyes were swollen, and one was completely shut. There he was in front of all the cast performing holding an ice pack to his face. Talk about guts!"

At Samuel's description of what Gary went through, Tony tried to hide his face. He looked at Gary with tears in his eyes and trembling lips and said, "Gary, how can you ever forgive me?" With that comment he got up from his chair and gave Gary a big embrace.

Samuel jokingly intercepted Tony's question about forgiveness and said, "Oh, it is not hard for Gary to forgive, he's a Quaker."

While eating cinnamon rolls and drinking coffee, they talked about reconciliation, the essay assignments, and why those topics were chosen. One of the assignments is an essay on "*The Value of Diversity in a Community*" Gary said, "We have had nothing but nonsense, waste, hurt, and trouble because of the lack of diversity in this community. That will be a fifty-word no-brainer" to write that one.

Another assignment is a one-hundred-word commentary on Fredrick Douglas's essay of 1852, "*What, to the Slave, is the Fourth of July?*" Gary again defined the point to be made, "It will take less than one hundred words to tell why slaves didn't celebrate Independence Day." Gary said, "The essay that I can hardly wait to tackle is the one about the American Indians hearing the Pilgrims say, 'Thank you, God, for this land you have given us.' Can't you just hear the Indians who were listening behind the trees looking at each other and saying, 'That's a bunch of bull-shit!'"

The three of them laid out a plan of how and when to meet with Mr. Gammon, how best to deal with the requirements, and who would help with what requirement. The specific plans they made were:

1. Gary, Samuel, and Tony will meet with Mr. Gammon as soon as possible to cancel the physical restriction order imposed on Tony.
2. Samuel will talk to Dr Bokima's accountant on paying a monthly amount toward the payment of the medical bill. (Tony will assume one half of the bill for a total of $750.00)
3. Tony will meet with John McDennis, member of the Grayville Community Church for resources to use in writing the fifty-word essay on *DIVERSITY IN THE COMMUNITY*. Mr. McDennis will coach Tony on the writing of the essay.

4. Tony will meet with Rev. Dr. Jack Stone for resources to use in writing the one-hundred-word essay on *FREDERICK DOUGLAS' ESSAY OF 1852*. Gary will coach Tony on writing the essay.

5. Tony will meet with Rev. Dr. Talbert Morgan to receive coaching and resources for the essay on thoughts the American Indians had at Plymouth Rock when the pilgrims said, "*Thank you God, for the land you have given us.*"

6. Tony, along with Gary, will see Tom Harris at the bus barn to schedule workdays for cleanup.

7. Tony will talk to Mr. Gammon's secretary to schedule Friday dates and times to see Mr. Gammon starting immediately.

8. Tony will talk to Mr. Gammon's secretary to set the time for the December 15 review and evaluation meeting with Mr. Gammon, Samuel, Tony, and Gary.

The next step, suggested by Samuel, was to set a meeting with Mr. Gammon.

XII. The Release to Move Forward

Because they would be meeting soon to begin the process of "coaching" Tony on meeting the requirements, Gary suggested they meet with Gammon right away. But before that meeting with Gammon, "We must have all our ducks in a row. We need to have our plans nailed down and what we want to accomplish, what our goals are. In fact, if we could give him a copy of what we plan to do and in what sequence, that would be extremely helpful. The most important thing we have to do is convince Gammon we are serious in wanting to help Tony."

It was surprising to note that Tony took a major part of the initiative to work out the strategy of meeting with Mr. Gammon. He made the suggestion that both mothers join them in meeting with Mr. Gammon.

He said, "We want him to know we are taking this next step of meeting the requirements seriously." Samuel glanced over at Gary and said, "What have we got here? This guy has turned from being an intolerant-hateful-red-neck-white-supremacist-radical-violent-militant-extremist-bigot to a Quaker?"

Tony offered an explanation, "I have this horrible image built about me of a person wrapped in a restraining order. Those kinds of persons project an image of being very bad for the community, society, and families. I don't want that image. That is why we should project an image of credibility and respect of what we are about. And, if our mothers were there, it will add to our credibility and authenticity."

"All right," said Gary, "it will be the five of us; me, Tony, our moms, and Samuel to see Gammon. Is that okay with you, Sam?"

"I think that is a good idea. All five of us will see Gammon."

"Now, let's get to work on our strategy."

"Gammon said the restraining order was the most important of all the requirements, so this will let him know we also see it as a very important element in Tony getting off his suspension."

Tony raised the question, "Who will call Gammon for the appointment? Gary, we will have to make sure it is a time when our moms can attend. As far as my mom is concerned, she will welcome this so much, she will take off work whenever we can get the meeting lined up."

Gary said the same thing. "My mom will take off work for this anytime. Who is going to call Gammon? Who **should** call Gammon?"

Samuel suggested that he be the one to call. "I am more of an observer to this whole incident. I am also considered a prime witness. I think if I called, Gammon would be more inclined to respond to me. Especially since my dad has so much at stake here. He is very much involved."

"Okay, then you call and let Gammon set the date and time. We will accommodate his schedule. That will be more of a statement from us that we are serious about this. We are doing as much as we can to cooperate with him."

When Samuel called Mr. Gammon, the principal, he asked Samuel if such a meeting would interfere with the pregame preparations against Clifton. "After all, this is an especially important game. A lot is at stake, a lot on the line. I certainly do not want our conversation to take away from the concentration and mental preparedness needed for the game."

Samuel responded with, "Gary and I think helping Tony is more important than the basketball game. The preparations and concentration for the work ahead for Tony is our main focus right now. In fact, it will help in my preparation for the game. What we are doing is very energizing."

The meeting date and time was set for after school the next day and the mothers didn't have to miss work to make the meeting. The agenda for the meeting was very specific and to the point. They would go over the requirements that Tony is expected to fulfill and then they would mention the goals they had established. They met in the same room where they met with Tony and Charles to give the sentence and requirements.

As they all were seated, Gary made the first comment. He told Mr. Gammon that in spite of the restraining order, Mrs. Pirello and Tony came to the Patterson's home to apologize for Tony's behavior. Gary told him, "It was at that occasion that I volunteered to help Tony meet the requirements to get off suspension. Tony agreed and I also told Tony that Samuel would also help in meeting the requirement laid out by you." Gary provided the following sheet which defined their strategy and the goals.

Gary, and Mrs. Patterson, Tony, and Mrs. Pirello, and Samuel will meet with Mr. Gammon:

1. In order to cancel the physical restriction order imposed on Tony for the protection of Gary Patterson.
2. Samuel will talk to Dr. Bokima's accountant on a payment schedule of a monthly amount toward the payment of the medical bill for treatment of Gary. (Tony will assume one half of the bill for a total of $750.00)

3. Tony will meet with John McDennis, member of Fairfield Glade Community Church for resources to use in writing the fifty-word essay on *DIVERSITY IN THE COMMUNITY*. Gary and Samuel will provide assistance where needed for Tony on the writing of the essay. Tony will submit the finished essay to Mr. McDennis for final approval. After final approval, the essay will be submitted to Mr. Gammon.

4. Tony will meet with Rev. Dr. Jack Stone for resources and advice to use in writing the one-hundred-word essay on *FREDERICK DOUGLAS' ESSAY OF 1852*. Gary and Samuel will provide assistance to Tony on writing the essay.

5. Tony will meet with Rev. Dr. Talbert Morgan to receive coaching and resources for the essay on thoughts the American Indians had at Plymouth Rock when the pilgrims said, *"Thank you God, for the land you have given us."*

6. Tony, along with Gary, will see Tom Harris at the bus barn to schedule workdays for cleanup.

7. Tony will talk to Mr. Gammon's secretary to establish Friday dates and times to see Mr. Gammon starting immediately.

8. Tony will talk to Mr. Gammon's secretary to set the time for the December 15 review and evaluation meeting with Mr. Gammon, Samuel, Tony, and Gary.

The following four goals are those that Gary Patterson, Samuel Bokima have established **with** Tony Pirello:

1. Have the restraining order removed.

2. Meet all requirements and meet them beyond the expectations laid out.

3. Have Tony removed from the suspension list.

4. Enable Tony to be reinstated as a member of the wrestling team.

XIII. The Next Game – Clifton at CCHS

A. The First Practice Since Shelby

It was Monday after a very busy weekend of conversations about the need for reconciliation and empathy. It was a weekend of meetings and conversations on how to transform attitudes and behavior. For teenage boys, the agenda for the weekend of heavy topics to deal with was necessary because the stakes were so high. The conversations on such significant points of interest were necessary due to the wide span of the effect Grayville's basketball team had on the country. It was a weekend of how to fashion the elimination of learned prejudices, racist opinions and ingrained mind-sets around intolerance.

There were a lot of anxious feelings in the locker room as the players were getting dressed for practice. It was the first practice and preparation for the first game since the Friday night Shelby forfeit. On the floor, just before practice was to begin, there were some nervous feelings during the warmups. Everyone was doing fine, just nervous. No negative words or downcast attitudes were noticed. Everyone did their best to provide an atmosphere of ease and "back to normal."

As they took the floor for practice, the coach called them together to warn them, "As you can see, there are several fans in the stands today for practice. We have never had that before. There are also some TV and newspaper people here. They all want to see how you relate to each other in the first practice since Friday. They want to talk to you to find out how you are feeling and behaving after all that has happened over the weekend. You are going to be on display.

"I could very easily clear the gym of all these visitors, but that would just add to the 'spectacle' of what is going on in Grayville. We will act like nothing is or has been going on. We are going to show them 'normal.' We will just go about practice and act like nothing has ever happened."

Practice went better than Coach Montgomery could hope for. It was the best practice they have had all year! They were fast and quick in their moves and loud as they called each other's name to encourage or get their attention for a certain move on a particular play. They yelled "good move," "good drive," "good shot," "way to go," "nice hustle." Coach Montgomery told the assistant coach, "This is the most spirited and motivated I have seen them this year." The team put on a great display to those who were watching in the bleachers.

B. The Strategy for Making a Statement

The coach cut the practice short in order for them to meet in the locker room because he had something important to discuss. After everyone had a drink of water and got settled down, he told them, "We are going to have a huge crowd Thursday night in the game with Clifton. Talk about being on display! You are going to be looked over, scrutinized, evaluated, judged, observed intently to see how much you hate each other. They will be looking to see how you show that hate. They will look for the prejudice they think you have. They will look to see how far you distance yourself from each other, how big the wall is.

"What we are going to show them (Coach slows his speech and clearly enunciates each word as he repeats.) what we are going to show them, is how much we love each other. How we care for each other. We are going to show them how a team that faced difficulty, how a team that faced what could have been a fatal blow, comes together as one, as a close-knit family. We are going to show them unity. We are going to show them balance and harmony.

"The problem is there will be many in the stands who want to see us fail. They will want to see animosity and hard feelings between us. They don't want to see that we are a team, or that we are restored to each other. They don't want us to be okay. They are people who have never realized their best selves. They don't want us to realize our best selves. They don't want to see us rise above the problem of last Friday night. They want to see us as failures.

119

"Thursday night, when we get on the floor, how can we show them we have risen above the problem of last Friday? How can we show them our best selves? How can we show them we are too mature for hate, prejudice, animosity? How can we demonstrate that we are somebody special? What can we do Thursday night to show them that we are winners?" The coach then waited for them to respond.

"David spoke up first. He seems to always have something positive to say and it is usually the right thing. He gives the impression that he is a mature responsible adult. "I thought tonight's practice was the best practice I have ever been a part of. And, I have been in basketball practices since the third grade. That is a lot of practices! The reason tonight's practice was so good was that we were loud! We made noise. We yelled at each other, but we yelled good stuff. When I stuffed that one dunk, Tom yelled 'Great shot' so loud I said to myself, 'What the hell was that?'"

Everyone laughed at his comment. "So, I got the message and when Joe dove for that loose ball, and smashed into all those chairs, I yelled like hell, 'Way to hustle!' If the fans hear us yell like a bunch of crazed banshees, with excited words of encouragement and support to each other, they will get turned on and excited, too. They will know we are giving it our best. And they will really get into the game. And they will get a real positive message from us."

David continues, "Chad and I were talking about the high five. We asked questions at lunch, where did the high five come from? What does the high five mean? When we see people give a high five it seems to mean a great deal. It means congratulations, good job, way to go, you are good, I appreciate you. Sweet. Nice."

Chad added, "When people see us give high fives, they see it as our way of giving support and encouragement. It has a way of showing that we care for each other. When I get a high five, it is very motivating and energizing. If the fans see us doing that, it will really send the message we want them to get. That no one hates anyone. That we know we made a terrible mistake but through forgiveness, grace, and love for each other we have become our better selves."

Wes responded with, "Man, for a minute there, I thought we were going to have to take up an offering after that sermon by Chad." He added his usual brand of light-hearted expertise. He said, "We are going to be so cool; the crowd will think a light bulb went off in our heads."

Ronnie, who is always on the quiet side, said, "I am always encouraged when you talk to me, when you yell out my name. Tonight, at practice, you kept yelling things to me. Encouraging things. Good things. Things that let me know I was included, that I was an important teammate. When Wes kept yelling, 'Ronnie! Ronnie!' over and over, it was great! He did it during warmups. When we were in line doing layups, he simply yelled my name! For no reason but to yell my name. He kept getting louder!

Sometimes he would yell 'Twenty-two!' my jersey number. So, I vote for talking to each other. To do the yelling, really yelling at each other during warmups, especially calling out our names. It made me feel like you were putting me on the radar. I was being announced! And loudly! So, I started doing it too. Then, I heard a couple of the people in the stands doing it. They started yelling out our names. They really got into it."

Coach said, "We have an especially important message to deliver to the fans Thursday night. All we do, everything we do as a team, as individual players, whatever the crowd sees, will be important in getting our message across. The message that we are taking seriously is that there is no room for discrimination, bias, or hatred. The message is that we seek to be sensitive to racial equality, thoughtfulness to other people, and being compassionate. And they should too."

C. Taking Precautions

Unknown to the players, was a meeting after practice in the principal's office that included the coach, the superintendent, Mr. Josh Stackhouse, the principal, Mr. Gammon, the director of school security, Mr. Foster, the principal of Stone Memorial, Mr. Jeffries, and a representative of the Grayville Clergy Association, Rev. Morgan. When they all gathered, Mr. Gammon told everyone that Coach Montgomery called the meeting. He turned the meeting over to the coach.

"I don't know what the expectations or plans are going to be of some people who attend the game Thursday night. All that has been going on in our country regarding race relations, all that we have experienced in our own community with the harassment and intimidation of one of our black families, one of our black students being beaten in the hallway, and the ugliness of last Friday, makes us vulnerable to some unpredictable behavior. I don't know how cautious we should be. I don't want to be an alarmist but there have been several unfortunate incidents which have targeted the Bokima family and the only other black student, Gary Patterson with harassment and intimidation.

"I would feel safe and secure if we took some preventive measures to be prepared for the unexpected. I would rather err on the side of being overly cautious. Non-descript safety measures. Not attention getting. Undistinguishable. Everything ordinary, not extraordinary. No one patrolling the parking lot or hallways or gym with automatic weapons. No militia dressed and armed to the teeth.

"I don't know if we will have anything like a demonstration. I don't know if some guy is going to show up to make his position known by bringing in a confederate flag, or a Black Lives Matter banner, or having an automatic weapon slung over his shoulder, or some extremist group disrupting the game, making a scene.

"Because that is a possibility, maybe not likely, but possible, I am thinking of having plain clothes police seated at different places in the crowd. We could also have some clergy placed in the crowd to serve as monitors, provide surveillance, and just keep an eye open for potential trouble. When anything comes up that is out of the ordinary, those persons could diffuse the situation right away.

"I talked to the sheriff about having uniformed sheriff's deputies patrol the parking lot as people arrive for the game. He was very cooperative and was in agreement with the idea. I told him if a carload of troublemakers comes into the parking lot they should be turned away before anything gets started. I would like to see at least one uniformed police officer at the four entrances to the gym. I may be overreacting, but we have become the news beyond Cox County on TV and newspapers. I can see uninvited guests come around just to create trouble.

"I also went to the state police station in Grayville to ask if we could have three or four state policemen in attendance, just to make their presence known. The officer in charge was receptive to the request and said he would have three patrolmen at the game." With that, Coach sat down.

The principal of Clifton said, "I think your suggestions are excellent as we approach the game. I am all for such precautions. I will be glad to have some of our school staff work with the police and the clergy to keep a sensitive eye on the crowd."

Mr. Foster, the security officer for the schools said he would be glad to coordinate the persons who would assume the surveillance roles.

The superintendent of schools, Mr. Josh Stackhouse said that he liked the idea of having uniformed police in attendance.

Discussion continued on the logistics and rationale. Everyone was in accord with providing preventive measures. Mr. Gammon suggested that Mr. Foster, be the one to handle the overall administration and supervision of the plan. Rev. Morgan said he would like to have Mr. Foster and some of the police officers meet with everyone, especially the volunteers before the game and give some "coaching techniques" on what to do if some suspicious person had to be encountered, or if the worst case scenario took place, that someone in attendance had to be escorted out of the gym.

Mr. Stackhouse mentioned that he would like to see the added security of having an x-ray machine or a metal detector to check if someone is bringing in a gun. He asked if a metal detector could be rented. He said that it would be terrible if some crazy came to the game to really cause a serious problem like that. Mr. Foster said he has access to a metal detector and he would meet with the city police chief to take care of that security measure. He said he knows of the police officer who handles such matters and provides police officers to manage each x-ray machine.

Mr. Foster went on to say that we would have a metal detector at each entrance to the gym which would help alleviate long lines of fans coming into the gym. He also added that if a person left the gym to get refreshments or go to the restroom, they would have to pass through another metal detector again.

Mr. Foster also suggested that we make use of the security cameras, placed in the hallway to the gym. He suggested we look into the possibility of adding to the security cameras already in place. He said he would check on the availability of that added security.

Rev. Morgan asked the question about persons attending the game and wearing inappropriate clothing such as a tee-shirt that says, "Black Lives Suck" or some other statement that could inflame emotions. Mr. Foster said that he would inform the uniformed police who would be present at the game to be on watch for such persons and ask them to change clothes or leave. Mr. Stackhouse and Mr. Gammon said they would also patrol the crowd to monitor such clothing issues.

Coach Montgomery said he was very pleased at their response and suggestions. He said he was no longer apprehensive about the crowd and what might take place. He said, "You have all been very thorough and helpful. I think we have everything covered in a very comprehensive way. Thank you."

Rev Morgan interjected one last thought. "I am sorry for this last comment I want to make; I know this has been a long and intense meeting. But the question I have is, what about Dr. and Mrs. Bokima and Mrs. Patterson and Gary? Should special attention be paid to them? Do you anticipate anyone to act out some unpredictable undisciplined manner of aggression or to antagonize? If anyone is a target, other than the three players, it would be those four persons.

Should someone pick them up and bring them to the game? Should they be escorted into the gym? Should we have someone seated with them and about them just for precautionary sake? My wife and I would be glad to accompany the Bokimas and maybe someone could do the same with Mrs. Patterson and Gary. As Coach Montgomery said, 'It is better to err on the side of being too cautious.' Sorry for the added agenda item."

Mr. Gammon responded right away. "Rev. Morgan, thank you for your added agenda. It was well worth the time and comment. My wife and I will be glad to be the escorts for the Patterson's. And, if each of you would tune in to where we are seated, that should provide some sense of security. Rev. Morgan, will that cover the need as you described it?"

Rev. Morgan said "I think that will be excellent. Thank you."

Mr. Foster and Mr. Gammon worked on the plans for the next two days. The plans included four Grayville uniformed police officers, and four uniformed sheriff's deputies. They would patrol the parking lot prior to the game as well as the hallways to the gym. Then they would be stationed at each of the four entrances of the gym during the game. Six plain clothes police officers would be seated strategically throughout the crowd. There would be eight clergy also strategically placed throughout the crowd. They would be looking for any suspicious person who looked like they were not really interested in a basketball game.

The officers who will be patrolling the parking lot will be on the lookout for a carload or vanload of people who are dressed like they might be looking for trouble. They will be looking for someone who might be planning on carrying a flag or banner with some message or symbol into the gym. That will be a serious "red flag!" Someone could come carrying a Confederate Flag rolled up and ready to be opened once in the gym. Hopefully, a police officer or one of the volunteers would spot the potential trouble and tell him to put it back in his car. They want to prevent anyone from trying to bring in a flag or banner or any sign that would cause a problem.

D. The Game

When the buzzer sounded for the game to start, they ran to the bench and the starting five had their sweats off in no time. They were ready to go. The Clifton team moseyed over to the bench and the starting five took their time getting off their sweats. The starting five GHS huddled, not only with Coach Montgomery, but with the whole team. No one looked anywhere but at the center of the huddle. They were tuned in to what was being said in the huddle. They were tuned in to what was about to happen.

When the starting five broke from the huddle and ran to the center of the floor, they were sent off by their yelling teammates on the bench encouraging and inspiring them on. They were at center court giving high fives and looking ready to go long before the Clifton starting five got to center court. When the Clifton five got to center court, they looked as though they were not sure what was going to happen.

At the tip of the ball to start the game, it was as if the Clifton players just wanted to watch. Joseph clearly out jumped the Clifton center. The ball went to the free-throw line of the Grayville side picked out of the air by David and without dribbling slammed dunked the ball for a quick two-point lead. The crowd erupted.

When Clifton brought the ball down court, within two minutes David intercepted a pass and made a quick pass to Chad who dribbled in for another quick two points. Then within thirty seconds, Mark stole the ball at their end of the court and dribbled up to the three-point line and over the outstretched arms of the defenders swished a three-pointer. In just a matter of less than two minutes, Grayville had a seven-point lead.

The crowd, on both sides, made itself known as they cheered loudly and constantly. Each side showed a spirited involvement in the progress of the game. They often would stand to give applause and appreciation for a great play and job well done to each individual player. It was without a doubt one of the noisiest, most aggressive, and most active of any crowd in the history of the Grayville High School gym.

But it was also, considering the social ramifications and potential racial powder keg as a reaction of last Friday night, a crowd under control. Considering the presence in the county of a white supremacist militant group, it was very fortunate that there had been no hint of a potential incident. There was no expression of any kind to demonstrate a racist message or any sign or banner to promote a movement. Considering the size of the crowd in this volatile political atmosphere, it was a very orderly, in control, disciplined crowd.

Why was there such an absence of a demonstration and why was the crowd so well behaved? Did it come as a result of the order and discipline of the team under scrutiny? What the crowd saw and experienced in the players from GHS was maturity and responsible behavior. The questions were; are these the same white players who spoke in such derogatory hateful racist terms of their black teammates? Are these the same black players who were the targets of such hateful remarks?

What the crowd saw and heard and experienced were the Grayville players giving expressions of support and encouragement to each other. What the crowd saw were teammates loudly cheering on each other. The noise the bench made in support of each other was as loud and animated as the student cheering section in the bleachers. The noise from the bench motivated the crowd to match their enthusiasm. And they did.

When a GHS sub came out of the game, the whole bench erupted with a cheer and all came off the bench onto the floor to greet him and give him high-fives. What the crowd saw was a team giving pats on the back, fist bumps, high-fives. They saw teammates standing up with enthusiasm to loudly cheer a great shot or pass or play.

What the crowd saw and heard and experienced was a team that showed how much they cared for each other. Expressions of support and encouragement were given at most every opportunity. The player's mood was upbeat, positive, energetic, full of enthusiasm, and became very contagious. If the crowd came expecting to see a team immersed in hate, they saw a team expressing joy with each other. If the crowd came expecting to see a team caught up in a racist tone, they saw a team celebrating their diversity. If the crowd came expecting to see a team tied up in resentment and animosity, they saw a team demonstrating the creation of a new beginning.

E. The Final Score

For the past five years, Clifton, the number one rival of GHS, had won all nine games by big margins. Everyone mentioned how GHS should have belonged to a less competitive league. Clifton was always dominant.

Tonight, one could predict what was going to be the outcome of the game. After watching the two teams in warmups, it was easy to predict who was going to win. Each player from GHS participated in the warmups with seriousness and enthusiasm as if it was a game. As a team they looked like they were really looking forward to playing. One felt a sense of urgency and energy about them during warmups. Everyone could see they were ready and anxious to play.

At the end of the first quarter, the score was twenty-eight to eight, GHS. And that was with substitutions being made along the way. Coach Montgomery substituted freely, to keep the score down. But it didn't matter, subs or not. It was as if every player from GHS was playing on a state championship team and this was the final game.

At the half, the score was fifty-four to fifteen. Joseph, who was ranked second in scoring in the state with an average of thirty-four points per game, had nineteen points at the half and six blocked shots. David, who was an excellent three-point shooter, had made four straight three point shots. At the half, he had a total of sixteen points.

During the game, the enthusiasm the GHS players showed, was contagious to the crowd. The GHS gym had never heard such noise. As the game went on and as the crowd witnessed the energy and "rebirth" of a team recently on shaky ground, the team felt a determination and resolve. With the hustle the boys showed, the crowd got into the game even more. With the high fives the boys gave to each other, the crowd became punctuated with high fives. When a sub came out of the game, the applause and greeting the bench gave him became motivations for the crowd to match their cheers. And they did.

The final score was not the victory. The final score was not the message the nine players of GHS wanted the fans to get. The message the team wanted the crowd to get was that change for the better had taken place. Good came out of what looked like a disaster just days ago.

The disaster of a few days ago was brokenness and divisiveness. When people experience divisiveness, it could come from hate, envy, sadness, abuse, or being shattered. Brokenness or divisiveness can be repaired, mended, and healed by people coming together as one. The final score the GHS team wanted to proclaim was that hate is never the last word, brokenness is never the last word, because love is more powerful.

The GHS team had averaged seventy-five points in its previous four games while their opponents averaged thirty-five points. GHS scored ninety-two and Clifton scored forty. Joseph increased his average points per game to thirty-five. He scored thirty-seven points against Clifton and he got his thirteen blocked shots.

The message that the GHS players wanted to convey to the crowd was in their pledge fashioned by Joseph; *Accept everyone as precious and of sacred worth; practice forgiveness over holding a grudge; love not hate; affirm each other; don't criticize; show empathy, not selfishness; replace prejudice with basketball; choose maturity over thoughtlessness; show compassion and care; think.*

Grayville High School Student Council served as hosts to the game with Clifton and passed out copies of the pledge signed by all the players.

Following the game, the team met in the locker room, Coach asked Chad if he would lead the team in prayer. Chad said yes and did.

STAGE THREE

XIV. Dark Side

But there were those at the basketball game who did not get into the excitement of the game. They didn't care. There were those who did not pay attention to the new energy and rebirth of the Grayville players. They didn't care. They were only interested in perpetuating their brand of hate and prejudice. The Aryan Patriotic Brotherhood (APB) was meeting at the Cox State Park, just outside Grayville, the weekend of the Clifton game. Some came to the game.

The APB had bigger fish to fry throughout the country, but what was taking place in Grayville, TN got their attention. During the past three months the black three of Grayville had generated a great deal of attention throughout the country. Before the Bokima family moved to Grayville, it was a town that didn't generate any kind of attraction to a group like the APB.

There were only two attractions in Grayville. One was the label it acquired as being the "Golf Capital of the Southeast." There are seven excellent golf courses in the area and the local Stonegap golf course has been designated as one of the "Top 100" golf courses in the USA. The other attraction is the Community Playhouse which is designated as "The best kept secret in Tennessee." Now that the black three are in Grayville, in a town with a population of 12,000, they generated a great deal of attention on national news and from the APB.

That is why the APB choose this place and this time to make their presence known with their annual conference at the Cox State Park. One would think that the Aryan Patriotic Brotherhood had bigger targets as witnessed by their many demonstrations and rallies throughout the county. In the past three months the APB has been in Seattle, and Portland to counter the civil rights demonstrations due to the death of George Floyd. They made their presence known in Minneapolis for five days while assuming the role of enforcer with a para-military image counter-protesting the Black Lives Matter movement and counterdemonstration for George Floyd. They have been to Grand Rapids, Michigan where they made their protests known to pursue their anti-black lives matter movement.

Grayville, a town that has no resident black family, now had a high-profile black family. The Bokima family had become a family and individuals of highest esteem and respect. The parents include a physician and an architect. The three boys are exceptional basketball players and make up three of the starting five for GHS. The singular factor that has drawn the attention of the country and the APB was the hateful, vitriolic, and racist comments made about the black three by five white teammates, not including Mark. The APB came to focus its attention on Grayville and exploit and take advantage of its unique racial crisis. They saw Grayville as a potential racial bomb going off to spread the cause of white power in a way that would generate a great deal of interest all over the country. They wanted to be the catalyst to cause the bomb to go off.

During the game Gary and Tony were sitting a few rows up from the GHS team bench when Gary saw a face in the crowd that he recognized. It was from a picture with an article about Tennessee hate groups that recently appeared in the Knoxville paper. He was seated up and off to the right in the bleachers higher than Gary and Tony, but Gary recognized the face.

It was Lester "Big Body" Boone, the president of the APB, all six foot three and three hundred and thirty pounds. Gary couldn't forget the face. He had a mountain-man beard and zombie like eyes that stared down at a person putting them in paralyzing fear. He had a face that matched his big body. He had a big nose, big ears, thick busy eyebrows, and a head of unkept hair to match his beard. After Gary recognized him, he watched him most of the game. Boone didn't stand when the crowd stood. He didn't cheer when the crowd cheered. He didn't yell at the referee when everybody else did. Gary was very curious as to why he was at the game and not with his Aryan Patriotic Brotherhood at the state park.

As Gary looked closer, he saw that Charles Jackson was sitting next to Big Body Boone! Why was Charles, a junior in high school, at the game with Boone? The only athletic events he attended were his own football games. Was Charles being recruited by the APB? Did Charles invite Boone so that he could deal with Samuel who broke up the fight? Or was Charles at the game with Boone so they could finish the beating Charles started? Surely not. Boone had bigger fish to fry, like the governor of Michigan. Gary figured the best guess is that with the racist flag flying after the Shelby game forfeit, Boone and the APB were here to pour gas on the issue and lite it.

Gary pointed out the two to Tony. He asked Tony, "Do you know the big bushy haired guy up there with Charles?" Tony looked in that direction and finally saw him. "No, but the way is he dressed I bet he is some kind of white supremist or a member of some kind of militant extremist group. I have noticed the last few weeks that Charles has been talking that white supremist Nazi shit quite a bit. Charles has really taken notice that Grayville has a black family and three of the starting five at GHS are black. So what does he do? He suckers me into helping him beat up the smallest black kid in school."

Tony asked, "Who is the guy?"

Gary said, "He is Lester 'Big Body' Boone of the Aryan Patriotic Brotherhood. The APB is one of the thirty-eight hate groups in Tennessee. If we look around, I wouldn't be surprised if we see a few other members of the APB."

The Southern Poverty Law Center (SPLC) reports that there are more hate groups in the US than ever before. There are nine hundred forty hate group recognized in the US according to the SPLC. Some of those hate groups are the KKK, Neo-Nazi, White Nationalist, Racist Skinhead, Neo-Confederate, Anti-Immigrant Force to name just a few. Mark Potok of the SPLC also reports that the number of hate crimes in 2017 was 7,775, up from 6,612 in 2016 and continues to increase.

Many law enforcement agencies in Tennessee believed that the extremist groups were becoming a thing of the past. The March 24 slaying of Jack Morris of Guthry, TN, and the investigation of that killing, revealed that the extremist hate groups are alive and well. The Tennessee Bureau of Investigation says that one of the worst characteristics about them is that "They have the effect of poisoning democracy."

It was unsettling to Gary to see Charles sitting with "Big Body" Boone. Not only was it a surprise to see them at a basketball game, but it is not good news that the APB was at the Cox State Park just a short distance away from the school. Since Charles had his encounter with Gary interrupted by Samuel, Gary felt some anxiety as to why they were here. Were they looking around the crowd for him?

Ever since the Bokima family moved to Grayville, they have felt the anxiety of racial unrest with them being the target. Never before had there been such a black presence in Cox County as with this family. After school started, the family began to settle in. Dr. Bokima, in just a short time, felt warmly received as he established his practice and Mrs. Bokima became a valued volunteer at the Community Playhouse. And the black three made their presence known in a big way on the basketball court. As the family assumed their roles in the community, they began to feel apprehension in the subtle messages of racial tension.

Although Gary was not related in any way to the new family, he had been targeted for harassment because he is black. The unwritten message was simply that there were too many blacks in Grayville.

The five white basketball players eventually got caught up in the anti-black family sentiments (except Mark) and then the top blew off. For a full week it was as if someone gave them the green light to turn on the heat of prejudice and harassment of the new black family in Grayville.

News of racial unrest travels fast. That was when the volunteers from all over came to the aid of the Bokimas. In that short time, after the Shelby forfeit, the volunteers came to make a statement, "There is no place for prejudice or bigotry in this community. Either stop the harassment or get out."

As the volunteers made their presence known and as they did their job of providing a watchful eye, escorting and general surveillance, the APB and "APB wannabes" slowed down the harassment and many left altogether. After the Clifton game, it was hoped that things would start to turn around.

Yet, there are people like Charles Jackson in Cox County who have a prejudice toward blacks and other minorities, and they don't belong to a white supremacist group. They have made their voices heard and their positions known. Some groups give illicit approval of hate and prejudice because they exist under the guise of a name like the Tea Party, or Bikers for Jesus, or Citizens for a Better Way. Ask any member about the details of membership and prejudice finds its way between the lines.

The message of the white players was that their expressions of hateful rhetoric was turned into expressions of reconciliation and affirmation toward their black teammates. That was not the message Boone, Charles, and others like them wanted to hear. But that was the message the white players proclaimed, not just to Cox County, but proclaimed throughout the country.

The victory over Clifton and the spirit with which GHS played, was an affirmation that prejudice will not be tolerated here. Since the Shelby forfeit, there were many steps taken, plans were made with careful and thorough details, and those plans were administered to make right the terrible wrong caused by the five white players from GHS.

Such steps in forgiveness and grace are contrary to the very essence of the APB. The motivating factor for the existence of hate in the APB and groups like them are the projections that by 2043, whites will be a minority in the US. That does not sit well with members of the APB.

As Gary and Tony were leaving the bleachers to join several people waiting outside the locker room door for the players to come out, Tony saw Jake from the Broken Drum. Jake came over to talk to them and said, "I am glad I saw you tonight. I have a question for you. I would like to ask you about Charles." At this point Tony interrupted Jake and introduced him to Gary. Tony was quick to mention that Gary was the student he and Charles beat up.

Jake stopped in his tracks. He looked stunned. "This is the student you and Charles beat up?" Jake was pointing at Gary. "I can't believe you both did something so stupid." Jake turned to Gary and said, "Gary, I am really sorry. I thought I knew these guys. I guess I don't know them at all." Then he turned to Tony, "What the hell were you guys thinking? I hope the school suspended you both."

"We got suspended. We each have eight responsibilities to meet if we want the suspension lifted. The eight requirements include three essays to be written on the subject of race relations and equality. And we have a restraining order to not go near Gary. If we violate the restraining order, we will get expelled from school and face criminal charges. But, as you can see, the restraining order has been lifted for me."

Jake asked Gary if Tony was assuming his responsibility in meeting the requirements the school laid out for him and Charles to do. Gary told him they were making plans to meet the requirements. Jake commented further to Tony, "I am sure that Charles is not doing anything required of him. To have a restraining order against you is one of the worst charges against anyone. It symbolizes a real degenerate person. You have your work cut out for you. You have a lot of serious strikes against you. You will need some help."

Tony added, "Charles may never get off suspension and finish school or play football again, unless he has a big change of heart and pays attention to the eight requirements laid out for him. I think he is into this white supremist shit. He was at the game with the president of one of the hate groups, the Aryan Patriotic Brotherhood."

"Well, that was the question I had for you about Charles, that white supremist relationship. Let's forget about Charles for now. Am I right in thinking you are getting your shit together? That Gary here is setting you straight? Gary, is he cooperating?"

Gary told Jake that Tony had begun one of the three essays. "I am helping him get the eight requirements met. It is important that Tony get back in school so he will be eligible for wrestling next year. I am going to help out as much as I can."

Jake said he was impressed that Gary had the attitude toward Tony that he did. Jake told Tony he hopes he keeps up this relationship with Gary. "You continue to listen to Gary and do what he says. It sounds like this is the best thing that has happened to you in a long time."

Jake said, "I am really glad to meet you Gary, and I think it is super what you are doing with Tony. I wish I had someone like you as my mentor when I made the decision to drop out of school. Tony, I am glad to see you working on getting back in school. Gary, if I can do anything to help out, please let me know. I hope to see you guys again sometime. Take care."

A. The Aryan Patriotic Brotherhood Met Their Match

Gary and Tony were waiting to see Samuel when he came out of the locker room. They had arranged to meet after the game and go to Cookville and Cinco Amigos for a late dinner. When Samuel met them, Gary told him about seeing "Big Body" Boone and Charles. Samuel said he had read an article about the APB meeting at the Cox State Park. After a few people greeted Samuel and congratulated him on a great game, the three of them left for the parking lot.

As they were walking through the parking lot, they noticed fewer cars as the crowd had thinned out quite a bit. Charles, "Big Body" Boone and two other suspicious looking men approached them. It appeared they had been waiting for them. They looked like they had done an extensive shopping spree at an army surplus store. They had green camouflaged uniforms, big heavy combat boots, pants tucked in the boots, berets, black heavy gloves, badges and flags and assorted patches sewn all over, big thick army belts, and crosses on heavy chains hanging from around their necks. The only thing missing was an automatic weapon cradled in their arms.

When they got close, Charles said to Tony, "What the fuck are you doing with this big ass nigger and this puny piss-ass nigger?"

As the four approached, Samuel stood in the middle of Tony and Gary and told them to keep quiet, "Just stay steady. I'll take care of this."

"Big Body" Boone said to Samuel, "Nigger, you ain't gonna take care of anything. We are gonna pound your fuckin head in."

Gary noticed that the two unidentified men had thick weighted leather cords about a foot-long hanging from their gloved right hands. Boone pulled out a black "six-incher" billy-club. Charles had a motorcycle chain wrapped around his gloved right fist with about a foot hanging down loose.

Unbeknown to Samuel, Gary, and Tony, five plain clothes policemen and Jake had been walking behind them when they were stopped by Charles and his "friends." While Samuel was standing still and Charles and Boon and friends were approaching him, the plain clothes cops continued approaching and surrounded them all. One of the cops said to Charles and the other three "You guys drop all the weapons and lie down on you stomachs with your hands behind your back."

"Big Body" Boone and his two thugs looked about them as if they were trying to figure a way out. As they were looking around, four uniformed state policemen came up to them with handcuffs and told the four, "Do as you were told and lay face down with your hands behind your backs." As the four were laying down, the state policemen cuffed them. This took place quickly and smoothly. There was no resistance or reaction of any kind. Not a word was spoken. It was over in no time as the state police led them off to a van to take them to jail.

Jake was suspicious about the APB being at the state park for a conference and got even more suspicious when he saw that "Big Body" Boone was at the basketball game. He assumed that Charles told them about Samuel, a black guy, breaking up the beating of a small black student. He began to put several pieces together and got suspicious of what Boone, his two thugs, and Charles might try to do tonight.

The first piece of the several pieces was that Jake learned that Charles had developed a big interest that leaned the way of white power extremism and Jake knew he had been in contact with "Big Body" Boone. The second piece that got Jake suspicious was that Jake knew Charles and Boone attended the basketball game when neither one ever had an interest in basketball. He suspected they were there just to "scout" around to see if and how they could get Samuel and the Patterson kid.

The third piece was that Jake knew that Charles was angry and frustrated that he did not get to finish beating Gary because of the big black basketball player interfering and now was his chance for revenge. The fourth piece was that with the APB with him, there was a likelihood of them "taking care of unfinished business," finishing the job Charles didn't. The fifth piece was knowing the three would be walking to their car in an almost empty parking lot with Charles and Boone lurking in the dark, and who knows who else, looking for some action.

The sixth piece was that Jake knew one of the plain clothes cops very well. He was a former teammate of Jake's and was a frequent customer of the Broken Drum. After Jake told him what he suspected, he concurred that there could be trouble, so they all began to follow. The seventh piece was to put it all together and it points to the ripe makings of a violent encounter.

Jake, his friend, and the other plain clothes police officers followed Gary, Samuel, and Tony and the rest is history.

B. When Making the Wrong Turn

Why was Charles Jackson with "Big Body" Boone at the basketball game? Why was Charles associating with a known white supremacist? Did he really hate blacks? Is that why he and Tony attacked Gary Patterson, who was much smaller than either one of them? Is there another reason why he would identify with white supremacists? What or who was the influence on Charles? How did he get to the point of such hate?

Even though Charles was on the varsity football team, he still lacked a great deal of self-confidence. All through grade school and junior high, he felt he was nobody special. The only identity he had was being somebody in football. That experience, although a boost to his self-image, didn't satisfy the level he wanted or needed to reach as to status or image.

Then he saw pictures of some white supremacy groups. He learned about the Aryan Circle, the Aryan Culture, Silent Aryan Warriors, Noble Elect Thugs, Neo-Nazi, Skin Heads, Christian Identity and many others.

He heard about the most visible and prominent one, the Oath Keepers, who are making the most noise on the political scene in America today. The Oath Keepers are making noise about the kind of transition we will have in the change in president of the USA. Charles has a need to be a part of such activity. Right or wrong, good or bad, he saw in them, the image, the status, the identity of what he wanted for himself.

Whether the Oath Keepers or any other white power militant group, what they wore really enhanced that image he wanted to project. They wear the military fatigues, head bands, combat boots, "White Power" t-shirts, ammunition belts, tattoos, they brandish weapons, gloves, sunglasses, and general facial demeanor which projects a mean spirit and dominance. The image of "being your own man" was evident. Being independent of anyone and anything was something they were proud of. The image that says, "No one is going to push me around" is the image Charles needed and wanted. "I am not going to take any shit from anybody." That was the power he wanted to display. With them, he would be somebody.

What they stood for; power, aggression, dominance, control, and authority were those things with which he could readily agree. He grew up in a home and culture that believed blacks were inferior and had no right to receive respect or opportunity. Beating up a black kid in plain sight of several students at school simply documented his position on the issue. He believed like most white supremacists; whites must maintain dominance over all people of color. It was all about power and that is what he was after.

Charles Jackson fit the white supremacists' mold. And Tony almost got sucked into that mold.

But why was he with "Big Body" Boone? When and how did he develop this relationship with Boone? Charles read about the APB in a rogue brochure put out by the APB. Charles found it to be like a favorite verse in the Bible. "This is just what the doctor ordered!" he told Tony on one of their think-tank discussions at the Broken Drum. It turned out that for over a year Charles had been in contact with Boone.

C. Charles and The New Dawning Light

Charles, Boone, and two members of the APB spent two nights in jail. Early Saturday morning the treasurer of the APB came to the county jail and paid the bond for Boone and the two thugs. Charles was left in jail. The APB, all twenty-five of them, left Cox County in a caravan of pickups and SUV's for their home base in Cleveland, TN.

Jake suggested to Tony that they go to the jail and visit Charles. The main thing Jake wanted to do was pick Charles' brain. He wanted to ask, "Why get aggressive and abusive toward blacks? Why drag Tony into joining you in beating up a lone black student, much smaller than you, in the hallway at school? Why get involved with the APB? Why risk graduating from high school, playing football, getting a possible football scholarship to college, and having your reputation dragged down into the gutter? Why risk it all?

Sunday afternoon Jake and Tony went to visit Charles. When the jail attendant ushered Charles into the visitor conference room, Jake and Tony saw he had taken on the look of a disgruntled and hard-core adult criminal. The image did not fit a seventeen-year-old high school student athlete. But he tried. He tried to talk like it. "What the fuck are you two doing here? Get your eyes full and get the shit out of here. Who the hell asked you to come here in the first place?"

Jake told him, "You can stop all the immature bull-shit. You are in trouble up to your ass. So, stop acting like a jerk and act like you got a brain in your head. We came because we care about you and want to find out what we can do for you. And there are other people who care about you."

At this point Jake spoke distinctly and loudly, "Like the mother of the kid you and Tony beat up. She wants to help you. Did you hear what I said? And the big black dude that stopped you two big athletes from beating up on a little black kid. He wants to help you, too. Did you hear what I said?"

"We got some questions, and we want you to answer like a responsible adult, not like an immature punk. Can you handle it? Or are you going to act like a stupid shit? If you are going to act like a stupid shit, we are out of here and you can rot in here. What is it going to be?"

After a long pause, Charles looks into Jake's eyes and then to Tony, he asks, in a quiet tone, "What is it you want?"

Jake said to him, "Charles, you are one step away from a wasted life. You are one step away from going downhill and never coming back. We are here to make sure you don't take that step. We want you back where you belong."

Charles interrupted any further comment Jake might make by saying, "It is too late. It is too late for me. I am in a hole and will never get out. Everybody has 'black-balled' me. Nobody gives a shit about me."

Tony gets angry and gets up from his chair and leans toward Charles and loudly spits the words out, "You stupid son of a bitch! What the fuck you think we're doing here? Didn't you hear a god-dam word Jake said?"

The jail attendant looks toward Tony and starts to walk toward him.

Jake puts his hand on Tony's arm and tells him to sit back down and take it easy. With that, again the jail attendant goes back to his position. Jake says to Charles, "We are here because we care. Not only us, but get this, the kid you and Tony beat up cares. And the mother of Gary Patterson wants to help. You saw her at the meeting you had with Mr. Gammon.

The big black dude that kept you and Tony from really hurting that little black kid wants to help. People who can make a difference and who are related to the incident at school care and want to help. Did you hear what I said?"

Charles just stares at his feet and makes no gesture of recognition of Jake or what he said.

With that, Jake got up and gestures for Tony to get up and get ready to leave. Jake tells Charles, "When we came here, I wanted to ask you questions about what you were thinking you were going to accomplish with those APB punks when you got arrested. Four of you, armed to the teeth. You were going to beat up the kid again? You were going to beat up Tony? You were going to beat up Sam? What the hell were you thinking?

"But I am not interested now. You have got to get your shit together. We don't want to waste our time on you if you're going to be an asshole. Listen to me! Listen! If you want to salvage your life, if you want to be responsible and act like a mature thinking human being, call me. You know how to contact me." Jake and Tony turned and left as Charles was still sitting on his metal chair dressed in his gray jail garb with "PRISONER" printed on the back.

After Jake and Tony completely left the building, Charles got up and the officer opened the door and escorted him back to his cell. Before the visit from Jake and Tony, Charles was served breakfast, but he needed to play the role of hard-ass and didn't accept the breakfast. Now he was hungry and had no need to play the hard-ass role. Jake and Tony kind of took the wind out of that sail. He asked the attendant as he was locking the cell door, "Could I get my breakfast now? I wasn't able to eat before."

The attendant said he would check on it. Soon the attendant came back with a breakfast tray and slipped it through the opening.

As Charles sat looking at the tray, he remembered what Jake said to him. "If you want to act like a mature thinking human being, call me." "Mature thinking human being." He began to eat his breakfast as he pondered that phrase, "Mature thinking human being."

As Tony and Jake were walking back to Jake's car, Tony asked Jake, "do you think Charles will call you?" Jake said, "I would be surprised if Charles calls me or you or Gary or even Samuel. But, let me tell you something. I would not be surprised if Charles calls Mrs. Patterson." He repeated the thought again, "I would not be surprised if Charles calls Mrs. Patterson."

"If Charles really listened to us, really listened, our visit to him could be a real turnaround for him. I think he is going to think now. I think your yelling at him got his attention. You really let him know that you are no longer a follower. You let him know you think. When you went ballistic, he surely got the message you are out to be a better Tony."

After Charles ate his breakfast, he called the guard over to give him the tray. He surprised himself as he spoke with some humility to the guard, "I sure appreciate you getting the breakfast for me. It was really good." The guard asked, "Wasn't it cold?" "Yes, but it tasted really good. Thanks."

Charles sat down and did more thinking. "Jake said I could just rot in here. Do I do such a thing as apologize to the kid we beat up? Is that what Jake would say is the first step? If there is anyone I should apologize to, it is the kid I was out to beat up. His name is Gary Patterson. Maybe I can find the name and phone number in the phone book. I will check all the Patterson's." As he went through the phone book, he noticed a "Norma Patterson." He asked the jail guard for the time to make a phone call. He was led to the phone in the hallway and made the call. The phone rang and Charles abruptly hung up. He asked to be taken back to his cell.

Charles sat and thought. "I better make sure I know what I am doing before I make a phone call. I better know what the hell I am going to say.

If Gary answers the phone, what do I say? 'I'm the guy who broke your nose when I was beating you up in the hallway at school. I'm the guy who night before last called you a fucking nigger.'"

"What if his mother answers the phone? What do I say? 'I'm the guy who beat up your son and broke his nose and almost put out his eye. And after the game the other night, me and three other guys were going to beat him up again and the other two guys with him.'"

After a few agonizing minutes, Charles comes to the conclusion that the only thing he can say is a very sincere apology. He really has nothing else to say. So, Charles asked the guard again for the chance to use the phone.

Gary answered the phone. Charles said, "Is this Gary Patterson?" "Yes" was the reply. He said, "This is Charles Jackson. I am calling from the County Jail. I am the guy that was with Tony Pirello who hassled you in the hallway at school." Before he could go on to further identify himself, Gary interrupted him and said, "Oh yeah, you were going to fight us in the parking lot after the game Thursday night. I remember you. You called me the N word. You had black leather gloves on and had a chain wrapped around you right hand that you were going to use on us. We would have been mincemeat if those plain clothes cops hadn't shown up because you guys had some rough looking weapons." Then there was a long pause of silence that left Charles not knowing what to say.

Gary continued, "I understand you and your friends were from the Aryan Patriotic Brotherhood. You said you are at the County Jail? Is that where the State Police took all four of you Thursday night? Are the other three still there?

Charles stumbled out a response, "They took all four of us to the county jail. But those three got their bond paid yesterday and left to go back to their home in Cleveland, TN. I am still in jail. I am not sure what the next step is for me."

Gary said, "My mother is standing here, and she asked me who it is calling. I told her it was Charles Jackson."

"Tell your mother I called to tell you and her, how sorry I am for attacking you in the hallway at school. I also am sorry for what took place in the parking lot after the game. That is why I am calling. To say I am sorry."

"I don't know if you have talked to Tony lately, but he and me and Samuel and our mothers went to see Mr. Gammon and had the restraining order lifted." Charles interrupted him immediately and with surprise in his voice and almost yelled, "You what? No more restraining order? Gammon made that most important. What happened? Why did you do that?"

Gary told him, "If Sam and I are going to help Tony get off suspension from school, the restraining order has to be lifted. And, if we can get you to join us, all the more to get the restraining order lifted.

"Did you know that Tony and his mother came over to our house the other night to apologize?"

"He what? Came to your house to apologize? Man, this is getting crazier all the time."

"Yes, the day we met at the principal's office for the hearing when they laid out the requirements you and Tony have to meet. That evening, Tony and his mother came over. Even before the restraining order was lifted."

"Wasn't your mother angry? Didn't she tell Tony to get the hell out of there? You and she talked to them? Did she let them in the house? Didn't either of you tell them to leave?"

"No, we were glad to see them. We had a very good conversation that evening. I am going to help Tony meet his requirements so he can get off suspension. And Samuel is also going to help. He is the big black basketball player who came to my rescue."

Charles was speechless. What could he say? He was completely surprised and caught off guard. "You got the restraining order lifted? Tony and his mom came to see you? Sam is going to help get Tony off suspension. And you invited me to be a part of that? This is fucking crazy."

Gary asked, "When do you get out of jail?"

Charles had been quiet during the time Gary was talking. He became very confused the more Gary told him about what he was going to do for Tony. Charles kept repeating, "This doesn't make sense."

He told Gary his time was up for a phone call and he had to go back to his cell. He lied. He wanted to get off the phone. He called Gary Patterson because he thought he was only going to apologize to Gary and his mom. But what he heard really confused him. He didn't expect to hear that Gary would be helping Tony get off suspension. And, to make it even more confusing, the black guy that intervened is also going to help Tony meet the requirements.

He had to get off the phone. He told Gary he was sorry again and hung up. He went back to his cell and just sat. He kept hearing Jake say, "Mature thinking human being." He didn't know what to think.

D. The Effect of Grace

Ronnie Miller had mentioned to the other players that he and Tony, one of the students who beat up Gary, were good friends, but not now. He didn't want to be identified with Tony after what Tony had done to Gary. To add distance between he and Tony, he wanted everyone to know, "I don't even know this kid Gary." Ronnie did not want to be identified with anyone who used racial violence. He figured he purged himself of racist behavior when he made his confession before his teammates. He added, "I don't want to be drug into anything that smells of racism, again."

His friendship with Tony began when they were in the third grade. They have become the best of friends after all these years. Ronnie has mentioned often since the attack on Gary, "I have never seen or heard from Tony that was any hint of a racist attitude. I was shocked to hear what he did to Gary because he never said a word that was prejudicial towards blacks. Even though he is a wrestler, there was nothing about Tony that would make you think he would be aggressive, let alone violent with anyone because of race. Ronnie kept asking himself "Why would Tony join another guy in beating up on a small black kid in the middle of the school hallway, in front of several students?"

Ronnie did not realize or have the slightest notion that Gary was now involved in Tony's life. Ronnie did not know of the reconciliation between Gary and Tony. He did not know of all the help Gary was giving Tony to meet the requirements to get off suspension. Ronnie was not aware of the grace Tony experienced from Gary and his mom. In spite of all the students telling Gary "Don't get taken in by that punk. Charge him with a hate crime and have his ass sent away." Instead, Gary and his mom had as their personal task to help Tony get off suspension and back in school and back on the wrestling team.

Ronnie saw no future for Tony, but Gary and his mom did.

More importantly, Ronnie was not aware of the change in Tony. He had no way of knowing that Gary was the biggest factor in that change. It happened in such a short time. Tony's mother marveled at the change each day. She often would say, "It is as if a light bulb went off in his head."

The change was really apparent in the desire Tony had to get back in school. The change was seen in small ways. In the past, as the captain of the wrestling team, being a ranked high school wrestler in Tennessee, big at six feet and one eighty-five pounds, good looking, not shy in any form, aloof, non-engaging, often charming, he was immersed in himself. He came off as arrogant, pompous, rude, and thoughtless. His favorite way of showing his humility was saying, "Enough about me, what do you think about me?"

He turned over a new leaf. When he gets back in school, kids who knew him will say, "He sure came down off his high-horse. That little black kid twisted a knot in his tail. He is nice to people, he asks 'how you doin,' he looks at you when you talk to him, when he talks to you, he looks into your eyes, I even heard him say the other day, 'excuse me.' He has been taking humility pills."

The change was really seen in the way he related to Gary. When Gary said, "I want to help you meet the requirements to get off suspension and back to school." Tony's response is always "Tell me what you want me to do." They have a mutual respect and trust in each other.

Ronnie had mentioned how he would like to meet Gary. David told him that he could arrange a meeting for the two of them to get acquainted since he was a good friend of Gary. David would ask Gary when a good time would be for them to meet.

There was no school on Tuesday due to a teacher's conference. So, David arranged for a meeting at Gary's house on Tuesday mid-morning. When they were to meet at Gary's house, Tony was there since Gary was helping him work on one of the essays. Mrs. Patterson was working at the hospital. Gary told Tony that Ronnie was coming over to meet him.

When they got to Gary's house and rang the doorbell, Gary and Tony both came to the door. David was first in the house after Gary opened the door. Ronnie followed David up the steps entering the house and was taken aback, actually shocked, when he saw Tony standing there next to Gary.

Instead of introductions being made of Ronnie to Gary or any greeting or conversation of any kind, Ronnie and Tony immediately moved to the side of the room and had their own conversation. They hadn't seen each other for a couple of weeks.

Tony was riding a high from all the good fortune which had been going his way and it was evident in the excited way Tony spoke to Ronnie. Tony mentioned that he had been following the crisis that the team was going through from Samuel and David. He mentioned how he had gotten to know the Bokima brothers very well. He talked about how he got acquainted with Gary and how that relationship was going so well and becoming so helpful. Tony congratulated Ronnie on playing so well against Clifton. Ronnie never had a chance to say much because Tony dominated the conversation after being so excited to see him. Ronnie had a lot of questions for Tony.

Finally, Ronnie stopped Tony's verbal adrenalin rush, which was almost like a caffeine high, by interrupting his emotional diatribe. Ronnie tried to speak quietly without sounding pissed off "What the hell are you doing over here at Gary's house? You have no idea what people are saying about you and Charles. Two big athletes beat up a little frail black kid. Two of you! You nuts? How in the hell can you explain that shit? What the hell is going on? I heard there is a restraining order against you that says you are to stay away from Gary. And, you are over here. What the hell is this?"

Tony began to explain, less excited and more toned down. "I am not sure I can explain it. I don't know what you call it, but Gary and Samuel showed me something I have never experienced. Mom says a light bulb went off in my head. It is more like someone hit me in the head to wake me up."

Tony continued to speak in such a way to let Ronnie know that he was serious about taking a new direction. "Gary and Samuel told me that whatever I needed to do to get off being suspended from school, they would help me. That is why I am over here now. Gary is helping me go through all the eight requirements to get back in school. That is what has been going on. What do you call it when suddenly things seem to fall in place in your life? I've heard people call it an "ah ha moment." He didn't expect Ronnie to answer his question. He knew Ronnie didn't know the answer. None of his friends knew about grace.

Ronnie said, "You have to introduce me to Gary. I really want to meet him."

They went into the living room where David and Gary were seated and in conversation. When Ronnie and Tony walked in, David and Gary told them "hello." They had overheard Ronnie lace into Tony and weren't sure what to expect when they came into the room. David said, "Gary, this is Ronnie, the guy I told you about and who wanted to meet you."

"Gary, it is a real pleasure to meet you. I don't know if David told you or not, but Tony and I have been good fiends for a long time. I came over here because I felt the need to apologize for my friend's attack on you. But, from what I hear, that is a bit late and unnecessary. Instead of me giving you an apology for Tony, I would like to hear about you helping Tony get off suspension."

"Tony and his mom started it. They came to our house the night of our conference with Mr. Gammon to apologize. Tony and I sat down, and he told me how he was really sorry for what he did. He said that Charles sucked him into helping him beat me up. I believe him. I told him I would do all I could to help him meet the requirements to get off suspension. So, here we are."

David was quick to add, "And Samuel said he would help also."

Ronnie said, "I asked Tony, 'what the hell is going on here?' Now, I know. Tony, it looks like you are in good hands. I need not worry about you anymore."

XV. Touching Lives for Good

2020 has so much chaos, disruption, and disorder that it needed a good dose of "sportsmanship." All that has been going on in Grayville is a mirror of the toxicity of our time and country. The confusing upheaval over the race issue is disheartening. People need a good dose of being nice and kind to each other.

Honesty lost its place as a virtue among the people. Talking about someone in a word of affirmation has lost its place as a virtue among the people. Giving respect and trusting people have lost their places as virtues among the people. People are quick to blame others. It has become easy to criticize, point fingers, make the other person a villain, and use divisive rhetoric and harsh words.

It is too bad that people, even friends and relatives, cannot talk about politics or religion or social issues. We live in a democracy where we should be able to express our stances, positions, and opinions without being afraid to voice them. But when people hate, insist on their own way, are prejudice toward other persons, make irresponsible racist comments, are intolerant of an idea that is new, or speak of another person or a group of people in a derogatory way we certainly limit the opportunity to exercise democratic freedoms. Caring, showing empathy, and dispensing love and compassion is so rare. People should resolve to be peacemakers.

A. Gary and Mom Visit Charles

That is why it was such a surprise for Charles to see Gary and his mother in the jail's visitation room. He called the night before to apologize to Gary and his mom. They must have realized what a struggle that must have been for him.

When the guard who monitored the visitor's room came to get Charles, he announced that he had visitors. Charles was surprised and curious, "Who are they?" The guard replied, "I don't know. It is a young black kid and a white lady." Charles wondered to himself, "Who on earth could they be?"

When Charles saw them seated in the visitor waiting room, he was shocked. Gary and his mom got up from their chairs and greeted Charles warmly and gave him welcoming smiles. Charles was speechless. He had no idea Gary's mother was white.

Gary spoke first and said, "Since you called last night and didn't have much time to talk we thought we would just come to see you."

Charles was still speechless. He could not understand that the kid he beat up and the kid's mother are here to visit him. And she is white! And they don't appear to be angry or resentful.

Mrs. Patterson spoke next. "Charles, we are really glad to see you. I am sorry you couldn't talk more last night. We thought it would be good to come on over and meet you. As the mother of the boy you beat up, I thought I should have the privilege to get acquainted and ask some questions. I am just curious about some things. You may think by asking questions I am prying, then just tell me and I won't ask any questions."

"Is it alright if I ask you some questions?"

Charles knew what kind of questions they would be. They would be judgmental and condescending. They would be of the flavor of 'holier-than-thou' about them to put me in my place. She would ask for an explanation on why I did what I did. I can hear her now, "My goodness, you are twice the size of my son. What on earth were you thinking? How could you be so mean?" Charles began to prepare by taking on a defensive mode. Who does this self-righteous woman think she is?

Charles was ready for Mrs. Patterson to lay guilt on him. He was prepared for her to talk down to him for hurting her little boy. He was ready for her to say, "Pick on someone your own size next time. Or is this the way you show people how tough you are?"

The first question Mrs. Patterson asked was, "We never saw your parents at the meeting at Mr. Gammon's office. I hope they were not sick or had a problem that kept them from the meeting. Are they okay?"

Charles was surprised and not ready for such a question. He looked at Mrs. Patterson and then to Gary. Then he attempted to answer the question. "They are okay, it is just that their interest in their kids is not like it should be. Dad is a drunk and is in a drunken stupor most of the time. He lost his job working for Jarvis Oil because he was always drunk. My older sister graduated from high school and left immediately to get away from both of them.

Our mom is not home most of the time. She works at the tavern out near Pomona. That is where she spends most of her time. When I want something to eat, I go out to Pomona to the tavern and she will fix me something."

Mrs. Patterson asked, "Does she know about the current trouble you are in? That you are suspended from school? That you are in jail?"

Charles said he has not told her. He said he had not seen her, yet. "She doesn't know I am in jail. I am not sure what her response would be. She would probably just shrug her shoulders and go about her business for the day. She doesn't care. I am sure she hasn't missed me not being at home this weekend."

"Charles we are very sorry. Would you want us to talk to her?"

"No, I would prefer you don't. I will call her and explain it all to her."

"That was one of the questions I had. I just wanted to find out about your parents. Another question I have is to ask you about your senior year at GHS. I understand you are on the football team and that a few colleges are interested in you. We heard that you have a chance for a football scholarship. Which colleges are interested in you?"

He said, "The colleges so far are Middle Tennessee State in Murfreesboro, Sewanee University, University of Tennessee at Martin, and Austin Peay. A guy I did some yard work for in Fairfield Glad went to Illinois Wesleyan and he said he would inquire there for me. I am a good long snapper. Center is the position I play. I haven't had any offers from a division I school because some think I'm not big enough. But my size shouldn't keep me from being a long snapper at a division I school."

Gary said, "But I heard you were into this white-supremacy movement. The other night I got the idea that was where you were headed, not college. In fact, I also heard that getting off the school suspension was not on your radar, that you weren't planning to meet the requirements that Mr. Gammon laid out for you and Tony. I heard that you didn't care if you went back to school."

"I know you know Jake. He and Tony were here yesterday to see me, and they tried to talk to me. Now you and your mom come here to talk to me. I don't understand. It is all very confusing to me. I beat the hell out of you and here you are. I attempted to do it again the other night and here you are. I don't know what to think. I don't know why you both are here. You should hate me. I feel like you are trying to trick me. I feel like you are playing with my mind. Everything is out of whack. I thought I had everything put in place. Now, they are not. I am screwed up."

"Guard, I have to go now." With that, Charles got up from his chair and didn't say a word to Gary or his mother. Not a "goodbye," "Thanks for coming," "I hope to see you again." Nothing. He just got up and walked over to the guard, never looked back and went back to his cell.

Gary and his mom just sat there surprised at the abrupt ending of their visit. Mrs. Patterson told Gary, "Let's think about this for a while. We have to do something to help Charles. But I don't know what it is or how. I don't think we can depend on his parents to take charge and help him to follow through with the requirements set up by the school to get off suspension. I feel bad that he thinks we might be trying to trick him and that he thinks we are trying to play with his mind."

Gary said, "It might be a gamble, but I am thinking that Tony and Jake could have more influence on him than anybody. We could try but if he is going to make a turnaround and get serious about school, Tony and Jake may be his only chance. Why don't we try to get them and a few others together, those close to Charles, under the pretense of a "get out of jail celebration party?

When we are together, we could individually make some comment about assuming responsibility to help meet the requirements to get back in school. We could slowly and without too much attention to it, plant some seed of thinking, of assuming some responsibility, of changing course. Under the guise of a 'get out of jail celebration' it will really be a 'consultation' to help Charles redirect the path he is on."

His mom said, "I am sure he would feel uncomfortable if we should spend time with him to try for some turn-around. I like your idea of getting everybody together as a 'get out of jail celebration.' Having Jake and Tony speak to him and some others, may be the best thing to arrange. Having you and Samuel present would show how much people care for him.

Gary let's go in that direction with the fact that those he is most familiar with join together to help him. Hopefully, they can impress on him the need to meet the requirements the school handed him and Tony. Maybe they can motivate him to do what he has to do to get off the suspension and get back to playing football. They might even help him fashion a new direction for his life away from those militant extremist groups."

Gary said, "Why don't we see an officer or someone about getting Charles out of jail. If we can take him this evening, let's call Samuel, Jake, and Tony and see if we can meet them this evening at the Broken Drum. I guess we should explain to them why we want to meet with them. They need to know that they may be the only ones who can convince him to get serious about working to get back to school. Tony got the message, maybe Charles will too."

Gary checked his contact list on his phone and found he had the number for each person he needed to call. He made the calls and they all gladly said they would meet them at the Broken Drum. Gary told each of the guys meeting with Charles that it would be a "get out of jail celebration" of just a few of his friends.

Tony, Jake, Samuel, Gary, and Mrs. Patterson could be the "coaches" during the "get out of jail celebration" consultation. If there is anyone has a right to offer Charles advice or want to "come down" on Charles, it would be one of those five. Gary said, "It might be a good idea to add Ronnie Miller to the 'coaches' list if he can. He has been an exceptional witness to the changes that have taken place in Tony. Charles said that nobody cares. To have all those guys there to have conversation with him, may be a big boost and encouragement to show Charles that people do care."

Gary called Ronnie. Everyone was on board and were to meet at the Broken Drum at 7:00 P.M. They understood they were to be there to join in a "get out of jail celebration" but mainly to gather their voices in a consulting kind of way to help Charles get serious about getting back in school.

Now, the task was to get Charles. He may not want to go with Gary and his mom. They just had to take their chances.

The person in charge at the information desk was a lady Sargent. Mrs. Patterson introduced herself as a friend of one of the inmates. "You have a young man in jail by the name of Charles Jackson. He is seventeen years only and was brought in Thursday night. What are the charges against him? Will he be having a hearing before a judge?"

The desk sergeant looked through a file on her desk and said, "He was with three men who were charged with threatening two young men of color. The charge states specifically they intimidated and harassed the two men of color. All four of the men were armed. The three men were arrested as adults and were released on bond yesterday.

Mr. Jackson will probably have a hearing before the juvenile judge. That hearing has not been scheduled yet. The record shows this is his first offense. So, likely the judge will probably take that into consideration. He may be released in the morning, but his parents have not made an appearance."

"Have charges been made against him?"

"No formal charges have been made against him by the persons he was threatening."

Mrs. Patterson said, "This is one of the young men Mr. Jackson and his friends threatened. And he is not filing any charges. If that is the case, could Mr. Jackson be released and when could he be released?"

"If you want him released to you, we will have to call the parents to have permission to release him in your custody. If that is what you want, we will call his parents."

"Please do."

The file on Charles had two phone numbers for his mother. One at home and one at the Pomona Road Hideaway. The sergeant called the tavern and Charles' mom answered the phone. After the sergeant talked to the mother, he received a quick "yes" and hung up. "I will send an officer to bring Mr. Jackson."

B. Gathering at the Broken Drum

When Charles was brought down to the intake desk, the sergeant told him that he had been released to the custody of Mrs. Patterson and that he was free to go. As he stood there in a shocked mode, he looked at Mrs. Patterson and Gary and hesitated, not saying a word.

Gary broke the ice and told him they were going to the Broken Drum and meet some of his friends and celebrate his getting out of jail.

Without moving, Charles asked, "Who is going to be there?" Gary was quick to answer, "Just some guys you know from school and others who have expressed an interest in you in the past few days. Tony and his mom, Jake, me and my mom, Samuel, Ronnie, Tony's good friend. And I invited David just to have some company.

Mom met a man at the hospital last week by the name of Jack Stone, a retired minister. In their conversation, he mentioned that he played football at the University of Illinois and he recruits for Illinois in the Kentucky, Tennessee, and Georgia area. She talked about you and he showed an interest when she told him you were the "long snapper" on the football team. She said she didn't know what a long snapper was. So, Rev. Stone explained what a long snapper is and does. She invited him to the celebration tonight. That would really be interesting if he would show up."

When they arrived at the Broken Drum, Jake was the first to greet them. He and Charles embraced, and Jake told him how great it was to see him. Jake led them all to a corner of the Broken Drum where tables were set up for a party and where Mrs. Pirello and Tony were waiting. Mrs. Pirello had made a cake as a part of the "celebration" for Charles. Tony gave him a big smile and hugged him and said, "This is a much better place to meet than the last time we saw you."

Soon, the Bokima boys came in, all three of them. The last time Samuel saw Charles was in the parking lot after the game when Charles and three others threatened Samuel. Samuel shook hands with Charles, hugged him and told him, "I brought my brother Joseph with us because he likes parties, I hope you don't mind." Charles finally spoke up and said, "I'm glad you brought him along. I like parties too."

The last time Samuel saw Charles, Charles stood as cast in a mold of arrogance and a voice of contentious hostile confrontation. Now, Charles met Samuel in a contrite sheepish manner, far removed from the aggressive and abusive verbiage in the parking lot. "Sam, sometime tonight, or in the next couple of days I would like to talk to you. I really need to talk to you. Will that be OK?"

"Sure, whenever or wherever you want. Just let me know what is best for you. In fact, my grandfather who lives in Pleasant Hill, not far from where your mom works, would like to meet you. He is a big high school football fan. He went to all your home games this year. He would rather see a high school football game on a Friday night than be on the fifty-yard line of a college football game."

"That is one thing I don't know anything about, grandparents. I have heard that grandparents can be the greatest thing in a kid's life. I would like to meet him. What is his name?" Again, Charles was surprised at himself. He never asked anybody about anything. Here he was interested in Samuel's grandpa, asking questions.

"He was a missionary to Nigeria. He is retired now. His name is Rev. Dr. William Norris and my grandma's name is Betty. He and my grandma adopted my dad when my dad was eight years old. Dad's mother and father died of AIDS. The family was a member of grandpa's congregation in Nigeria. So, he and grandma adopted Hiram. That is my dad's first name."

"Is your grandpa black?"

"No, my grandparents are white. They are originally from Pennsylvania. After college he went to seminary to train to be a missionary in the United Church of Christ denomination. He and Betty got married when they were in college."

Sam said to Charles, "Maybe we could get together here tonight for a few minutes after all the excitement calms down. Would that work for you?"

"Yes, that would be fine."

Just then, Ronnie came in and gave a special greeting to Tony and his mother. Then he went to Gary and asked, "How is the student doing?" As he nodded toward Tony. Did that fifty-word essay get to fifty words or does he have to lie some more?" Tony, in overhearing Ronnie, walked over to Ronnie and said, "I not only wrote fifty-words, but I added extra words to show how academically sound I am. The rumor is the essay may get published!" With that the group had a big laugh.

As each person exchanged greetings and casual conversation, Gary was observing Charles. Charles seemed to be taking it all in with interest. It was if he was saying to himself, "All these people are here because of me? And there are four black people here."

Tony came over to where Gary was standing and said, "The Charles we are seeing now is a different Charles than the one that greeted me and Jake when we went to see him in jail. He really tried to act the part of a hard ass. He practically told us to get the hell out of there. Can you believe he is the same six two two hundred twenty-five pounder who beat the hell out of you?"

Gary quickly responded, "No more than I can believe you at six feet and a hundred and eighty helped him beat the hell out of me." At that comment, Tony reached over to Gary put his arm around his neck and hugged him tight and said, "I am really sorry for that stupid move. But one thing good came out of it, you got a whole lot of sympathy from all the ladies."

About that time Rev. Stone came in and walked over to where everyone was gathered. Mrs. Patterson greeted him with a hug and she began to introduce him to everyone. She purposely left Charles last to meet him. She said, "Charles, this is Rev. Stone who I told you about and who played football at the University of Illinois. Thanks to him I now know what a long snapper is."

Rev. Stone shook hands with Charles and asked how he was doing. Charles told him he was doing fine and, uncharacteristically of Charles, returned the question, "How are you doing?" Charles has always been so self-absorbed and so dismissal of others, he surprised himself by asking how he was. He has never shown any interest in anyone else, except himself.

Rev. Stone surprised Charles when he said, "I noticed in the statistics of last year's GHS football team, that your long snapping percentage was close to 87%. That is pretty good for a high school long snapper." Charles was very surprised that this man he doesn't even know had so much information about him. Information he didn't even know. Rev. Stone went on with more revelations of Charles's stats. "The average percentage of successful snaps in high school is about 75%. You had perfect snaps on twenty-three of twenty-five extra point snaps. You had perfect snaps on nine of twelve field goal snaps. You had twenty-six perfect snaps on thirty punts. That is fifty-eight out of sixty-seven which is an impressive 87%."

Charles was amazed!

"When did you start playing center?"

Charles was surprised Rev. Stone knew the statistics of his long snaps. Charles told him, "When I was in the seventh grade, I tried out for the junior high football team. The coach asked if someone would volunteer to be center. No one raised their hand, so I did. I had no idea what that meant. I have been playing center ever since. By the time I was a freshman I had grown four inches and gained twenty pounds. The more I grew the more I found out it is helpful to be a bit bigger if you are going to play center. So, I kept playing center and kept getting bigger.

"Then I found out the center must snap the ball for extra points, field goals, and punts. The first time I ever snapped was for a punt. I snapped the ball over the punter's head, the other team recovered the ball and ran for a touchdown. It was then that I knew I had to learn how to snap and really started seriously practicing snapping the ball."

"I understand you got into some serious trouble recently at school. I heard it may have some consequences with school and football. Is that true?"

"Yes. I got involved with some people that I shouldn't have. They steered me the wrong direction. I wasn't mature enough to tell them to go to hell. They are bad people."

Rev. Stone asked Charles how it was going to affect school.

"Tony Pirello and I both are suspended from school for beating up Gary Patterson." Rev. Stone interrupted him and asked, "Is that Tony Pirello, the wrestler? He got suspended too?" Charles nodded his head yes. "Two star athletes at GHS are suspended? When I was in the hospital last week, Mrs. Patterson told me about you beating up on her son, but I didn't know it was both of you."

"I told you I had some bad people steer me in the wrong direction. I really did a dumb thing. Bad decision."

"What is next?"

"Most everybody here tonight said some things about supporting me, encouraging me, helping me get off suspension and back to school. And some have done some things for me that don't make sense. I don't know why the hell I am here. Pardon the French. Gary, the guy Tony and I beat up, he and his mom came to see me when I was in jail. They didn't come to make me feel bad or guilty. They weren't mad and looking for revenge. They came to ask what they could do for me. Can you believe that shit? Pardon my French. They also got me out of jail.

Gary says he wants to help Tony and me get off suspension so we can get back in school and back to wrestling and football. It doesn't make sense to have people do that kind of stuff. It would make sense if they all told me how much they hated me.

And that Samuel Bokima, the big black guy who plays basketball, who jumped on Tony and me when we were beating on Gary, he says he wants to help us. He cleaned our clocks. Now, he said he wants to help us get back in school. He says his goal is to get me back in football and Tony back to wrestling. I don't understand all this. So, to answer your question, I don't know what is next for me. Everything is messed up.

And, to make matters worse - you won't believe this. After the game Thursday night, I was with two members of the Aryan Patriotic Brotherhood and their president. We were waiting in the parking lot after the game for Gary, Samuel, and Tony to beat the hell out of them. We had weapons to make sure we did the job right. That is when the local police and the state police intervened and we all four got locked up. The APB treasurer came Saturday morning and paid the bail for the three APB then they left to go home to Cleveland, TN.

That all took place Thursday night. Here it is Monday, and all this is happening to me. After all the shit I caused, these people, they are here to let me know they care. I don't understand what is happening. What's the word I want to use? Bewildered? Fucked up? I don't have a clue about what direction to go." Then he takes a long pause. "These people here have saved me, I know that. But I don't know why." He said this as he looked at all the people gathered around the room.

Then, he looks intently at Rev. Stone and says, "I don't know what is next. That is what you asked, 'What is next?' Rev. I will tell you the truth, I don't know what the fuck is next. I don't have a goddamn idea. I am so screwed up. I am really screwed up."

Rev. Stone put his hand on Charles's shoulder drew him close and assured him in a pastoral tone, "The truth is, you have been touched by the love of these friends. They have given freely to you, no strings attached. When that happens, people become whole. John Shelby Spong is probably the most respected contemporary theologian and biblical scholar in the country. He said, 'Wholeness comes to the world when one's life is freely given away to others.' Wholeness is being realized in you because of the love of all these people so freely given to you."

About that time Tony and his mom said they had to leave as well as Gary and his mom. Mrs. Pirello and Mrs. Patterson gave Charles a big hug and Mrs. Patterson told him she had arranged for Samuel to take him home. She said she had to be at work at the hospital early in the morning.

Gary told him, that he, Samuel, and Tony are going to get together soon to talk about working on the rest of the requirements to get Tony off suspension. "Of course, we expect you to be a part of that, but we are leaving that up to you. If and when you want to, we are ready. We will be working with Tony anyhow, so it would work out well. Just let us know." He shook hands with Charles, and they all left.

Ronnie and David were next to say "goodbye." They told Charles that they would have to get together in the next couple of days. With smiles on their faces, they congratulated him on getting out of jail.

Rev. Stone was next to leave and before he did, he told Charles, "I know you will find the right direction to go. I know you will because I see in you a young man with a good head. I look forward to hearing the word that you are back in school. If I can do anything to make it happen, please call me. Here is my card. I am an old, retired guy with lots of time. You have a lot of good things ahead of you. It is time now for responsible and mature decisions. You can do it. I want to help any way I can."

Jake and Joseph stopped to tell Charles goodbye and Jake left to take Joseph home. Before Jake left, he whispered in Charles's ear, "The irony of this whole shittin' mess is that the little black kid you and Tony beat up may be the biggest promise of hope you have. I can tell you have been thinking. That's good. Think about joining Tony, Gary, and Samuel. Good things are happening there about getting back in school. You are doing good. Keep it up. See you later."

Samuel was sitting in one of the easy chairs in front of the fireplace in the corner of the big room where all the gathering took place. Charles went over to Samuel and pulled up a chair.

"Tell me about your grandpa. How old is he?

With a surprised look on his face at the unexpected question, Sam answered, "He is eighty-five."

After a long pause, as if Charles was thinking what to say next, he asked, "Could I meet him?"

"Yea, most any time. He and grandma are retired, and he is free most of the time. Why do you want to meet him?"

Again, a long pause, "A lot of things have happened the last few days. It is all very confusing. Nothing makes sense. I feel like something is different in me and I don't know what or why?

"You for instance, I can't figure you out. And Gary. I can't figure him out or his mom. Twice in just a few days, I had serious run-ins with you. In the fight in the hallway at school you slammed me against a locker and bent my arm behind me and slammed my face against the locker. You held me in that position for all the time you were talking to that teacher. After he took Tony and me to the office, the assistant principal had to take me to the hospital. You had separated my shoulder, dislocated my elbow and my right eye swelled shut.

"Then after the game Thursday night, I was with "Big Body" Boone and two punks from the APB when we stopped you guys in the parking lot. We were going to beat the hell out of all three of you. I hated your guts. I was going to get even. You had roughed me up, you sent me to the hospital, you stuck your nose in my business, you tried to show everybody you were better than me.

"Boone told you he was going to pound your face in. You didn't flinch. You told Gary and Tony not to worry, you would handle it. There were four against you and we all had weapons. Still, you didn't flinch. But what made things so bad, and why I hated you so much, is that you are black.

"Now, (Charles goes into a long pause.) things are different. The confrontation in the parking lot seems so long ago. It was such a stupid thing to do that it seems like a nightmare. Something is going on in my head. I don't feel like I am in control. Something is happening to me and I can't figure it out. The one important thing I know is, I don't hate you. I don't feel bad that you roughed me up. I deserved it. I deserved more than I got. I feel sorry for what I did to Gary. I feel sorry for approaching you Thursday night. I feel ashamed of myself. I don't like that person.

"Jake and Tony came to see me when I was in jail. We got into a yelling match. Jake told me I had to be responsible and mature and 'act like a mature thinking human being.' He repeated it again and enunciated every word slowly and clearly. 'Act like a mature thinking human being.'

"I went back to my cell and that is all I could hear, 'Act like a mature thinking human being.' Then, I looked back on all I had been doing and I thought, 'What the hell have I been doing?'

"Talk about being messed up in the head, talk about things not making sense, I got the crazy notion to call Gary Patterson. Why? Talk about being screwed up in the head! Call the black kid I beat up? Where the hell did that come from?

"I don't know your grandpa. But I am sure he is the guy I need to talk to. You see, Sam, I don't see black anymore. I know he sure as hell doesn't see black. I have to find out why. I think your grandpa can help me understand."

Sam began to speak as if a light bulb went off in his head. "You know what would be great? If you and I could go see grandpa and grandma in the morning for breakfast. Grandma makes the most fantastic biscuits and gravy in the world. You like biscuits and gravy, don't you?"

"Oh yea."

"I will call them right now and see if we can go over there tomorrow morning. All right? Charles nods his head yes. "Hello, grandpa? This is Sam. Sorry to call so late, but I've got a favor to ask of you and grandma. What are you and grandma doing tomorrow morning about breakfast time?" He listens. "OK, how about Charles and me coming over for breakfast?" A pause takes place. "OK, but here is the catch. How about we have grandma's biscuits and gravy? Another pause. "Super, Charles and I will be there about 8:30. Thanks."

"Charles, you are in for a special treat! Her biscuits and gravy always have a way of making things go great. It is almost like they have a healing agent in them."

Then, Sam gives a look of turning serious. "I don't know what to tell you about the stuff going on right now in your life. I am only a seventeen-year-old black man and young black men learn stuff early on. We learn fast because we face hate more than most people and we sure welcome love when it enters the picture. I know from experience that people get messed up because of hate, then someone comes along and offers grace, and tolerance, and kindness, and love, you wonder, 'What's this all about?'

"Well, it is happening now. Before you got to jail, all you had were big doses of hate. All around you, hate. All the people around you, like the APB, hateful. And the consequences were all bad. Jail. Suspended from school. Hell, I never knew about the shoulder and elbow and eye!

"In jail, of all places, some good happened to you. I know what it is. It is called grace. I've learned a lot about grace from my grandpa. It is people caring. And tonight, you were surrounded by grace. Now, everybody here tonight, even Rev. Stone, well, maybe not him, had a right to hate your guts. But, instead, you found out people love you, they showed you that they care for you, you were embraced emotionally and physically.

"Of all people, Gary should hate your guts. Gary's mom should hate your guts! But she really cares for you. Does that make sense?

"I will tell you why it makes sense. It makes sense because they are Quakers. Of all the Christians in the world, I believe Quakers show more grace and love than any follower of Jesus."

"Sam, you help make everything get in focus. You make all the sense in the world. You ought to be a psychiatrist. No, you ought to be a minister. I can hardly wait until tomorrow morning.

"You ready to go home? I am beat to death and I haven't seen my folks in four or five days. And, I haven't had clean clothes on for about the same time."

"Then let's go. You probably will stink up my car. You better take a shower before I pick you up in the morning."

Finally, Charles laughed out loud for the first time in days.

C. With Grandpa and Grandma Norris

"Good morning, Grandpa." At the same time Sam greeted his grandpa, Mrs. Norris entered the living room, went over to Samuel and gave him a big hug. "Grandma, what is that fantastic smell coming from the Kitchen?" His grandpa told him it was a new broccoli casserole she is trying for breakfast. Samuel caught the humor and told Charles, "Well, there goes the biscuits and gravy."

"Grandpa, I want you to meet Charles Jackson. Charles will be a senior next year at GHS. Charles is the center on the football team. He wanted to meet you because he's having to rethink some of the baggage he has grown up with about black people." Looking to Charles, he said, "Did I describe the issue correctly, Charles?"

Rev. Norris interrupted before Charles responded and said, "We will have plenty of time to talk about that, right now, I want to talk to Charles about football. I heard about you from a friend of mine, Rev. Jack Stone. He also told me about Gary Patterson and Samuel and the Ayran Patriotic Brotherhood. We can talk about that later, too."

"But I want to talk about you and football. I saw you play this past season. You are a very good high school center. Rev. Stone said that if there is anyone who plays the position like they should, it is you. Not only can you block, and control the line, but you are probably one of the best long snappers in high school football. Rev. Stone ought to know, he played college football at the University of Illinois. Being an avid high school football fan, and seeing you play, I am really glad to meet you."

"Thank you, I am glad to be here and meet you. I appreciate Sam arranging for us to come over this morning. I really wanted to talk to you especially, after I got acquainted with Sam and heard him talk about you."

"I will do whatever I can. Hopefully, my experience and knowledge will be of help. But we can discuss that later. I saw all your home games and a friend of mine here in Pleasant Hill and I went to a couple of your away games. So, I am interested in Grayville High School football. As you can imagine," as he points toward Sam, "I am also into GHS basketball, but I enjoy football more. Sorry, Sam."

"I am curious about some things. For instance, how many boys went out for football? When I went to the games this fall, it looked like they didn't have many boys on the sideline. What can you tell me about the coach? You had a good record this season. What are the prospects for next year? Do many of you starters return? Are you satisfied with your individual performance this past season? Those are just some of the questions I have had on my mind."

Charles said, "To answer your first question, I don't know how many went out for football. It was the smallest number since I have been in high school. Soccer has become a popular sport for a lot of guys. Football is a lot different from soccer. I think the main problem is a lot of guys don't have the interest in a physical contact sport and they don't want to have to go through all the tough practices. At least I have heard that in conversation with some guys. Sam, what do you think?"

"That's the way a lot of guys think. And, as you said, soccer is really getting to be a popular sport, even here in conservative Cox County."

Rev. Norris asked him, "Why do you have the motivation or willingness to work hard and participate in a contact sport?"

"Most of my life, I have been nobody. Because of football I am somebody. Football is all I have. I am not close to my parents. They never seemed to care. I have never felt they cared. Neither one ever told me they love me. I don't remember ever getting a hug. I never knew my grandparents. When my dad's mom died, back in Indiana, he never went to the funeral. My mom's parents lived in Knoxville and when her dad died, she didn't go to his funeral, either. They never took my sister and me to visit our grandparents.

"I don't have many friends. Lately, I have gotten involved with some people who scare me. I don't have a girlfriend. I would feel uncomfortable in a church. I have never felt I was special until football. With football, I found out that I can be somebody special playing center. I found out I am good at it. I get recognition and people give me complements. With football, I feel like I am special."

Rev. Norris interrupted and said, "I heard you spent the weekend in jail because you aliened yourself to someone you thought would make you feel special. And last week you beat up a black student to make yourself look special? Samuel said it had something to do with race? Is that why you were in jail? Something to do with race?"

"Yes sir. I have made some bad decisions the past few months. Sam is right, I have a lot of baggage that I am carrying with me. I need to get rid of it because it will just get me in more trouble. I don't want to get in more serious trouble. I have to get back in school.

"In the last two weeks I have experienced hate, I felt hate. And in the past two days, I have experienced love, acceptance, and support from people. They should hate me. But they don't hate me. Sam calls it grace. Because of hate, I've had some very bad things happen. I was thrown out of school and because of that, football is in jeopardy."

He didn't need to tell Rev. Norris about beating up on Gary and hanging out with the APB, he knew all that. Rev. Norris said. "Charles, I don't think you are messed up at all. Samuel said you were having problems with all that has been going on in your life the past two weeks. You have been confronted with good, love, and as you said, grace. And now, if you don't mind me using a little of the Bible, you have experienced the 'old passing away and the new has come.' In theology that is called "transference." That is also confusing sometimes.

"Now, you just hang around the people who love you, and soon you will be free of any confusion you feel or any problem you think you might have. Stay away from people who scare you."

Then, Rev. Norris yelled to his wife, "Betty, we have been waiting for thirty minutes, when is breakfast going to be ready?"

"Before we go to the kitchen, let me tell you Charles, you have shared your feelings in the most mature, responsible way. You are a very articulate intelligent young man. I hope you don't mind me saying this, Jesus would be very pleased. Jesus would say the same thing about my three grandsons. But they know I am the only one they have to please." At that, Sam said, "Or else!" They all had a good laugh at that.

Rev. Norris got up from his chair and the three went to the kitchen. They sat down with Mrs. Norris. Rev. Norris asks Samuel to offer the grace. Without hesitation Samuel prays, "Jesus, thank you for your many blessings to each of us. Thank you for the chance to have Charlie join us around this table and becoming a part of our family circle. Thank you for this meal we are about to share and grandma's touch to make it such a joy and your presence at this table to make it such a blessing. Amen."

Then Rev. Norris said to Charles, "Now, Charles, we can talk football and you can answer my questions." He noticed Charles starting to tear up. Rev. Norris went on with his question. "First of all, tell me about your coach. I especially want to know if he has encouraged you to think or even talked to you about playing at the next level, college."

D. A Pattern to Touch Lives for Good

After a hearty breakfast of biscuits and gravy, eggs and bacon and after a conversation of GHS football, Rev. Norris asked about the next step. Charles said he was invited by Gary, Tony, and Sam to join them as they worked on meeting the requirements to be removed from suspension and the restraining order. "Sam, if that offer is still on, I want to do that with you guys."

"Good! We meet tomorrow at Gary's house to plan the next assignment. I think we should talk to Mr. Gammon to tell him our next phase which would include you."

Rev. Norris said, "Charles, would you be open to the idea of us, you and me, going to see Mr. Gammon?"

"Yes, I would appreciate that."

"Samuel, would you and Gary and Tony mind if I went with Charles to see Mr. Gammon? We will tell him that Charles will be working with the same plans you are using for Tony to meet the requirements. That way, Mr. Gammon will know what is going on each step of the way for both Charles and Tony. He will know what expectations, goals, and time-line we all have for Charles and Tony."

Samuel told his grandpa that they had such a meeting with Mr. Gammon in regard to Tony. "If you meet with Mr. Gammon, just tell him we are adding Charles to the same plan and we could all work together using the same plans and strategy. I will give you the copy of our plans and goals with Tony which we shared with Mr. Gammon."

Rev. Norris said, "Charles, that sounds like a solid plan. What do you think?"

"Sounds great! Would you call Mr. Gammon and arrange the meeting? I am ready to get started and get back in school. Sam, I can hardly wait to meet with you guys." With a half-hearted laugh and sarcasm, not to be taken seriously, Charles said, "I want to get into this assignment with this Douglas guy."

"How about if I call Mr. Gammon now?" Rev. Norris got up from the table and picked up the phone and phone book.

After Rev. Norris talked to Mr. Gammons, he told the boys the meeting was all arranged. On the way home, Charles thanked Sam with a serious tone, but also with great enthusiasm and joy. The meeting was going to be Monday after school in Gammon's office conference room, the same room in which Charles and Tony tried to be belligerent hardnosed "can't hurt us" kind of guys.

Rev. Norris told Charles to be dressed in such a way as to impress Mr. Gammon. On the way to Gammon's office, Charles told Rev. Norris how he acted at the last meeting with Mr. Gammon. "I tried to be a real hard ass, a 'couldn't care less' kind of punk. I tried to be as uncooperative as I could. I am sure he thinks I am the worse student he has ever had at GHS."

"OK, all the more to blow him away with the new Charles Jackson."

As they entered Gammon's office, the first thing Charles did was to approach Mr. Gammon, reach out his hand to shake hands with him, and smile. He said, "Mr. Gammon, it is good to see you again. This is Rev. Dr. William Norris, Dr. Bokima's father and Samuel Bokima's grandfather. Dr. Norris, this is Mr. Gammon, the principal of GHS." The two shook hands and both looked at Charles as if to say, "What got into this kid?" The look on Mr. Gammon's face was one of "Is this the same punk kid that was in here with Tony Pirello after having beaten up a little black student?"

Mr. Gammon walked behind his desk and asked Charles and Rev. Norris to "Please have a seat. What can I do for you gentlemen?"

Rev. Norris began by saying, "We are here to talk to you about the suspension and restraining order of Charles and how we plan to meet the requirements to have them removed. As you have found out from my grandson, Samuel Bokima, he and Gary Patterson are helping Tony Pirello meet his requirements to be removed from suspension and the restraining order. They have invited Charles to join them in that venture. We wanted to check in with you to receive your permission for Charles to join them."

Directing his comments to Charles, he said, "How do I know you are not doing a con job on me? How do I know you are serious about getting back in school?"

"Dr. Norris and Gary and Sam will follow me every step of the way. They will know if I am doing a con job on them and you. They will let you know. I could say, 'I give you my word.'" But I know my word means nothing. But my word will mean something sometime. And I will earn your respect and everyone who helps me."

"All right. That is good news. Here is my proposal. Rev. Norris, you can be my witness and the courier to Samuel, Gary, and Tony and to Tony's mother of my proposal.

"My proposal is that I will immediately, this very moment, drop the restraining order relating to contact with Gary Patterson. My proposal concerning the school suspension is this; there will be a lifting of the suspension on both Tony and Charles on two conditions. One, Charles and Tony will sign a contract that they will finish all the requirements as originally established by simply signing the original sheet outlining the requirements. Two, Charles and Tony will sign the same pledge signed by the basketball team. Rev. Norris, I will put you in charge of getting those two documents to me. When I receive them, I will lift the suspensions immediately. Both Charles and Tony will be reinstated as full-time students. Until I receive those two documents signed by Charles and Tony, the suspension will be in force. Is there anything either one of you would like to say?"

Rev. Norris looked at Charles and said, "Charles, things look very clear. What do you say?"

Charles rose from his seat, put out his hand to shake with Mr. Gammon, and said, "Mr. Gammon, thank you very much. You won't be disappointed."

Rev. Morris said, "Then, let us get to it. We will go talk to Tony, Gary, and Samuel and tell them Mr. Gammon has made a very timely and gracious proposal to remove the suspension and restraining order. Mr. Gammon thank you for your time and gesture of kindness toward Charles and Tony." Shaking Mr. Gammon's hand, he said, "I will be seeing you soon with the signed documents."

"Thank you, Rev. Norris. Charles, it has been a real pleasure seeing you again. I look forward to seeing you in school."

XVI. Making All Things New

A. Charles and Tony

Rev. Norris contacted Rev. Stone and told him the wonderful news of the proposal offered by Mr. Gammon. He told him the documents Mr. Gammon wanted to have were, submitted to him and both Charles and

Tony are off suspension from school and were now full-time students. He also reported to Rev. Stone that both boys have not only met, but far exceeded the requirements that Mr. Gammon determined. They met the requirements way ahead of the December 15 deadline. Samuel and Gary did a great job of tutoring and "coaching" them to meet the requirements, especially with the three essays.

Although Tony joked about the essays being published, they were. A quarterly bulletin by the Southern Poverty Law Center requested the essay on Stephen Douglas by both Tony and Charles. The Association of High School Student Councils published in their monthly editorial the essay by Charles Jackson on *The Value of Diversity in the Community*. When it was publicized that two former student athletes committed a hate crime by beating up a smaller black student in the hallway of their school, then made the dramatic change from prejudice and hate to tolerance and empathy. Many requests were made of their writings on the issue as well as several speaking engagements.

Several local and regional newspapers and four Protestant denominations published their articles. The United Church Youth Forum Bulletin and the youth newsletters of three mainstream denominations published their articles.

Tony and Charles also received unexpected negative responses to their writings on racism, hatred, tolerance, and diversity. The unexpected responses were a stark contrast to the accolades and acceptance that so many people gave them. The contrast was manifest in the amount of hate mail they received from several hate groups, extreme right-wing conservative organizations, and individuals that championed white supremacy and anti-Semitism.

Charles received a letter from "Big Body" Boone, of the Aryan Patriotic Brotherhood, who stated their position clearly, "You have denigrated yourself and your self-respect. You have abandoned the only hope you have of being the voice of reason and order. As you compare your yellow skin to the darkness of their sinful degenerate ways, you will embark on a declining slope of emptiness that will consume your life."

The more they received these malevolent messages, the more they also received support, appreciation, and affirmation from the Patterson and Bokima families and the many persons who have read their contributions on equality and justice. When they first began to receive the hate mail, they discovered a new closeness, appreciation, admiration, and respect from Rev. Norris and Rev. Stone who had been serving as their mentors and "coaches."

They had received accolades and letters of appreciation from all over for the quality work of their essays. They became interested in writing more. They were invited to write more. They become proficient and began to show talent in their creative writing. They were able to express in their writing the "why" they could write so effectively on the topic of racism. "All we have to do is think about the stuff, the baggage, the culturally induced milieu of racism that ran through our brains as prejudiced and bigoted teenagers and compare that to the new revelation of our best selves."

Rev. Norris gave Charles an idea for an article. "Charles, why don't you write an article on *'Focus On the Task for a Perfect Snap.'* You can mention the naïve way you first approached snapping the ball as a center on a football team. That the first time you realized you had to snap to a punter, you were in a critical point in a critical game. You snapped the ball over the punter's head and then you realized, 'I have to focus on this to improve.'

"You can write about the confusion, unsettledness, and lack of direction that a prejudiced person experiences. And when you realize that hate distorts life, one needs to focus. Then, well, you can write the rest."

Rev. Norris also gave Tony an idea for an article, using his position as one of the leading wrestlers in the state of Tennessee. "Tony, you ought to write an article on *'How Cardio Makes a Champion.'* Compare a wrestler who is not in shape, with a racist individual. They both just exist, they are just mediocre, they don't excel, they will just amount to average, if that. But, a person who trains, and trains seriously, is like a person who becomes tolerant, gracious, and openminded. They, like the wrestler who trains seriously, can be at his best longer. So, fashion your life….. well, you can write the rest."

As they accomplished so much in their writing, they also excelled in the many opportunities when they were invited to speak. In each speaking engagement, they talked about their personal journey from hearts filled with hate and prejudice to hearts and lives filled with empathy and compassion for all persons. They received excellent help and advice from Rev. Norris and Rev. Stone, and when they used that and fashioned it around their message of their personal experience, they captivated many audiences.

What made their speaking engagements so interesting and enjoyable to the audience was the occasional presence of Chad, Samuel, Jake, David, Joseph, and individual members of each team. During the question/answer time after the presentation, they would call on one of the guys who accompanied them.

On one occasion at a Men's Fellowship Conference of the Great Rivers Presbyterian Synod just outside Chattanooga, a gentleman asked Tony, "What did you think when Samuel threw you across the hall into the lockers?" Tony said to the group, "My head was ringing and my shoulders were hurting and I looked over at him, all six feet six inches and way over two hundred pounds, and I said to myself, 'Leave the big black dude alone.'"

As time went on through the wrestling season, and Tony's accomplishments on the mat became news, his speaking engagements became more frequent. During the last few weeks of the football season, college recruiters were seen in the hallways GHS seeking an appointment with Charles. As he became one of the top recruits in Tennessee high school football, his calendar got filled also with speaking engagements.

They both developed a mature, responsible, and quality presentation. Rev. Stone and Rev. Morris helped them prepare by focusing on their personal story and how that could fashion the message without them being the center of their presentation. The "coaching" and mentoring of Rev. Stone and Rev. Morris was more for helping them, not in the substance in their speeches, but in their presentation.

They helped Charles and Tony look like responsible teenage boys. They wore suits, ties, dress shoes, and were coached to stay away from useless words and phrases like "You know?" "Things like that," "And everything." "And, uh."

What really made their presentations interesting and enjoyable was when they interjected their experiences from their respective sports into the message. Often after Charles's presentations, individuals in the audience told him, "Son, you ought to be a minister."

In one presentation Tony was the principal speaker before the Women's Club of Jamestown. After the applause at the conclusion of his presentation, the moderator said, "After such a fine presentation by Mr. Pirello, I am almost led to take up an offering. You ought to be a preacher." With that comment, he got a standing ovation!

Charles and Tony not only had their suspension removed, but they also excelled in their senior year academically at Grayville High School. They also received league and state recognition in their respective sports. Charles anchored the offensive line for the football team which finished with a seven – two record, the best in twelve years. He received "All Conference" honors as the center for the all-conference team. Tony was ranked in the top ten most of the season in the one-eighty-pound class in the state of Tennessee, finishing as the fifth ranked wrestler in his weight class in the state and finishing third in the state wrestling. tournament.

B. The Word from the Players

The GHS basketball team not only demonstrated the message with their oath but also with their lives.

Their oath was the pledge they all signed at the team meeting at the Morris home. Not only did they fashion a dynamic and powerful message with their pledge, but they also witnessed to their message with the game against Clifton and every game after. Every move, every word, every expression each player made conveyed a genuine feeling of love and appreciation for each other. The essence of that message is and will be who they seek to be and what they seek to demonstrate with their lives; *I accept each person as sacred worth. I seek to forgive, be unselfish, love not hate, affirm the other person, show empathy and compassion, think, and not let prejudice stand in the way of playing basketball.*

The fans who came with skepticism about the change in the players had that skepticism erased. The fans got the message loud and clear. This team was in one accord, one unit, one voice, one intent, and one purpose – let it be known that love for each other accomplishes great things. The harmony and good will among them, in every game, were dominant. The support and encouragement given back and forth to each other were contagious as the crowds became involved in the games with enthusiasm and energy.

There were fans who came to the Clifton game with a big chip on their shoulders, waiting to see any gesture that showed the white players still resented the blacks. They came expecting to see the black players show signs of resentment and ways to get revenge. Instead, the players gave such a sign of a mutual caring for each other and genuine enjoyment of playing together, that the opposing fans joined in cheering them on. It was if people were in a church service and heard a testimony of regeneration, renewal, and rebirth of a person whose life had reached the bottom.

That is about what happened with the GHS basketball team, they almost hit the bottom. The worst thing that a teammate could say about another was said. Hatefulness and words of vitriol had raised their ugly heads. The prospects of renewal and change were nil. But, through grace, honesty, thinking, empathy, maturity, and exercising the need for reconciliation, all things became new and the crowds saw and felt it.

XVII. Evidence of Change – "The Council on Respect, Empathy, Compassion" (CREC)

A. Rationale for a Statement

Charles Jackson was looking around in the Christian Bookstore for a book that would help him understand the change that was happening to him the past few weeks. He did not know theology, or biblical passages but somehow, he recalled "conversion" and "redemption" as words that might fit his inquiry.

Recently, Rev. Morris happened to mention that the change in his outlook toward people of color was a very positive change. Charles suggested to Rev. Morris "Maybe it is this new self-image that is causing the change. I've always put myself down. I never figured I was good enough. I figured no one cared. I am six feet two inches tall and have a good build at two hundred twenty-five pounds. I am not ugly. But I have never been satisfied with myself.

"My folks never said anything to make me feel good about myself. They have never given me a compliment. My mom or dad have never told me they loved me. They never went to any of my school open-house programs. They never met any of my teachers or coaches. They never came to any of my football games. Whenever I got any recognition for anything at school, they never complimented me on it. At the prospects of going to college on scholarship, they couldn't care less." Charles just starred ahead as if really contemplating. Rev. Morris let him finish his contemplative gaze. Finally, he said, "In fact, I never felt they ever cared about me."

Rev. Morris said, "I am sorry you have had that experience with your parents. But thank goodness," at this point Rev. Morris puts his hand on Charles's shoulder and tells him with a big smile on his face, "You have people around you who really care. It is wonderful to find grace in the gift of love people give us.

If you don't mind, I will throw in some Christ-centered theology. Jesus said, 'Love God first, and your neighbor as yourself.' That is how we find grace, by loving. We find grace when we love our neighbor. We find grace when we love ourselves. Loving ourselves is healthy. It enables us. It builds us up. We also find grace when we are loved. When we are touched by grace, we are transformed, made new."

Charles said, "I must be getting a huge dose of grace. Sam, Gary and his mom, you and Mrs. Norris, Rev. Smith, Jake, Tony have been piling it on me. You said, 'it is healthy.' You said, 'it builds you up.' I feel that."

Charles had lunch with Tony recently and Tony told Charles, "I am amazed at the difference I have been seeing in you. You never cared about people. You never said or did anything that made me think you cared about anybody. I have never heard you ask anyone 'how you doing?' The first thing you said to me today was 'Glad to see you, Tony. How are you?' You never did that before.

"You are a big guy. Physically big. I've always been intimidated by your size. But, anymore, I am not threatened by you. I am not afraid of you. You are different. You are quiet, humble, nice. You are someone I like being around."

"Like Rev. Morris told me, 'When we get affirmed by people, it changes us.' I got the first taste of that when Gary and his mom came to see me in jail. Why? My mind told me they came to talk down to me. I figured they came to do what everybody has always done to me, tell me what an asshole I am.

His mom said she had some questions for me. I figured here it comes. Just a bunch of bullshit. 'You ought to know better.' 'Who do you think you are?' She didn't talk like that to me at all. She asked about my folks! She asked about me and getting back to school, and football, and the colleges that showed interest in me. It blew me away. Of all the people…. she should hate me. But she was interested in me.

Talk about being screwed up. I was so upset. It threw everything in my world upside down. Something was wrong. I had to get back to my cell. That started me thinking.

You said something nice to me. That you like being around me. Nobody ever said that. Thanks, Tony. I can't explain it to you. Like I said, everything in my world is upside down. I have always been around losers. You and I were losers. We did stuff that losers do. We thought like losers. We talked like losers. I seemed to gravitate to people that would pull me down. People that made me feel intimidated.

Now, we both are around people that lift us up, people that care for us, people that want the best for us. We are coming out of this as different persons. I don't know about you, but get this, I feel blessed. At least that is what Rev. Stone says, 'You have been blessed.' I don't know what the hell it means, but it feels good."

As they were eating lunch, an exceptionally large lady, holding the hand of a little girl, stopped at their booth and she said to Charles rather loudly and with a bit of anger, "Aren't you a member of the Aryan Patriotic Brotherhood? I think I saw your picture in the paper when you were arrested with the president of the APB."

"No mam, I am not a member of the APB. But you are right, that was me you saw in the paper. I was with the president of the APB. It was the biggest mistake I have ever made in my life. I am sorry I got involved with them. You can rest assured; I am not involved with them anymore."

She said, "I am glad to hear that. The newspaper or the Chamber of Commerce or the Grayville Council of Churches ought to make a statement that those groups are not welcome in the city of Grayville or Cox County. We have had enough of their hatefulness. I am glad you saw the light. Just stay out of trouble." Then she and the little girl walked away.

Tony said, as she walked away, "Charles, she has hit the nail on the head for both of us. 'We have seen the light.'"

Charles added, "She also made another great point. She said that some group or organization from Grayville or Cox County should make a statement about racial equality that would represent Grayville and Cox County. I think you and I should jointly write an article suggesting that.

We should write that there ought to be a committee or council in Grayville that fashions a statement that we are a community that will not tolerate racism or discrimination of any kind."

The lunch hour extended into three hours. They discussed how to get a council together to address the racial issue, who would be on the council, what to call the council, and create a mission statement for the council.

Charles and Tony talked it over and decided to speak to Mr. Gammon about it as well as Rev. Morris. In conversation with those men, they mentioned their questions and suggestions. Both men endorsed their "proposal" enthusiastically. Next Charles and Tony visited the mayor of Grayville, the county mayor, the president of the council of churches, the president of the chamber of commerce, the president of the school board, the sheriff, and the chief of police.

The spial they gave to each of them and to the many others they happened to talk to was fashioned into a formal petition which they gave to the local papers, the papers in Knoxville and Nashville.

We have in Cox County a legacy and history that contains references of racial unrest due to prejudice, the desire for segregation, oppression, and hate. The history we have feeds the potential of perpetuating racism.

After the racial incident at Grayville High School and the demonstrations of prejudicial behavior in our neighborhoods, we need to fashion a mission statement for our community that will be in stark contrast to the racial climate of the past. It should be a statement that defines a welcome, acceptance, an open and affirming recognition of all persons. The statement should state that discrimination will not be tolerated and that there is zero tolerance for prejudice and hate in Grayville and Cox County.

In spite of the overwhelming affirmation of their statement, there were voices of discontent and the attitude of "keep things just as they always have been." Meaning "there is no room for negros in Cox County."

Of the seven community leaders Charles and Tony talked to separately, they all gave the boys the greenlight to proceed with their idea of creating "The Council on Respect, Empathy, and Compassion." When the seven were asked if they would serve as members of the Council, they all said "yes." After receiving enthusiastic endorsements from these seven leaders, Charles and Tony asked Rev. Morris and Rev. Stone to help them put some meat on the bones of the CREC structure. The organizing committee of the CREC was put together and now work was to be done.

A. The Council at Work

The seven community leaders, the four black students, and Charles, Tony, Rev. Morris, and Rev. Stone made up the council of fifteen members. The first order of business at the first meeting was to elect the chair of the council. The mayor called the meeting to order to conduct this first task. Immediately a motion was made by Rev. Stone that Rev. Morgan's name be submitted for chair. The motion was seconded by Josh Stackhouse, president of the school board. Another motion was made by Rev. Morris that the nominations for chair be closed. The second was made by Police Chief Tom Clark. The motion passed. Rev. Morgan was elected as the chair of the CREC.

The second order of business was taken up by the chair, Rev. Dr. Morgan. He said, "We need to make official recognition of Charles Jackson and Tony Pirello for taking the initiative to move forward to form the Council on Respect, Empathy, and Compassion. Many communities make the statement of being an open and accepting community. But seldom do those communities have the fortitude to make an official printed statement to stand behind. Because of these two young men, Cox County and Grayville will make an official statement and take an official stand against discrimination and hate. To these two gentlemen, we offer our sincere thanks and appreciation. At that point, the council members stood and gave Charles and Tony a standing round of applause.

As a sign of respect, Rev. Morgan asked Charles and Tony if they had any suggestions as to the next order of business. Their suggestions were, 1. *Make a statement - WHY establish a Council on Respect, Empathy, and Compassion. 2. Develop a Mission Statement.* Rev. Morgan said he would like to entertain a motion to the effect of adopting those two suggestions. Charles made the motion and Tony seconded it. The motion passed!

Rev. Morgan immediately formed two committees and appointed members to each one. As if setting the tone of the urgency of the work of the new Council, Rev. Morgan did not ask who would like to be on which committee, he just arbitrarily appointed seven members to each committee. One was to fashion a statement on WHY establish a Council on Respect, Empathy, and Compassion. The members are: Gary Patterson, Joseph Bokima, Wayne Gibson, Grayville Mayor, Josh Stackhouse, President of the School Board, Del Moore, Sheriff, and Tony Pirello, Rev. Jack Stone.

Chairman Morgan then appointed members to the second committee, the Mission Statement Committee. The members are: Samuel Bokima, David Bokima, John Scott, County Mayor, Tom Clark, Chief of Police, Martha Simpson, President of the Chamber of Commerce, Rev. William Norris. Charles Jackson.

The committees were given four weeks to formulate, fashion, and administer, official statements for each responsibility. The statements were to be official in that they would be presented to the City of Grayville City Council and the Cox County Commissioners for approval and adoption as the official word regarding the position on racial equality.

B. Statement on "Why establish a Council on Respect, Empathy, and Compassion."

***Whereas,* Cox County and Grayville, Tennessee have a history of segregation, discrimination, and oppression of black people and**

Whereas, the history of Cox County and Grayville has practiced separation and exclusion of black people from the civic and civil boundaries of the city of Grayville and

Whereas, the history and legacy of Cox County and Grayville endorsed the banishment of blacks from access to Main Street and the convenient gathering of persons in the urban sitting and

Whereas, the history and reputation of Cox County and Grayville designated Grayville as one of twenty-four Sundown Towns of Tennessee and

Whereas, the history of the City of Grayville has an intrusive denial of civil liberties by systemic racism by not allowing blacks to enter, engage in, and participate in places of business for pleasure and

Whereas, the history of Cox County and Grayville has been open and conciliatory to hatred, racism, and white supremacy attitudes and practices,

Therefore, let it be resolved, that a Council of Respect, Empathy, and Compassion be formed to make a new and bold statement for racial equality, human rights, and social justice in Cox County and Grayville.

Be it further resolved, that all laws, written and unwritten be expunged that deny the basic rules of decency, freedom, and convenience to ALL persons.

Be it further resolved, that all citizens, places of business, organizations, institutions, public facilities, and points of private access be open, affirming, accepting, and inviting to ALL persons.

This is an urgent time, a time for unity and an end to those tools, voices, and behavior that create divisiveness and chaos;

a time to end hatred and expressions of discrimination;
a time to journey toward reconciliation and healing;
a time to recognize the human need to be accepted, loved, and be made whole;
a time to demonstrate security, not fear;
a time to offer a hand of welcome, not rejection.

With a vision of justice to all and the hope of RESPECT, EMPATHY, AND COMPASSION as the character of this time and place, we offer this crown jewel of order and direction.

C. The Mission Statement

The Mission of the Council on Respect, Empathy, and Compassion is to assert that in Cox County and Grayville, Tennessee racial prejudice will not be tolerated. The CREC will assume the task to inform, educate, and keep before the people the adverse effects of racial discrimination. The goals will be to replace the effects of hate with love, despair with hope, sadness with joy, anger with patience, exclusion with acceptance, violence with peace, a contentious attitude with gentleness, brokenness with healing, and oppressive behavior with compassion.

For over a year those who had a hand in issuing the statement of the end of racial prejudice, began to see the changes. The changes were not grandiose. Black families did not flood the entrances to Grayville with moving vans to move into Grayville. The sports teams at GHS did not all of a sudden have black athletes dominating the scene. Signs did not go up all over town welcoming blacks to Grayville. No new black businesses began to open up storefronts. Main street did not get repainted with BLACK LIVES MATTER in front of the courthouse.

The Aryan Patriotic Brotherhood did not hold a meeting at the State Park. Gary Patterson never had any confrontation his senior year in, out, or around the school. The Bokima family never had anyone drive in their yard, trash their driveway, or send hate letters throughout the last year of school for Samuel and David. Charles and Tony had to have Tony's mother maintain a schedule for their speaking engagements.

The whole environment took on an air of tolerance and "Lets not go through using the N word again." The message the basketball team gave, especially in the Clifton game, made a lasting impact. They had experienced the low. They had reached the point that hate draws a person. None of them liked the result. No one likes alienation from friends. No one likes being identified as a person who is base, filled with a lack of human decency, contemptable, and mean-spirited.

Charles Sykes, in his book, *How the Right Lost Its Mind*, made a statement that provides a good summary, "When you look back on your life you will want to know whether you made a difference. You will also want to know whether you stood for what you believe to be right. You will win some and lose some. But what you shall find most important is whether you stood firm in the truth."

XVIII. Years Later

Some people suffer from the "Florence Nightingale Syndrome." The FNS is manifest in a person when that person wants to solve all the world's problems and heal people who are hurting and ill. When someone upsets or offends another person, they want that person to come to their senses and apologize, make things right, correct the wrong and make all the bad feelings go away. They think everyone should be like them; selfless, giving, humble, not insisting on their own way, wanting to make things right, be peacemakers.

It seldom happens that people who are closed-minded, stubborn, selfish, and have little regard for the welfare of others, will do an about face and show empathy and compassion. There are politicians who will not speak or vote on behalf of doing good or standing for high moral principles because they don't think or don't care. High standards, strong moral judgments, and virtues that are valued are trashed.

Some people don't want to hear the facts. There are some who find lying much more accommodating than truth because with truth one has to think. It is encouraging to find someone who seeks to understand, is sensitive to others, has a regard for facts, knows when they are being lied to, and recognizes the high standards of good.

A racist attitude is hard to break through. A racist attitude is often etched in concrete. A racist attitude is not interested in facts or truth. A racist person is prone to demonize persons of a different color and those who accept people of different colors. People who are racist have their own facts, narratives, and truth.

So when someone like that makes a change for the good, that is cause for a wonderful celebration. People who see such a change in persons who were once comfortable with racially charged rhetoric, are astounded but grateful. It happens. Change does take place. People do abandon their hate and their "white supremacy" attitude. They do tune in to what is right. They do have a "light bulb" go off in their heads. Truth does matter to them. Facts are important. Good, right, love become valued and embraced.

It happened to the three white basketball players, Chad, Tom, and Mack after they made their racist remarks about the black three. It happened to Charles Jackson and Tony Pirello after they beat up a smaller frail black student, Gary Patterson. All five had their lives deeply touched by the giving, empathy, and love of caring people. They had their lives transformed by grace.

XX. Lives Transformed by Grace

A. Chad

When the news finally broke as to why the Shelby game was called off, persons from all over the country labeled Grayville, Tennessee the latest hotbed of racism and hate. The most repeated question asked by commentators and individuals was "Did the players guilty of the racist remarks directed at the Bokima brothers and the two athletes who beat Gary Patterson have any feelings of remorse or shame for what they said and did?"

Chad made the confession that it was he who started the name calling and racist talk toward the black three. He confessed to the coach and apologized to his teammates. He was especially contrite with the black three.

Chad and Joseph, the oldest of the black three, became best of friends. Chad never again repeated the immature irresponsible hateful rhetoric that was used in the locker room on the night of the Shelby game. Instead, people saw and heard from a young man who had risen above the use of thoughtless lightning-rod racist verbiage.

At the GHS graduation Chad was recognized for his high academic standing. The next morning Joseph and Chad were having breakfast at Glider's. Joseph asked Chad, "Would you join me and about fifteen others from church in a mission work camp of the United Church of Christ in Biloxi, Mississippi. It is a mission where we will help rebuild a dam and levy to help restore a small community of Hispanic and black families as they encountered some terrible flood damage. It will be a ten-day trip, we will be living in a dorm-like facility, eating in a cafeteria, and be supervised by some local engineers."

Without hesitation, Chad answered, "Yes, I would be glad to go. That sounds like a really important project." So, that is how Chad's journey began which enabled him to grow into a responsible thinking adult. After his transformative senior year at Grayville High School, he told Joseph that he felt he was "about to begin a journey that will have a consequential effect on the next several years of my life.

"I plan to attend Belmont University in Nashville. I have been offered an academic scholarship to Lipscomb. And, I have been invited to be a walk on with the basketball program. I have been doing a lot of thinking about the choice of a college. I choose Belmont University because it is close to home yet far enough away that I will feel 'I am away at college.' I realize it is a Baptist school, but I don't expect that to be a problem. What I do know about it and what I need, is to experience the spiritual environment in an integrated community.

One thing that sets it apart from other conservative religious campuses is that it has a mixed-race couple which coaches women's basketball. The head coach is a black woman and her assistant coach is her husband, who is white. That is the kind of focus which will be the catalyst for my growth and maturity. I need to experience healthy and wholesome race relations after what I have been through this past year at GHS."

"I need to accept the way things are going to be, that our country is becoming more racially diverse, and more like a melting pot than it ever has been. Although Grayville has taken a giant step forward, there are too many voices that say, 'We are not ready for this change.'"

One of the first social get togethers that Chad experienced at Lipscomb was a cookout for all the players at the home of the head basketball coach. It was there that he met three principal individuals that would draw him closer to his need to become more understanding and empathetic to the racial issue, especially at Lipscomb.

Ray Sheets immediately found a friend in Chad. Ray Sheets was from Zanesville, Ohio and attended Christian Academy, a Southern Baptist high school. Christian Academy had a tradition in Ohio of being a basketball powerhouse. And Ray Sheets was the star of last year's team. He led the team in scoring and was ranked number five in scoring in the state of Ohio. He led the team in rebounding and assists. He did this on the court as a point guard. He was a rare high school point guard because he was six feet six inches tall.

Chad began to understand the depth of Ray Sheets convictions when he, in a private tone of voice, drew Chad away from everyone and said, "Did you know we were going to have to have two N teammates? Those two monkeys over there, pointing in the direction of the two black players, are going to make this season a bad experience."

When Chad first talked to the coach about walking on, he asked about having teammates that might be black. Chad was quick to add to his question that he was hopeful and wanted to have black teammates. He mentioned to the coach that he had learned a great deal about race relations in Grayville because of three black teammates and he wanted to continue to learn and understand.

"We have Clarence Beckmon from Cleveland. He is a six-nine center who played at Ascension Lutheran. He was outstanding last year at Ascension. The other is Mohammad Sadaam, from Holy Cross in Springfield, Illinois. He is six four and plays guard. He is a Black Muslim but his parents wanted him to come to a Christian school so he would be safe from discrimination and hatefulness. They didn't want him to go to a black college because they wanted him to be exposed to the mainstream of an integrated campus.

The first thought Chad had was, "I have to keep Mohammed and Clarence away from Ray Sheets." That was the task that Chad set out for himself. But he had to come to the reality of accepting the education, the tradition, and the cultural confines of the making of Ray Sheets. "After one season with Clarence and Mohammed, if he is still a prejudiced person, I have to accept that. My only option is to love each one, and if I err, I will err on the side of grace."

Chad thought that his strategy to bridge the gap between Ray and Clarence and Mohammed would be to have all three teammates become acquainted. Gradually, Ray would come to trust and show empathy to Clarence and Mohammed.

Chad started with Clarence at a campus coffee shop. He told Clarence the history of his racist attitude and why he was suspended. He told of his friendship with Joseph and all they had accomplished as far as adopting a community of mutual love and respect. He also told of the pledge that each player made as a message to send to the community. Then he told Clarence, "I want you to meet Ray Sheets."

A few days later, at the same coffee shop, Chad had arranged a meeting with Ray and Clarence. "Clarence stuck out his hand and told Ray, "Glad to meet you."

Ray did the same. Clarence looked at Ray as if he knew him. He said to Ray Sheets, "Are you from Zanesville, Ohio?"

"Yes, how did you know that?"

"I attended the basketball camp at Ohio Northern University and you were there. You were the dominant dude. You were voted the most valuable player there. I voted for you. And I think everybody else voted for you. This is going to be great that we will be together here at Lipscomb for the next four years. It is going to be great playing with you."

Ray said to him, "Do you know the other African American, the guy from Springfield, Illinois? He played at Springfield Central and he took them to the semi-finals of their District Tournament."

"Yes, I talked to him at the coach's party. He is in the same dorm as me and lives two rooms down from me. He said he plays guard too. Man, we will have two big guards! You are six-six and Mohammad is six-four. Ray, this is going to be fun."

"You know what, Clarence, Belmont will have to do a new schedule when we are sophomores. They will have to add some Big Ten schools and Mid-American schools." At that they all laughed and Ray said to Chad, "Chad, aren't you glad you came to Lipscomb?

As Chad heard this exchange, he only remembered Ray using the words, "African American" when he referred to Mohammed Sadaam.

B. Tom

For a long time after the forfeited Shelby game, Tom dealt with guilt and shame for his contribution in making that night infamous. He and Chad and Mack had made their confessions and asked for forgiveness and had made a significant statement on the need to put an end to hate and prejudice. Tom should feel free of that burden of causing hurt and brokenness. Everything turned out very well for everybody.

Tom had another burden to carry. In addition to that experience which can be put aside and forgotten, he was also hiding behind something which was causing a personal conflict. Tom struggled to find a way to come out of this personal dilemma without completely destroying himself.

"I have got to get away from here. Graduation will have to be my departure date from Grayville and Cox County, at least for a while. And, it will have to serve as my entrance into maturity and new life. College choice will be very important. Someplace to start the new experience of life, to be myself, to unveil my personal 'yoke' and be set free."

About a month after graduation from GHS, Tom spent two weeks visiting college campuses. He had picked out a college when he visited college campuses as a junior. But now, he felt the need to make a change. Not only did he take in the landscape or the physical campus setting, but he also inquired as to the student life on campus. Most notably, does the college have a good, healthy, and religious tolerance of the LGBTQ population? Is it a struggle to be a LGBTQ student on this campus? Is there a wholesome fellowship of LGBTQ students? How does the faculty relate to the LGBTQ community and to individual students? Is the campus a safe place for a gay student from the Bible-belt of middle Tennessee?

Tom had to get away from Grayville and find his niche in life. He wanted to have a solid beginning in finding that niche and he wanted the assurance that being gay did not keep him from accomplishing anything he set out to become. Most of all, he wanted to become a person who gained respect and appreciation from people for contributing to the welfare of the community where he might live.

He had felt nothing but shame and guilt in his last two years of high school. It wasn't until after his sophomore year that he finally had to come to grips and accept who he was and what he was. He didn't want to be gay. He knew it was a terrible wrong. He learned at church that homosexuality was "abhorrent in the eyes of God." He had heard his dad and mom talk about it. He overheard his dad say, "If one of our kids ever came to me and told me they were gay, I don't know what I would tell them."

Tom had thought about the time to "come out" for months. Who would be the first person he would come out to?

Tom "came out" to his closest friend. He talked to Matt just a few days after graduation. He had never admitted it to anyone before that he was struggling with the prospects of being a gay man. He and Matt knew each other since third grade. They were very close. Tom trusted Matt. For over two years Tom had been harboring this secret. Now, as he was about to begin his "new life and new identity," he should "test the waters" and see what the first reaction to his openness would be.

He figured the best way to say it is to be perfectly honest and to the point. So, he met with Matt at Matt's house. As they sat in the kitchen eating Matt's mom's apple pie. "Matt, I have something to tell you."

Matt responded in a joking attitude, with a smile on his face, while continuing to eat his apple pie, "What the hell, are you going to tell me you're a fag?"

Tom was shocked at Matt's response. Never did he suspect Matt harbored such an attitude toward gay people. Tom said, "Yes, that is it exactly. Only I would say that I am gay."

Matt, bolted out of his chair and with a mouth full of apple pie said, "You fucking me? Don't fuck with me! I don't want to hear that shit."

Without further comment or any reaction to Matt's comment, Tom got up from his chair and headed for home. He knew he had better tell his mom and dad before Matt began to spread his venomous message of hatefulness. Now, more than anyone of the white players from that Shelby game, Tom knew and understood the feelings of Joseph, Samuel, and David. And he felt the pain of Gary Patterson. He felt the feeling of rejection and being denigrated.

His mother was in the kitchen and his dad wasn't home from work. He told his mom, "Mom, I need to talk to you. Could we sit down?"

"Sure, what is it? You look very upset."

Without any thought of what to say or how to say it, Tom got right to the point. "Mom, I am gay."

They were sitting at the kitchen table and his mom didn't say a word, she just looked at him with an expression on her face that offered, "Son, do you really know what you are saying?" Tom said, "You don't look surprised. Why don't you say something? Yell at me or something."

"Why would I yell? Yes, I am surprised but not angry. You have to admit this news is very surprising for a parent to take in. My first concern is you. All I want is knowing that you are OK. Are you sure? How do you know? Have you talked to anyone about this?"

"Mom, I am OK as long as you are OK. I want you and dad to be OK with me. I have been so worried and afraid to tell you both. It is something I have been struggling with for a long time. I have to be who I am. I know it will be difficult. But, I have to be honest with myself."

"Don't be worried and don't be afraid. Your dad will be surprised too, but he will come to understand and be OK."

That evening, after dinner, which was under duress and filled with anxiety, Tom asked his dad if he could talk to him. His dad said, "Of course. But, if you are going to tell me you are gay, your mother beat you to it. And it is OK. It is OK with us, but we are concerned about you. We want you to be OK."

"But I heard you not too long ago say that if I ever told you I was gay you wouldn't know what to do."

"Tom, I am sorry for that." His dad paused for a moment, leaned over and looked straight in Tom's eyes with a look of compassion and love. "Tom, I can't imagine what a difficult time this has been for you. I know it must be a real challenge to accept and have to handle this personal dilemma. But I admire and respect the way you have handled it. Your mother and I will try to do the same. It is a big adjustment for all of us. We have a lot to learn. We love you. We will always love you. We want to help you and be with you in the next step. And I know it will all work out."

C. Mack

Since the tenth grade, Mack had been dating Barbara Stills from Pleasant Hill. Barbra always had to ride the bus to school. It was on the bus that some of the guys teased Barbara and asked her if Mack was the first boy she ever kissed. She said, "Yes and he is the only one I want to kiss." They asked her, "Do you know who the first girl was that Mack ever kissed?" She turned around and threw a pencil at them and said, "I better be the only one too."

After graduation from GHS, Mack stayed in Grayville and attended Rhone State and studied criminal justice. He wanted to be a sheriff's deputy. Barbara attended Tennessee Tech University and studied to be a nurse.

It turned out as Mack hoped. He became a Cox County sheriff's deputy and Barbara became a nurse at the Cumberland Medical Center. They were married shortly after Barbara graduated from nursing school.

They had Rev. Jack Stone conduct the wedding service at the chapel at Rhone State.

After about a year of living in Grayville, Barbara read in the paper that Kids On The Rise needed mentors for at risk children in the Cox County schools. She inquired and applied to be a mentor. She was paired with a second grader from Martin Elementary by the name of Wanda Martinez. Wanda was the youngest of five with a sister and three brothers. The oldest brother was Ralph, an eighth grader, and he seemed to have the most difficulty of the Martinez children with schoolwork and relating to others. He had hardly any friends. The family was from Mexico. Her father worked for Grayville Carpet and Flooring as a carpet layer. Mrs. Martinez did house cleaning for six families as her regular clients.

They were a close nit family and they seemed to be well cared for by Mr. and Mrs. Martinez. The only problem was that they spoke little English at home. That made it difficult for the five children to do well in school. Therefore, Wanda's teacher applied for a mentor for Wanda.

After they got acquainted, Barbara spent a great deal of time with Wanda and they built up a strong bond and had a trusting relationship. About three months into the school year, Wanda began to put on a sad demeanor. After school one day, Barbara and Wanda went to the Dairy Queen for Dilly Bars and talk. Barbara kept asking what was wrong and she found out that Wanda was very worried about her older brother Ralph. "He has been bullied after school by three boys and last Friday they beat Ralph and hurt his ear. He had stitches taken and now can hardly hear out of that ear. The doctor said he had a broken eardrum. I am afraid he will keep getting beat up and really get hurt." Wanda began to cry. Barbara hugged her and tried to reassure her by telling her, "Wanda, don't you worry anymore. I promise you that Ralph will not be bullied ever again. I will see to that."

That evening, Barbara told Mack about the problem and how disturbed Wanda was. She told Mack that because Ralph is Hispanic and dark, a bit smaller than the other boys, and seems kind of slow, he gets picked on. Mack excused himself, got in his pickup and left.

Mack had spent some time with Barbara and Wanda as they spent their time together. Mack also knew the other siblings in the family, especially Ralph. Ralph reminded Mack of Gary Patterson who also was bullied because of his size and because he was black. Ralph seemed to be caught up in the same victimization.

Mack headed for his church. It was the first night for the organization of the youth fellowship and he gave a special invitation to Ralph. Mr. Martinez said he would take Ralph to the meeting. When Mack arrived at church, he pulled his pickup near the front door. He walked in and immediately saw Ralph. Ralph was walking fast and leaving the church and was near the front door. Mack asked him what he was doing. Ralph said he was leaving to go home. He started crying as he went into the parking lot to begin the walk home.

Mack called after him, "Ralph, wait up." Ralph stopped but did not look back at Mack. Mack asked him again, "What happened that you want to leave? The meeting hasn't even started yet."

"The three boys that beat me up are in there and they told me to leave or they would rip off my good ear." Ralph began to cry even more.

Mack squatted down so he was eye to eye with Ralph. He said, "Ralph, would you go back in there with me? We will just go in and you stand next to me and we will just listen to what is being said and just act like nothing happened."

"If I can stand by you."

"You bet."

Mack had his deputy's uniform on as he and Ralph walked into the room where the meeting was about to begin. He and Ralph stood near the back of the room. He saw three bigger boys looking at Ralph with astonished looks. They had expressions on their faces as if to say, "He has a deputy sheriff with him. And he is looking at us." Soon, Ralph and Mack noticed they turned away from looking at them as if they were trying to be nonchalant and act like they didn't care that Ralph was with a cop. In fact, they were paralyzed with fear.

After the meeting was over refreshments were being served. Mack said to Ralph, "Lets mosey over toward them and the refreshment table. Act like nothing has happened and that you are their best buddy." The three boys saw them coming and they began to move behind the table of refreshments. They couldn't move much because the crowd kept them gathered around the refreshment table. When they got to the table, Mack asked the three boys, "What do you gentlemen recommend? My friend Ralph and I want to make sure we eat the good stuff."

Ralph sensed from the three bullies they were nervous and really intimidated by the presence of Mack. Seeing Mack's gun in the holster contributed to their look of fear and intimidation. What was interesting is that Ralph took on a whole new demeanor. The tears were dried up, he had a smile on his face, and a confident look that suggested, "Now, what are you guys going to do? You still going to rip off my good ear?"

Ralph approached the three bullies, "John, Rex, and Wayne I want you to meet my mentor from Kids On The Rise, this is deputy Mack Diles." Ralph didn't look up to Mack to see his reaction or expression on his face. He made the statement and now it was if he was saying, "Now Mack, the ball is in your court." He said to the three boys, "Deputy Diles said he wanted to meet some of my classmate."

"John, Rex, Wayne, really nice to meet you gentlemen. Mack reached out his hand to shake theirs. They watched his hand extend out and after a long look they took turns shaking Mack's hand. "As Ralph said, I am his mentor. Are you in the same classroom as Ralph?"

The three weren't sure how to respond. Rex spoke for the other two and said, "We know Ralph from school. Yes, he is in our class."

Then, Mack let the hammer down. "Ralph, aren't these the boys that hurt your ear real bad and forced you to get a hearing aid?"

"Yes."

Mack looked into the eyes of the three boys and was talking to Ralph, "It cost your folks a lot of money to get your ear taken care of. That hearing aid is very expensive. All that trouble and all that expense because of these fine-looking boys?

"Yes."

Still looking straight at the three boys, Mack went on to say, "But your mom said your lawyer told her that will all be taken care of." Mack is still looking straight into the eyes of the three boys. "Your mom said he will be contacting the lawyers of these boys?" as he nodded in the direction of the three. This may be far removed from the truth, but maybe not! Ralph saw a bit of worry in the boys faces and nervous behavior and kind of reveled in it. Mack put a footnote before the three bullies when he directed this statement to them, "Even eighth graders are not too young to think. Too bad you boys didn't think."

Mack and Ralph walked away and left the three boys to digest what was said. As they were walking out to Mack's pickup to take Ralph home, Mack said to Ralph, "So, now you have a mentor. That was a slick way to get me in the Martinez household. You got a mentor and got rid of three bullies all in one evening. Ralph you are a piece of work."

D. Charles

Charles had a great senior season at Grayville High School. He won league honors as first-string center. He was named honorary captain at the start of the season. He was named offensive player of the week by the Knoxville Tribune four times. He was credited with providing leadership which inspired and motivated the team to an 8 and 1 record.

The biggest factor that demonstrated the change in Charles was the way he carried himself. His facial expressions oozed with confidence. His behavior drew in the attention, the commitment, and the focus of the team by the way he looked at, spoke to, and gave the physical touch that pulled it all together, becoming effective motivation.

With this new level of maturity, with his looking into each person on the team, and with his contagious enthusiasm for doing the job rightly, he provided the window for each player to reach a new level of participation. As his coach said to Rev. Stone, who served as a "consultant" to the coach because of his valued experience at the University of Illinois, "Charles speaks a different language than he did last year. He uses vocabulary that is filled with hopeful words. He carries himself differently because he stands up straight. He relates to his peers as a mature adult. It is as if he found some wisdom someplace.

Charles received football scholarship offers from nine schools. Notably, the University of Tennessee, Auburn, Mississippi State, Vanderbilt, and Kentucky. But, with the efforts of Rev. Stone and three members of the coaching staff at the University of Illinois, Charles was one of the most enthusiastic recruits Illinois ever had. At Illinois he was superlative as the long-snapper. His junior and senior year at Illinois he was named to the All Big Ten Team.

Academically, he excelled as well. His major was history with a minor in Greek! He took seriously all those comments he received when he did his speaking back home to groups on race relations and the need for peacemakers, "You ought to be a minister." After graduation from Illinois, Charles enrolled at Garrett Theological Seminary on the campus of Northwestern University.

It was at Garrett that his elementary theology and limited biblical knowledge began to be more developed and extensive. One day he was walking to class and he was mulling over in his mind two of the biblical scholars he had just learned about, Crossan and Borg. And, he began to think how far he had come since watching the Clifton basketball game with "Big Body" Boone.

Charles found that his minor in Greek at Illinois really prepared him for the opportunity to share deeply in the New Testament theology class and in the study of the Gospels. Soon, he was involved in a cadre of like Greek scholars for significant and meaningful discussions. Because of that circle of exposure to academic dialogue he became acquainted with other pockets of theological discussions. Many students began to appreciate the thoughtful and penetrating level of knowledge of Charles. He began to appreciate their contribution to his widening horizon of new concepts of theology and ecclesiastical understanding.

In one such discussion over the lunch hour, he was more of a distant observer than a participant. But a comment from one of the students caught his ear. "I am certainly glad I was not privy to what took place in the Bible-belt a few years ago. Cox County Tennessee took on the persona of George Wallace. 'Segregation today, segregation always.'"

Another student from Chicago asked, "What took place in Cox County, Tennessee?" At that question, Charles quickly moved his chair closer and leaned in to hear better. As Charles moved his chair closer, a female student moved her chair over and told Charles to move in closer and join in the conversation.

A student with a thick southern accent said, "I will tell you what happened in Cox County. It was at Grayville High School, and all hell broke loose."

A student from Nashville broke in on the conversation with comments of his own. "We lived down there when that took place, it is about two hours east of Nashville. "Grayville seldom had a black student. Historically, they banned all blacks from even living in Grayville. Grayville was one of several "Sundown Towns" in Tennessee. There were signs on the outskirts of town that said, 'If you are a negro, don't be in the city limits after the sun goes down."

One of the women students referred to a previous comment, "Jeffrey, you said all hell broke loose. What do you mean?"

"What happened was a small frail black kid got beat up by two huge stupid white athletes in the hallway at Grayville high school. It happened about four or five years ago. Students watched these two big brave athletes jump this little black kid and beat the hell out of him. It made the headlines all over the country. People all over called those two white guys 'red neck' 'villains,' 'hate-mongers,' and 'bullies for Jesus.' I sure as hell would hate to be one of those athletes. They got expelled and sent off to jail. I don't know where they are now. I wouldn't mind if they are rotting in prison."

"Charles, pull your chair up closer." Charles was invited to join in the discussion by the student who wouldn't mind if he would be rotting in jail.

Everything got quiet. It was if some great mystery is to be revealed. "I may not have a southern accent, but I am from the south. In fact, I am from the Bible-belt that you talked about." Charles nodded his head in the direction of the two students who told about the racist problems in Cox County."

"In fact," here Charles gave a long pause. "I am one of the two athletes that beat up that small frail black student."

Everyone stopped any movement they were making. Those who were in eye contact with Charles held a gaze that defined them as saying "This is unbelievable."

"The other athlete that joined me in beating up that one hundred thirty-pound black kid went to Iowa State on a wrestling scholarship. He got married to a black gymnast from Iowa State. They live in Grayville and teach at that school where we beat that kid up. The kid's name is Gary Patterson. He and his mom are Quakers.

"Does that give you a clue why this horrible racist animal, Charles Jackson, is at a seminary? That Quaker family and many other good Christian folk sought me out. They offered me grace and a chance to reconcile where I had caused brokenness. Gary and his mom got me out of jail. They did not condemn but loved. They and so many other good Christian folk made sure we worked through the suspension from school. They were our advocates to help us get reinstated to our sport. And, doing so, we both received scholarships to compete in our sports.

"Have you ever gone through the drive-through at McDonalds and paid for the person behind you? Have you ever had the person in front of you pay for yours? That is what happened to me with those people in Grayville.

The other athlete was Tony Pirello. We both were saved by the generous grace of others."

E. Tony

Tony began to realize, during his senior year at Grayville High School, that his mother has done more for him in giving him a sense of direction, than anybody else in his life. She is the one who insisted they go to the Patterson home and apologize to Gary and his mother for Tony's part in the beating of Gary. Because of his mother's insistence that he apologize, Tony and Gary became the best of friends.

Gary Patterson is a close second to Tony's mom for giving Tony a sense of direction for his life. Not only that, but Gary enabled Tony to end the suspension, return to school, and also renew his participation on the wrestling team as captain. A huge of factor of influence is that through the efforts of Gary, Tony not only returned to school and the wrestling team, he also earned a wrestling scholarship to Iowa State University.

Tony had a very successful year as captain of the wrestling team. He was ranked in the top five in the state each week during his senior year. He was named to the All-League Team in his weight class. He was second team All-State in his weight class. He was second in the state wrestling tournament. And, at the conclusion of the season, he was ranked second in his weight class in the Mid-States Confederation. He finished with a record of thirty-four wins and three losses.

Rev. Dr. Jack Stone made an aggressive try to recruit him for the University of Illinois. The Illinois wrestling coach even made a trip to see Tony and talked to the wrestling coach at Grayville. But Tony had a deep desire to go to Iowa State. He had heard about the coach and some of the wrestlers and wanted to be a part of that atmosphere. The Grayville coach, Tom Dankins, wrote to the Iowa State coach and sent tapes and a biographical sketch of Tony. The assistant coach at Iowa State made a trip to see Tony and that was all it took. Tony was very excited to be a Cyclone.

Tony took special note of members of the Iowa State team. The competition was going to be tough. In his weight class there were six wrestlers who all had great credentials from high school and from their competition in the first few years of college. But Tony was very confident that he would be more than competitive in his collegiate career. He set five goals for himself as a Cyclone. 1. He would have one season where he would be undefeated. 2. He would participate in the NCAA Tournament all four years. 3. He would be All-American his junior and senior years. 4. He would be in the top five in the nation in his weight class each year. 5. In his four years of collegiate wrestling he would hold the record as the winningest Cyclone in wrestling.

In late August as he began his freshman year at Iowa State, he met the wrestling team and the six wrestlers in his weight class. After one week of working out with the team and wrestling against three in his weight class, he adjusted his five goals. He set only one goal for his collegiate career. He set as his goal to just earn his letter "I."

His experience at Iowa State was very enjoyable, exciting, and proved to be a time of unexpected good fortune. At the beginning of his junior year at Iowa State, he met a girl that put a new and life-changing mood over him. She was a gymnast on the Iowa State women's gymnastic team and was from East St. Louis, Illinois where she attended a predominately black high school. Her name was Moquema Williams. She is black. She is beautiful. She is the former Illinois High School All-Around Gymnastic Champion. As a sophomore at Iowa State, she earned All-American honors. And, after meeting Tony Pirello, from Grayville, Tennessee, she fell in love. It was mutual.

After graduation, Tony and Moquema were married. They were married in East St. Louis at Moquema's home church, the Ebenezer African Methodist Episcopal Church. Her pastor, her father, married them.

Moquema's best friend, a fellow gymnast from Iowa State, Jill Morrison, who is white, was her maid of honor. Gary Patterson was Tony's best man.

At the wedding reception and before the traditional toast by the Best Man, Moquema told the story of Tony and Gary with great pride and respect for Tony. "But to Gary, I give the highest place of respect and appreciation. I want you to know that without Gary's commitment to what is good and right, Tony would have never made it to Iowa State. You need to hear the whole story of Gary being beaten, the visit of reconciliation of Tony and his mother to Gary's house, the gracious and unselfish giving of Gary to Tony's high school career, and the resultant admirable relationship they have for each other. I think it is the story of the ages. That is why it is so easy to love and respect Gary Patterson and why I love, so much, Tony Pirello."

The audience erupted in a standing ovation with tear streaming down the faces of most everyone.

After everyone returned to their chairs, Gary, as Best Man, made a toast. In toasting Moquema and Tony, Gary said, "You all have heard the story of why I am here. Only this time, Tony is not beating up a black person, (there were only a few white persons present for the wedding reception) he has married one!" Again, the audience gave a standing ovation with a long spell of laughter. After everyone was reseated, Gary continued, "And, it must be noted, Tony is not bad-mouthing a black person, he is telling her he loves her. This is not a newly discovered Tony Pirello, he has been a fantastic guy for a long time. He has been a mature thoughtful young man for a long time. He is a wise man (at this point, Gary begins to sob, clearly tears of joy) a wise young man who is responsible and loving. Now, now, (Gary gives a big pause) Moquema is going to make a man out of him!" With that the crowd erupted in laughter.

Moquema received her degree in elementary education. Tony received his degree in physical education. In their senior year they had discussed at length where they would go to teach and live. What kind of community did they want to live in? What kind of school system did they want to teach in?

The more Moquema learned about Cox County and Grayville, the more she saw living there as a real opportunity to contribute to the realization of racial justice. She and Tony saw living and teaching in Cox County a real opportunity to be agents of change. They made inquiry to the school administration and presented their credentials. Gymnastics had never taken off, but the school officials saw the hiring of Monquema as the time to introduce gymnastics as a grand orientation to a new program. The wrestling coach was looking to retire soon and Tony would be the perfect replacement.

Moquema taught at Pleasant Hill elementary. She was the first black faculty member at Pleasant Hill. In fact, she was the first black faculty member in the Cox County School System. To the students she was a very unique attraction. What was so revealing and such a surprise was that the students, very soon, ceased seeing her as a person of a different color, but accepted her presence as one of them. They fell in love with her. Her smile, her beauty, her sense of humor, her many displays of affection and caring touched the lives of several children.

Before the Thanksgiving break, she was asked by the principal to display her gymnastic skills at a school auditorium presentation. "How many times do any of us have a chance to watch an All-American gymnast perform? In fact, we will open the demonstration to the Pleasant Hill Community." In the presentation, she enamored the children and many adults who attended. They saw her in an activity for which she excelled in high school and college.

Monquema was not looking for a home, but she found one at Pleasant Hill. Monquema was not looking for affirmation, she didn't need it, but she found it at Pleasant Hill. Monquma was not looking for inclusion or acceptance, she already was, but she became a part of the family in Pleasant Hill.

Mr. Gammon, the high school principal asked Gary Patterson when he saw Gary at the last basketball game, "How can we describe the transformation of Chad, Tom, Mack, Charles, and Tony?" Gary said, "If we are going to err, let's err on the side of grace."